Valiant
Journey

Doris English

DEDICATION

I dedicate this work of fiction to the love of my life, my husband, for without his urging and encouraging this book would still be lying in my desk drawer.

ACKNOWLEDGEMENT:

My deepest appreciation to my daughters, Donna, who spent hours editing and formatting, and Dawn, who spent hours proof reading as well as contributing her photography skills for our cover. Thanks again to grandson, Jimmy, for the lovely cover art and my granddaughter, Jen and grandson, Caleb for donning period clothes and stepping back in time to grace the cover.

CHAPTER 1

The smell of the sea laced a soft breeze that rustled across the plain, caressing Joel's sunburned face. He slouched in the saddle that had been his home for the last two days. From before sun up until it was too dark for him to see his way, his exhausted mount lumbered on. They crested a small knoll, their pace slowing. Joel pulled on the reins and paused. Just below him the lights of San Diego twinkled against an indigo sky, which he knew met the sea beyond.

Joel leaned down and patted the lathered side of his powerful stallion, "Only a few miles to go, old boy, before you can have a meal and a clean stall to bed down in. I wish I could say the same for me."

The young man shook his head, as he tried to clear it of the troubling thoughts which had pestered him most of his lonely trek. Lingering for a moment, he stared toward his destination. The nearness of it did nothing to relieve the reluctance which had dogged his long journey. Only respect for his ailing father forced him onward.

He dreaded the encounter with his brothers, that is, if he could even find them. It was not the first such mission his father had sent him on, and unless his brothers changed it wouldn't be the last. He sighed, every bone in his young body complained. He lifted the reins and horse and rider moved out.

Dust boiled from beneath Joel's horse as he entered the town. Light spilling from a few doorways caught on the mist and bathed the street in a golden aura while loud, boisterous sounds mingled with music greeted him. Low hovels made of dense, sun dried bricks lined the western side of the street blocking the ocean breeze and allowing the sour smell of cheap whiskey mixed with sweat and horse flesh to assault his nostrils. He cantered by the darkened general store and turned his mount, his eyes fixed on the most prominent brothel and the adjacent saloon, knowing his search would begin there.

He felt more than saw a movement in the shadows. Now fully alert his body tensed while his hand moved toward the weapon resting beneath his right knee. Joel's fingers closed around the cold steel of his father's 54-caliber Kentucky rifle and pulled it from its supple leather holster as his eyes scanned the shadows. They rested on a young woman leaning against a post just below him. He swung off his horse, rifle in hand and she reached for the reins, looping them on the hitching post in one liquid movement.

Joel's face flushed in the semi darkness as light from the cantina fell on her. He jerked his head away, averting his eyes from the soft flesh that spilled from her tight golden dress. The sight and scent of her did strange things to his nineteen-year-old body and his breath quickened. She paused, waiting. Like a magnet his eyes returned to her and a knowing smile lifted her scarlet, pouting mouth as she stepped in to him and spread her fingers against his chest. His heart thundered. Her low sultry laughter competed with the pounding of his heart to fill his ears. His head roared and felt as if it would explode

She stepped back and her gaze slowly took in every inch of his tall lean frame. Approval ignited her eyes.

"Hi, handsome. Are you looking for a good time?"

Joel closed his eyes and shook his head, releasing his breath in one ragged shudder, "I'm looking for my brothers, ma'am."

"Brothers?" She puzzled.

"Yes, ma'am. Four of them. Aaron, Jim, Simeon and Ben, the youngest."

"Are they anything like you?" She chortled.

"No, ma'am. We had different mommas. They're tall and ruddy."

"And you're dark and handsome."

Ignoring her remark, he explained, "Bright blue eyes they have."

"That could be anybody." She shrugged, lowering long lashes.

"No, you'd recognize them. They're a head taller than most and always together."

"One of them has red hair?"

"That'd be Simm."

"Maybe I've seen them around." Her answer came hesitant, evasive.

"I'm sure they wouldn't have missed a pretty girl like you," Joel observed, knowing his brothers, their habits.

"So you think I'm pretty, eh?" Pleasure lighted her eyes and she pressed closer.

"No doubt about that, miss," he agreed, straining away from her

"Then what would you want with your brothers when you can have me?" She crooned, as she stepped closer again placing both hands on his shoulders, then her left hand trailed toward the weapon he clutched in his right hand.

With his free hand, Joel captured hers, gently pushing her away, "I don't want to offend you, ma'am,"

"Jessica," she corrected, a hard glint touching her eyes.

"You're wasting your time with me." He stammered, hoping she'd get his message.

She tossed her head, her long red locks catching the light like a fiery cloud, her eyes sparked, outrage in them, "What's the matter with you? Are you a boy in a man's body?"

"Whether I'm boy or man is not in question, ma'am. 'Tis a man's job I've come to do tonight and I intend to do it. Now I'm tired, hungry and dirty so if you'll pardon me, I'll be about the business I came to do." And he walked away, struggling with emotions that wanted to betray him.

Joel hurried past the brothel, forgetting his horse. His encounter had left him unwilling to begin his search in the expansive building that was little more than several whitewashed huts strung together. Just then wafting through the night air, Joel caught the smell of ham frying and his empty stomach rumbled. Torn between what he had to do and the demands of his tired and hungry body, he followed the aroma and turned into a small hotel. The narrow, two-story building wedged between saloons appeared out of place with its air of genteel refinement among the rough adobe hovels squatting in the dust.

The young desk clerk who was pudgy and short of stature with a face much too pale for this part of the country, fixed fearful eyes on Joel's rifle. Then gradually, he glanced upward to meet Joel's steady gaze before asking in a high pitched voice, "Something I can do for you, sir? Don't have a bed left in the place."

"Don't have time for one anyway, but I would like a meal and a bath. Think I could get one?"

Relief flooded the pale blue eyes that held Joel's. "Sure. I'll give your supper order to Sue."

"Sue?" A smile creased Joel's dust crusted face.

"She runs the cafe." The young man hastened to explain.

"And a bath?"

"You can bathe while supper's cooking." The clerk's eyes widened and perspiration beaded on his upper lip as if he were still uncertain of Joel.

"Would that be satisfactory?"

"Couldn't be better."

"Whew, you're pretty easy to please mister." He said with a crooked smile while his pale eyes held Joel's in a steady gaze, satisfied now that the cowboy wouldn't prove a problem.

"The baths are available then?" Joel grinned.

"Yea, the trail drivers have come and gone." The clerk raised his eyebrows as if to convey an unspoken message.

The young man jerked his head, motioning toward the door, "You know, down the street."

Joel knew only too well. Then a thought occurred to him, "Perhaps my brothers were in here."

"I haven't seen anybody who looks like you."

"They don't.

"Could you describe them?" He stammered, uncertainty firing his eyes again.

"Four of 'em. Tall, ruddy and blue eyes."

"One of them has red hair?"

Joel nodded.

"You're right, they're nothing like you."

"So you saw them?"

"They've been here for a couple of days. Tonight I heard them say they were going down to the Palace for a little fun and games."

Inwardly Joel shuddered. They'd lose all the gold in their pockets then gamble the money from the cattle sale, money that was his father's only hope to buy a ranch. It had been a slim hope from the start. They had captured a wild herd of cattle and driven them north, hoping to trade hides for enough to salvage their future. It seemed an impossible dream to Joel but he was just the "kid" and nobody asked him for his advice.

When his father fell too ill on the drive to continue. Joel was the only one willing to stay behind to look after him. His brothers went on to finish the drive and sell the herd. When they hadn't returned in the expected time, his pa feared the worst and sent Joel after them. Now he waited over two-day's journey away, not knowing the fate of his sons.

Joel reached for the clean, white towels. Anticipation of a warm bath and a good meal pushed his worries to the back of his mind. When he felt refreshed, he would be better equipped to handle his brothers and any temptation that might come his way. He whistled an old rover's tune as he made his way down the narrow hall toward the public bath.

The smoke-filled saloon reeked with perfume, sweat and cheap rum. In the back corner, a tense game of cards captured the attention of a third of the inhabitants while the loud music softened and a shrill voice began to warble the sad strains of a love gone wrong. A strange mixture of seamen from the docks and cowboys from the trail sprawled at separate tables, their usual hostility muted by the lateness of the hour and the amount of rum they had consumed. The stories bandied about had turned from accomplishment to sad tales of woe.

A young woman dressed in gold, her cloud of Titian hair cascading down her back, slipped in beside a tall, blond stranger who watched the action at the table closely. The muscle in his face twitched as he clinched his teeth. She looked from him to the young giant with flaming hair holding his cards near his chest and smiled knowingly. Lifting up on tiptoe, she cupped her hand and whispered something into the stranger's ear, diverting his attention from the tense drama unfolding at the table.

He grasped her arm and jerked her with him as he stepped back, motioning with his head to two other men   propped against the bar, their eyes fixed on the card game.

Although they moved with one accord toward him, their gaze lingered on the scene behind them. The girl yelped, trying to jerk her arm free, but the blond giant only tightened his grip, his fingers digging into her soft flesh.

"Jessica has just brought me some bad news, boys." Aaron growled.

"I haven't told you everything." She railed. "It's gonna cost you."

Aaron bent toward her crooning in her ear, while grabbing her other arm, "You forgotten who you're talking to. This is Aaron, remember?   The good times we've had?"

"What's she talking about, Aaron?" The taller of the two demanded.

"Seems like our esteemed little brother has arrived in town."

"Wha---How could that be possible? We left him to look after Pa. I'll have his hide if he let anything happen to our pa."

"More'n likely he came to see about us. Ain't the first time Papa's little saint tried to rescue us from our life of sin." A mirthless chuckle rumbled from Jim.

Aaron's face darkened and with a slight gesture toward the gaming table remarked, "If that's not a winning hand Simeon has, we've got a lot more to be rescued from than the quality of our lifestyle."

"W-what do you mean, Aaron?" Ben asked, his keen blue eyes pinioning Aaron's.

"If I'm not surprised, he's just---------." Aaron broke off suddenly at the cunning lights firing Jessica's eyes as she took in a conversation not meant for her ears.

Suddenly he flung her across the room where she landed in the lap of an appreciative seaman who grasped her tightly around the waist with one arm and grabbed her hair with the other to pull her head down for a sloppy kiss.

Grinding her sharp heel into his foot, Jessica managed to twist away from him. When he flinched in pain, she threw his arm away from her waist with one hand while administering a sharp slap to his face with the other, and screamed, "Why can't you stinking swabbies ever take a bath?"

Stunned, blood rushed to the sailor's face and he roared like a bull. Just as the sailor staggered to his feet, Aaron stepped between him and Jessica, a sly smile curling one side of his mouth, "Sorry, old fellow, I involved you in a fight with me girl. You know how it is now don't you?" Aaron winked knowingly, his voice smooth as silk. "She just took out her anger with me on you. She's quite a wench, you know."

The short stocky man took in the giant from head to foot before relenting, "So she's yore wench, eh?"

Aaron nodded.

"You'll be having a battle on your hands if you expect to tame the likes of her."

Aaron chuckled as his eyes slowly slid over Jessica from head to foot, "That's the fun of it, mate that's the fun of it."

His arm slowly captured Jessica and he pulled her to his side, holding her firmly against him. With the incident defused he moved back to his brothers, dragging her with him.

Ben frowned and Jim objected, "Aaron, we've got business to discuss that don't need her ears."

Aaron smiled down at the young woman still pinioned to his side; "Jessica's our friend. She's going to help us with our business. Now aren't you, honey?"

Defiance flared in her eyes as she retorted, "There is a price for my assistance."

Aaron answered, his voice silky smooth, but his eyes had turned the color of cold steel. "Now is that any way to treat a friend?"

"A friend?" Sarcasm laced Jessica's voice.

"Didn't I just save you from that sailor?"

"I didn't need you." She tossed her curls, hand on her hip.

"Then I'll just give you back to him." Aaron threatened.

Jessica stared into his eyes, taking his measure, "What do you want?"

"I want you to find that little brother of mine and

delay him."

"He's in the hotel and you know Sally won't let us go over there." Jessica objected.

"That's because Sal doesn't want to lose any of her business."

"Besides that little pip squeak at the desk won't allow it," she added.

Aaron's eyes slid over her like hot liquid, before his lip curled in a derisive smile. "And you can't tame the likes of him? Your charms must be failing, Darlin'."

A flush burned Jessica's face, the memory of Joel's rejection just outside in the warm night still stinging, "There's not a man alive I couldn't charm, Aaron Isaacs. I just don't want to make trouble for myself with Sal."

A grin broadened Aaron's full mouth and his blue eyes warmed. "I didn't know you and Sal were such good friends that you wouldn't want to offend her."

"Friends?" Jessica then growled as unwelcome memories tightened her lips, a slight shudder trembled her shoulders. "Not friends, you trail buster. Right now she's my only ticket out of this hole, and I don't want to mess my plans up by getting involved with the likes of your business."

"Never mind about Sal. You just do what I tell you."

"I guess you don't hear too good, Mr. Aaron Isaacs. I don't work for you, therefore I don't take my orders from you."

Aaron pulled her into him, his hand on her arm, twisting it behind her until she winced. "Darlin', now you know you'd rather work for me than anybody else. Besides, I'll make it right with Sal." He chuckled in her ear, "You know, Sal kinda has a soft spot fer me. I've seen it in those beady eyes of hers. All it'll take is a little sweet talk."

So Jessica's will buckled. She knew what Aaron said was true. All it took was for his handsome frame to swagger down the street and women inside and out of the brothels vied for his attention, hoping he'd pause and fix that vivid blue-eyed gaze on them, favoring them with his lazy smile. Although Jessica was not immune to his charms, her desire to escape was stronger. Now her heart pounded trying to decide her best course of action. So she shrugged as if the decision had been hers all along, "Guess it might be fun to fool that tenderfoot at the hotel." A smile spread across her scarlet lips suddenly as she found the game more appealing by the minute, plans spouted in her own mind. Plans that might help her as well as him.

Aaron gave her a long speculative look and suggested, "It wouldn't hurt you to change that dress and fix your hair different. Why, I bet you could look like a regular lady, if you'd just mind what you do with those eyes and that sashaying walk of yours."

"You trying to say I don't act like a lady?" Jessica smiled, and, thrusting one hip out, lowered her lashes.

Aaron chuckled, charm oiling his voice, "Honey, when a real man looks at you he doesn't care if he ever sees another lady."

"Even you, Aaron?" For a brief second, a wistful light softened the green fire in her eyes.

"Why me most of all, honey. Now you go get dressed."

Jessica chuckled beginning to warm to her task, "Just remember, a favor begets a favor."

Aaron turned her toward the door, giving her a little shove, "Be on your way, you've not much time."

As soon as she was out of hearing range, Jim demanded of Aaron, "Now tell us what's going on over there at that gaming table."

"If I'm not badly mistaken Simm has just wagered the last of the cattle money." Aaron explained his voice barely above a whisper.

"How did he get it?" Ben demanded. "You know Pa was counting on that money to buy a little spread somewhere."

"I went by the hotel safe to check on it and that dandy told me Mr. Simeon had already requested it. By the time I found him, he was in the middle of this game. We'll just have to hope his luck holds out."

"What luck? You know soon as he gets paid, he finds some poker game to lose it in." Ben sighed.

"This time seemed different, he won a pot yesterday. I reckon that's what egged him on."

"Aaron how can you be so calm about it?" Ben questioned while Jim just frowned, his eyes glued to his brother.

Aaron shrugged, "What could I do about it? We all have our weaknesses -- Jim likes his bottle and don't you have an eye for a pretty girl, Ben?"

"Me, Aaron? I don't hold a candle to the way you chase skirts."

"Me, chase skirts, Ben? Don't confuse the two of us. The difference between me and you, little brother, is I haven't seen a skirt yet I had to chase." Aaron reminded softly, his lip curled.

Ben clamped his jaws together, biting off his retort, "That's beside the point, Aaron."

"My point, brother, is, except for that saintly little half-brother of ours, I don't know a man alive that, come now and then, don't give in to a weakness."

"It'll kill Pa if Simeon loses his money." Ben exclaimed, his handsome face troubled

"It's not lost yet."

"And if it is, Aaron?" Ben pressed.

"Been thinkin'. We'll have to make up a story about how we never made it here. Could be we got attacked and they took the cattle. You know, we barely made it out alive. Maybe they took us captive and we had to escape. That's why it took us so long to get back. You know Pa heard all sorts of tales about how bands of rustlers were preying on the drovers. They kill all of 'em and take their cattle on to market. You know he wouldn't have even taken that chance except he needed the money so bad."

"If'n these outlaws kill the drovers, how come we escaped? You said they took us prisoner. That don't make a bit o' sense." Jim piped in, his attention finally captured.

Aaron smiled at his brother, "You're right, brother. Guess we had to play dead and they were in such a hurry, they left us."

"Then how come we're so late?"

"Simple. They took our horses. Now coming across that desert on foot takes a long time."

"If we could even make it," Ben drawled, his eyes doubting.

"Never mind the details. Pa will be so glad to see us, he won't even consider those."

"Without his money?"

"Sure. We'll start over in a new place. We'll just have to convince him that we'll help him to a good start. I was kinda getting little wanderlust anyhow. A routine day in and day out existence ain't the life for me. I need a little adventure in my life. I like to ride on new ground. All we have to do is convince Pa when we get back." Aaron persuaded.

"You're forgetting Joel."

Aaron frowned, irritation darkening his face, "That little trouble maker has never been anything but a thorn in our side since the day that he was born. The only good thing was that Indian woman up and died. Seems Pa can't see no good in anybody but that little varmint. He's made a difference between us and him all his life."

"But Aaron, don't you think it was because he was such a little shaver when his mother died?" Ben asked, his face troubled.

"No, the truth of the matter was our Pa loved her more than he did our ma." Jim sided with Aaron

"Even if he did, he didn't just set out to love her more. Anyways what determines how much you love somebody? Don't it just happen? " Ben argued.

"But she was an Indian, Ben." Jim insisted.

"Is that why you hated her, Aaron?" Ben asked, turning to his older brother.

"Yes, and her little half-breed, too."

"Why?" Ben insisted.

"Don't you remember the way people looked at us? They probably called Pa a squaw man. That's what he was. She ruled his life, didn't give us any time with him." Jim chimed in.

"Jim, she was a good and decent woman who treated us with kindness."

"I hated the airs she put on because she could read and write, said she learned it at the mission. And all the time praying, as if God would hear her, an Indian married to a white man." Aaron added, bitterness darkening his face.

"Aaron!"

"All I regret is when she died that little runt didn't go with her."

"And you hate Joel like you did her!" Ben accused. "Why?"

"He stole pa's attention that rightfully belonged to us. You never saw him seeing to it that we got educated like the runt has. No ciphering and reading wuzn't even enough, it had to be the classics, whatever that is, and such." Jim piped in defending Aaron.

"Now wait just a minute, Jim. Pa tried to get us to like that stuff and all we wanted was hunting, riding, shooting and fishing."

"Made a man out of us didn't it? Look at how that runt turned out. He don't even know how to have fun. I bet if Jessica sidled up to him out in the dark, it'd scare the britches off him." Jim laughed at the thought. "And as for holding his liquor, I doubt he's even had some."

Ben snickered, "He's still young, yet. Give him time."

Aaron stared at Ben, his blue eyes cold, "I believe you're taking up for that little wimp."

"Yea, Ben. You sound like an Injun lover." Jim agreed, adding. "People here will throw you out on your ear if they know yo're kin to an Injun."

Aaron pursed his lips and corrected primly, "Indian, Jim, the word is Indian. Now you wouldn't want to appear uneducated."

Jim responded, "Injun, Indian, I don't care, the problem now ain't what to call him but what we are going to do with him if Simm looses Pa's money. That tale you made up ain't gonna hold water when that half-breed gets back and tells what he knows."

"Then he just won't get back." Aaron shot back.

"And how are you gonna manage that, Brother?" Jim drawled, his cornflower blue eyes unbelieving.

"Kill him."

Ben gasped and even Jim gulped as he responded, "Now, whoa, Aaron, I don't hold to that. Murder could get us a California collar, and my neck don't feel like getting stretched."

"We won't kill him. We'll have him killed carry his bloody clothes back to Pa and claim we found him , or what was left of him, in the desert between here and there. He'll just assume an Indian done it."

"An Injun, er, Indian killing an Injun? Do they do that?" Jim wrinkled his forehead, perplexed.

"Are you plumb crazy, Jim? Nobody knows he's half Indian. With that pale skin and dark curly hair, he looks more like a Frenchy. Anyway, Indians, don't ask for identity papers before they scalp you."

"I won't go along with killing him, Aaron." Ben stated crossing his arms.

"Just because you're the youngest one of our ma's kids do you have to be the dumbest?" Aaron hurled, his eyes icy blue daggers, "Can't you understand that it's either him or us?"

"Maybe it won't have to go that far. Just maybe

Simm won't lose this time." Jim suggested his eyes uneasy.

A loud commotion erupted from the corner as the tabled toppled and Simm shouted, "You cheat, there's no way you could have beat my hand."

An ominous quiet followed. The click of a pistol hammer shattered the silence and a smooth voice responded, "Would you like to accuse me again?"

Simm's eyes, bloodshot and wide with terror, turned to Aaron who spoke for him, "My brother is a little overwrought from too much ale and not enough sleep, will you overlook his insult?"

The trim stranger smiled beneath his mustache and picked up his black sombrero, never lowering his gun. "If he apologizes, all will be forgotten." Then turned eyes like flint on Simm.

Aaron stepped forward, "Apologize to the man, Simm."

Simm nodded a reluctant head and muttered an unintelligible apology.

The handsome stranger chuckled and picked up his winnings, "Apology accepted".

Three pairs of blue eyes impaled Simm's as the full realization of what he had done permeated his consciousness. He closed his eyes and shuddered.

CHAPTER 2

Aaron awaited Jessica outside the garish green and gold brothel. Had he not expected her to walk through the door, he would have failed to recognize the demure beauty in a green merino, her flaming red hair, under control caught up in a fashionable chignon and held in place by silk netting the color of her dress.

Aaron's approving whistle softly parted the damp night air. And Jessica whirled around in a graceful circle, stopping in front of him in a deep curtsy.

Despite the worry that burdened him, he smiled at her transformation.

"Where did you borrow that dress?"

"It's mine." She snapped.

He quirked one amused eyebrow, "How did you get it?"

Jessica pulled her shawl tightly around her and dropped her head, shielding her eyes from him. She murmured. "I bought it."

"Whatever for?" Aaron's eyes twinkled in the light from the window as he reached for her.

Jessica pulled herself to her full height, her body rigid to his advances. "I thought I might need it someday. And seems I do, wouldn't you say?"

Aaron sensing her anger, erased the amusement from his face and countered seriously, "Why you look like a church marm, Jessica."

"A church Marm?"

"A young matron on her way to worship," He explained, his tone disarming, all teasing vanished.

"I wouldn't know how that felt," She countered. "Like at the hotel, I figured I wouldn't be welcome."

"It's just as well. A life like that would be too dull for the likes of you."

"What makes you so sure?"

"You were made for the pleasure of many men, my lovely."

"To be used, you mean."

"You would get bored with one man

"Not if he loved me. Hidden away in every girl's heart is the dream to be really loved by one man."

"Even a girl like you?"

"Especially a girl like me." A wistful tone crept over the usual brittleness in her voice.

"Maybe it will happen for you some day, Jessica." Aaron's tone threaded with tenderness.

"What about you, Aaron?"

"Haven't given it much thought."

"That's because you've mistaken temporary pleasure for happiness. Problem is that doesn't last more'n a few minutes."

"It's always been enough for me."

"Someday you'll need a woman. I mean a whole person, not just a body to use and discard. You might even need a woman to love you."

"Me? Need a woman? It's women who need men." He laughed derisively while his voice faltered, some of the usual certainty missing.

"You need me tonight, don't you?"

"Well, yeah."

"We'd make a handsome couple." She observed, her eyes large and liquid in the soft lantern light.

Aaron started to laugh at the absurdity of it, and then thought better, "Intriguing thought, Jessica. You are quite beautiful and dressed up in that soft green dress buttoned up to your chin. Who would ever know the trade you've plied? But what if we ran into one of your customers? That would ruin your little game."

"We could move far away." Jessica suggested, a half-smile playing at the corner of her mouth.

"That's a possibility, but before I can even plan my future, I have to rid myself of an inconvenience."

"Your brother?"

"You're smart as well as beautiful," He exclaimed placing his hand beneath her chin and lifting her eyes to his before placing a gentle kiss on her full scarlet lips.

"What do you want me to do?" She asked against his lips.

"I need a gun." He smiled, still holding her chin in his hand.

"You have one."

"I don't mean mine, I mean someone I can hire."

Her green eyes widened in the darkness and she stepped away from him, "You want to kill your brother?"

"Of course I don't want to kill him, it's just come down to his life or mine. He's come to take me back to hang for a crime I didn't commit." Aaron lied.

"Why would your brother do that?" Doubt darkened her eyes.

"Because he's not my real brother and he hates me." Aaron spat out, his bitterness making the lie seem true.

"That's not what he told me. He seemed like a nice fellow, maybe a little straight laced" She chuckled as she remembered Joel's discomfort outside the cantina. "I think I scared him."

"Naw, you didn't scare him. That's part of his act. He's a wily one. Comes across as a saint, but he's not. I wouldn't be surprised if he killed that drifter himself just so he could pin it on me."

"Why does he hate you?" Jessie pressed.

Aaron's pulse raced, frantic to find the believable lie, "Because our father has always loved me best. He's got a powerful jealous streak in him."

"But do you have to kill him?" She resisted in the soft light, her mind exploring an alternative that would be good for him and provide a solution for her.

"What else could I do?" He shrugged; his eyes pleading and vulnerable, melted the last vestige of Jessie's resistance.

"Send him far away." She murmured, her countenance uneasy as if she had said too much.

"But how?" Aaron frowned, puzzling at what she meant.

"Maybe you'd better handle getting rid of your brother. I don't think I want to help a man who wants to do away with his brother." She dropped her head as if considering while her heart thundered.

Aaron took her hand and crooned, "Jessica, darling, I told you how he is. It's my life or his."

She shook her head, looking down so he couldn't see her eyes, the eagerness firing them "No, I don't want any part of it."

"But you just said we might not have to kill him." Aaron reminded.

"And I said too much." She answered, her voice crisp, turning back toward the doorway.

Aaron grabbed her arm and jerked her around, "You listen to me, you little trollop, you promised to help me, and help me you will or else."

Her eyes widened in the soft light and she

whispered, "Or else what?"

"You figure it out, and start with the fact you know too much." He threatened, his blue eyes cold as steel.

She jerked her arm free, defiance in every line of her body, "Don't threaten me, Aaron. You won't get my help that way."

"Oh, you've changed your mind? You'll help me?" His voice persuasive, his eyes hard, his mouth fixed in a tight smile.

"Maybe I'll help your brother. You know I could turn the table on you, Aaron. Say he wants you real bad? Yeah, maybe I'll just help him." Her eyes narrowed, a smile played at the corner of her mouth as she watched the tension in Aaron mount. She was enjoying the game. It felt good to be in control, watch a man squirm for a change. Then she added, her sultry voice suggestive, "Maybe there's a reward, I could use the money. Maybe earn me a little nest egg to help me get away from this place."

Aaron started to reach for her again and then dropped his hand while a slow, seductive smile lifted the corner of his mouth, his eyes moving down her body, his voice persuasive, "Now, little one, you and I both know Joel ain't the man for you. Remember? This is Aaron you're talking to." And he moved in and took her in his arms, his hands moving down her back, pressing her to him.

She pushed against him with both hands, but he held her in his powerful grip. Bending his head down he nuzzled her neck and whispered, "You do fire up a man, my little beauty."

She resisted, jerking her head away.

Aaron chuckled and placed her hand over his heart, "Now see what you do to me?"

Jessica closed her eyes, "Don't try to play with me, Aaron."

"Believe me, I'm not playing, honey. You think I could make my heart thunder like that?"

"Maybe fear could." She suggested.

"Or excitement?" Aaron countered.

"Whatever it is, we have an issue to settle here." She reminded, standing firm.

"And that is?" He whispered, his lips near her ear.

"Am I going to help you with your brother?"

"Are you?" He crooned, his fingertip tracing her pert, turned up nose.

"I don't know." She twisted her head away and leaned back in his arms, a cold smile on her lips.

"What do you mean by that? You trying to tease me, Jessica? I'm a man with a big problem. What you and me are discussing is a matter of life and death with me. You mean you don't want to save my life?" his voice syrupy.

"I don't believe that cock and bull story you told me about your brother. The man I met didn't resemble the one you described to me."

"Seeing him one time out there in the dark and you think you know him."

"I know you, Aaron. Your tales fit your needs."

"Then I guess what it boils down to, is do you want to help me or my brother? Who's more important to you?"

She twisted away from him and turned as if to go back into the building, flinging over her shoulder, "The question is which would benefit me more."

He reached for her and she slipped beneath his fingers. She lifted her skirts gracefully and bounded up the steps, Aaron right behind her. When she reached the top, she turned toward him, her eyes eye level with his. Green sparks flashed from hers in the light filtering beneath the half doors just above her. "What's in it for me, Aaron?"

"What do you mean? You know I'm about broke. Whatever I have I'll have to pay whoever we get to take care of the problem."

"Maybe it's not your money I want." The plans that had been racing bits and pieces through her mind crystallized and she could scarcely restrain the triumphant smile that played around her lips, rioting within her and turning her eyes to green fire.

"What then?" He hesitated, sensing the change in her. A touch of fear melted the ice in his eyes, threatening his arrogant façade. For one brief moment Jessie saw the real Aaron and he touched her woman's heart.

Resisting the unwelcome emotions he stirred in her and knowing her future was at stake, she answered quietly, determination lacing her voice, "Your name."

"My what?" He all but shouted

"Marry me. Take me away from this life, give me a home and respectability. I can make you happy, and if not happy, at least safe from your brother. "

"I'm a little young, yet." He disclaimed.

"You must be at least twenty-four. That's old enough for a good size family. Fact is you're late getting' started."

"What about love?" He hedged, grasping for anything that might dissuade her, his heart hammering inside his chest at the very thought.

"Love will come later. Respect and a future are what I want now."

"Respect? You?" Aaron laughed.

Green fire from her eyes impaled him, "That's the bargain, take it or leave it."

He took a deep breath and let it out slowly as if considering her conditions. Then he bargained, attempting a delay. "O.K. but first help me with my problem."

"Your problem will not be solved until I become Mrs. Aaron Isaacs."

Aaron sighed, his hands dropping to his sides in defeat, "Do they have a preacher here?"

"A padre just outside of town."

"Come on let's go." He said, resignation in his voice.

"No, I want a proper wedding." she insisted.

"Then when will we take care of my problem? I'm in a hurry. I have an ailing father waiting for me."

"You haven't been in a hurry so far so a few more days won't matter. Anyway I thought the law was after you at home."

"Uh, er, no. Joel wasn't going to take me home. He was going to take me back to Missouri. That's why we came to Wyoming; my dad was trying to protect me. Joel tracked us down."

"So there, there's no reason you can't wait until I have a proper wedding."

"First you tell me what your solution is." He demanded, growing tired of the charade.

"I won't help you murder your brother."

"What else is there?" He asked, irritation raising his voice.

"Let's just say it won't cost you any money."

"How?"

"There's a lot going on at Sal's besides appealing to man's baser pleasures."

"Yea, what?"

"Ships need men, men don't always want to go to sea. There's a lot of persuasion going on in her cellar."

"You mean get him shanghaied?"

"I'm admitting nothin'." She lowered her voice. "It's something that we don't talk about. Not good for our health."

"Why you little devil."

Jessica shook her head, "I haven't participated in that action yet. 'Course if anybody really bothered me, then he might wake up on his way to China."

"Maybe I'll just deal with Sal direct." Aaron threatened

"Ha! You deal with Sal direct and you'll find yourself on a boat. I'm your only solution."

"How do they work it?"

"Some of the girls entice 'em, drug' em and off to sea they go. They don't even know what hit them till they're out of sight of land."

"You'll never get Joel in there."

"All the more reason you need me."

"You think you can entice him?"

"Don't underestimate me." Jessica flinched as thoughts of Joel's earlier rejection stung her memory. The thought of revenge left a pleasant taste in her mouth, not to mention the coins in her pocket she would demand from Sal. They would be a kind of insurance if things didn't work out with Aaron. She continued explaining vaguely. "Enticing him is not my plan. It is a bit more complicated, but fool proof. However, it depends on your going through with our agreement."

"I'm not sure I like the plan----about shanghaiing

him. I'll always be in danger of his showing up again. If I know he's shut up for good then I could rest easy."

"Those sailors are gone a long time. Many of them don't survive."

"I guess I could move Pa somewhere he'll never find us. Leave without a trace. Fact is, we won't have a place to return to because Sim lost the money Pa was going to use to buy us a spread." Aaron mused, his hand stroking his chin.

"This is a big country, a lot of places to hide." A touch of yearning threaded her sultry voice.

"Yeah, maybe the Seattle area." He stepped up to the step where she perched, his tall frame towering over her and placed both hands lightly on her small shoulders.

"Maybe Oregon?" She asked breathlessly.

"Opportunities are breaking out there."

A subdued excitement now captured Aaron's voice.

"For me and for you. Sounds good leaving our past behind." She murmured, her eyes dreamy. Her brittle facade breached for a moment.

"How can we do it?"

"Go to Oregon?" Jessica asked, her eyes puzzled.

"No, get Joel into Sal's."

"The girls will give us a little party after our wedding, then we'll drop something in his punch and the rest will be history. You'll be minus one brother and

I'll have one husband."

"So what about tonight? You going over to eat with him?"

"Changed my plans. Why don't you go to the hotel and tell him the good news?"

Aaron looked doubtful.

"He won't grab you before you get married. Tell him to grant you a little time with your bride." She laughed at Aaron's expression.

He grinned and nodded. "Guess he'll be so surprised to hear about me marryin' that he probably would delay the trip. Long as he knew he could keep an eye on me."

"Sure he will, now you run on, I've got to plan my wedding." She exclaimed and, reaching up on tiptoe took his face between her small-gloved hands and kissed his lips, murmuring against them, "You'll be happy that you married me, Aaron Isaacs, just you wait and see."

In the darkness she felt his body stiffen and strain away from her.

Joel slipped into the dim, coolness of the mission and took a seat on the last row of rough sawn benches, now polished to a rich patina from human use. He leaned his head against the tall back and closed his eyes, trying to sort out the thoughts and feelings that tumbled through his mind. His body was still tired from yesterday's long ride and his bones ached from the precarious sleep on a bedroll in Calaban's stall last night. However his less than desirable lodgings hadn't hindered his sleep as much as the astounding news his brother had given him.

Aaron, getting married? He still couldn't believe it, but maybe that was just the thing his brother needed to settle him down. Given the right woman, many a man had abandoned his errant ways. Anyways that's what Pa had told him. Said it had taken a good woman to put him on the straight and narrow.

Thinking of Pa, Joel smiled. This would be good news to him. He'd wanted to see his sons married and families on the way before he died. However, relief battled with apprehension for control of Joel's mind. That courtship had been the reason for his brother's delay eased his mind some; yet the whole business seemed out of character for Aaron. Joel grew anxious to meet the girl that could capture his brother in any kind of permanent commitment. Maybe if he met her, then he'd understand. He sighed, there was nothing to do but wait. And maybe nap.

Voices intruded and he opened his eyes with a start. He had drifted off. Light filtered in from the open door at the side of the altar and an old wizened padre entered, dressed in a drab robe. Behind him came

Aaron with Jim, who would be standing up with him as best man. The door slammed, blown by a stiff western breeze, only to be opened by Simm followed by Ben whose head turned toward a woman at his side.

Joel strained to get a better look but now she was in the midst of the men and all he could see was the back of an ivory dress and a lace scarf covering the woman's hair and shielding her face. He sighed. Soon enough he'd get to meet this miracle worker first hand and then maybe he'd understand the source of her magic.

Her voice was low and musical, strangely familiar to Joel as she vowed her love and faithfulness to the man at her side. Aaron's voice, rather strained and subdued, sounded altogether different from the blustery confidence he normally conveyed. Joel smiled to himself and thought, "Well ole' Aaron is entering uncharted waters for him, must be an unnerving experience. I just hope the filly is up to the task."

An awkward silence greeted the Padre's last words as the bridal party stood transfixed, not knowing what to do next. Then the young woman turned toward Aaron and Ben laughed, "Well, dummy, kiss your bride before I do it for you."

Jim snickered and reached for her, "Here, Aaron, I'll show ye how a real man does it."

Aaron glared at him and knocked his hands away from the girl, "You keep your hands to yourself, Jim Issacs. No other man is gonna go pawing my wife."

Jim's eyebrows lifted in surprise and he stammered, "Well jest saying them words in front of this here padre, don't change what's she's been."

Aaron leaned across the girl, grabbing Jim's arm, and spoke between tight lips, "But it changes who she is, and don't you, Simm, or Ben ever forget that fact."

Suddenly a shaft of sunlight spilled through the high round opening above the altar bathing the young woman in a shimmering radiance as she turned toward her new husband, her soft full lips parted to receive his kiss.

And Joel groaned inwardly as her scarf drifted to the floor.

"Well, Brother Joel, what do you think of your old married brother, now. About time I settled down, eh?" Aaron quizzed Joel, a strange light in his eyes.

Joel nodded his head even while nausea churned his insides.

"Don't you think she's a pretty little wench?" Aaron nodded toward the punch bowl where Jessica laughed and talked with a bejeweled woman whose heavy set body appeared captured in a green satin gown designed for another time and another place.

"I had no doubt that the woman you married would be pretty." Joel agreed as his eyes took in her beauty from across the room.

And beautiful she was. A radiant happiness seemed to eradicate the earthy sensuousness he had encountered the night before. She looked vulnerable and no older than he. Joel marveled at the transformation, wondering what events had brought her to this moment in her life.

"You think Pa'll approve?" Aaron's voice cut through Joel's musings.

"Approve?" Joel hedged.

"Me getting married."

"He's wanted you to settle down for a long time, Aaron."

"Yep. Reckon it's time I started some young ones running around him." Aaron looked pleased with himself, anticipating their papa's reaction.

Joel nodded, "He has wanted some grandchildren."

"And I'm just the one to give him what he needs." Aaron's broad chest swelled with the thought of his own importance.

"And the cattle drive, Aaron? How did that go? Pa would be especially proud to have a ranch for his grandchildren to grow up on."

The smile plastered across Aaron's face faltered and Joel caught a hint of alarm in his brother's bright blue eyes, "Don't you worry about that, little brother, I'm taking care of things for Pa. That's what an oldest son is for."

"He's sick and worried about you, Aaron. You've been gone so long."

"I know, I know, but when he sees my little Jessie,

he'll forget all about that worry. You know a guy can't go courting in a half a day's time."

"But you could have sent Ben, Jim and Simeon on home with the money." Joel insisted.

"Me send them off by themselves?" Aaron drawled. "You know, little brother, you and I are the only ones in the family with a dab of sense. Why if it weren't for the two of us, Pa'd be in a heap of trouble."

Joel shivered inwardly but replied pleasantly, "I guess you have a point, Aaron."

Aaron pummeled Joel on the back. "Sure I do, now come on over and meet my lil' bride."

Joel moved with the blond giant across the room, "I can hardly wait." And he realized he meant it.

Jessica looked up into Joel's eyes, amusement firing green sparks in hers, "So this is your 'little brother', Aaron. I can't believe so many handsome men came from one family." A dimple teased her cheek in an innocent smile as if last night had never happened.

Aaron's face darkened in a mock frown, "Now, little gal, you're a married woman and you mind you keep those compliments for your husband."

Jessica lifted her head, a challenge in her green eyes, "But, darling, you don't go blind when you get married."

Aaron stepped closer to her, his height dwarfing her petite frame, "As long as you're my wife you'll not go admiring another man, not even my brothers."

Joel sensed the threat in his words and feared

her response. Surprised, he watched her as she turned those glorious eyes to her husband, an inward radiance sparkling from them and whispered, "That will be my life's pleasure."

Suddenly Joel realized that this woman loved his brother and an uncanny fear for her gripped his heart.

Aaron patted her arm saying, "Why don't you get better acquainted with my brother, Jessica, while I make our guest feel welcome." With that he headed for a bevy of laughing girls surrounding the punch bowl.

"I'm amazed." Jessica whispered.

Joel quirked one eyebrow, questioningly.

"That you've kept your peace." She explained.

"I only make trouble when it's necessary."

Now it was her turn to throw a questioning glance his way.

"You're married. That's a fact, I would do nothing to cause trouble in a marriage. Besides I assume he is aware of who you are." Joel explained.

"Were." She corrected.

"Were?" Joel questioned.

"I'm Jessica Isaacs, wife of Aaron Isaacs. Jessica Walters is behind me, dead as far as I'm concerned. Unless you wish to make an issue out of it."

"Why should I make an issue of it? Your life and Aaron's life are your concern, not mine."

"I wish I could believe you."

"Believe it. I only want what's best for you, him and our entire family."

A brittle laugh washed away the former radiance as she looked at him with hard eyes. "Don't pretend with me, little Joel. Aaron's told me why you're here."

"What has he told you?"

"That you've come to take him back."

Joel frowned, not understanding how he had raised her ire, "Well, in a manner of speaking, I have."

She leaned in to him, her green eyes like daggers, "Understand this, you will no longer ruin my husband's life."

"I? Ruin Aaron's life?" Incredulity creased his forehead and he leaned back against the wall, crossing his arms.

"He's told me all about you."

"And what might that be?"

"Don't play innocent with me. I can see through you."

"You can?"

"Aaron told me how charming you could be. But understand this, I see through your charm and I will protect my husband at any cost."

Joel threw back his head as laughter rolled unimpeded from deep within him, "You're going to protect Aaron from me?"

"And you'll leave him alone," Jessica insisted

Joel sighed, completely mystified, "Jessica, I couldn't think of anything I'd relish more than to leave him in your exclusive care so I can get on with my life."

As if a curtain had suddenly fallen on her anger, a half-smile parted her full lips, revealing perfect, even teeth. "Is that a bargain?"

Joel shook his head, a relieved sigh issuing from him, "Lady, that's a bargain I'd relish."

She looked up into his face, a cunning charm on hers, "Aaron won't let us seal it with a kiss, so how about a cup of punch instead?"

CHAPTER 3

Joel's stomach churned with the roll and the pitch of the hard planks beneath him, while pains, dagger sharp pierced his head. He sat up slowly, his hands to his head. A heavy darkness permeated with the smell of sweat and tar closed in about him.

He shook his head and the pain exploded, just as the floor took a sharp rise before the bottom fell out from under him. In the darkness he heard a moan, a thump, then retching. His own queasy insides threatened to follow suit and he placed a restraining hand over his mouth. He attempted to lean up against something stable enough to brace himself against the strange rocking and reeling of his dark prison.

Instead he encountered soft, cold flesh and he knew whoever was behind him, would have no worries about his whereabouts. Above the fetish odors assaulting his nostrils, Joel smelled the sea and he knew where he was-------locked in the belly of a ship somewhere at sea. But where? How? The last thing he remembered was toasting Aaron's bride with a strange tasting punch. Understanding dawned and he groaned.

A door creaked and a dim lantern parted the darkness above him. He saw a ladder and the outline of a lumbering body climbed down followed by a wiry, short form who walked with a limp.

Joel squinted as the lantern swung before his eyes. A raspy voice spoke in the darkness behind the light as a boot nudged his leg, "This'n be awake, he is. And a mighty fine looking lad. Look at the shoulders on him, would ye mate?" One invisible voice spoke to the other.

"Looks like we made a fine haul of manpower, and we'll be needing it on this long trip. Especially if'n the Santa Rosa catches up with us." A chuckle parted the gloom behind the lantern, "Wonder what those boys thought when they got back to those hides they had stored and they wuz gone?" The burly sailor boomed.

"A business, I tell you true, I don't be liking. If'n I'd known the cap'n's intentions, I'd ne'er have signed on board." The wiry sailor answered in a hoarse whisper.

"Ye'd have signed on all right, jest like these dumb blokes did. With or without yer permission. That's the way our cap'n carries on his affairs. He gets what he wants. You'll see him in action if'n the Santa Rosa catches up to us."

"Shut pan. That's nothing we need be discussing right now." The wiry man warned as the circle of light illumined Joel's alert eyes.

"Don't shush me, they'll know soon a plenty what their role will be."

"That tankard of ale you guzzled has loosed your tongue."

"Twarn't a tankard of ale and you know it. 'Twas no more than our daily ration of rum."

"Yeah, yours and four more to boot, I watched you giving it out. You cheated the men and drank it yourself." The smaller man accused.

"Ah, Jim, me boy, you know some of those guys can't handle their cup and you don't want yours so I jest helped them out a wee bit. "

"Hmp! Helping them out like Sam Hill, you were. But that be yore problem, as fer me I don't care what you be doing with me portion. All I want is to get me time in and get off this ship and its chicanery."

"Ah, it ain't so bad, mate. If'n you do what the cap'n says and stay out'n his way when he's a havin' one of his bad days."

"What you like is there's plenty of rum. Now me, I'm different. There was a time when I could take pride in going to sea. To see a ship cutting through the waters, her white sails full of the wind with her deck scrubbed, her bright work polished and gleaming in the sunlight is a sight prettier than any woman I ever saw. But to serve on this pig sty with a cap'n whose not interested in anything but wine, women, and ill gotten gold, takes the pride right out'n a man."

"Careful, Jim, me boy. That sounds like mutinous talk to me."

"Abe, I ain't one to mutiny. If I signed on with a cap'n then I'll be his man 'til I get off, even if'n I don't like the way the ship's run."

"Then why you aboard?" The raspy voice asked.

"Cause of this gimpy leg. No one else would hire me 'cept as a cook, and I'd die stuck down in the galley or forecastle, never feeling the excitement of a good blow."

"Well, you'll be getting plenty of that when we go 'round the horn."

"So they say. The cap'n said to check the cargo and the men and we'd best be doing our job." Jim reminded with sigh. "Uh O, this'n gone to meet his maker. It'll be the sack and over board for him. Then I reckon you expect to have a few losses."

"Eh, the Cap'n Donner don't hold to wasting his money. Sal'll be hearing about this 'un. Me and the cap'n told her only the healthy ones could make it around the Horn. He'll be demanding his money back, he will." And then Abe snickered, adding, "And maybe a little something to boot."

"All right mates, be up and about. Ye're sailors now so go mid ship and get you some gruel and proper clothes before ye start your four on and four off."

"I didn' sign up fer no tour o duty, and I ain't gonna work," came a garrulous growl from the far corner.

Joel watched as the lantern bobbed away from him and lifted high to bathe a dark bearded man in drovers' clothes in a ring of light. A malevolent chuckle issued from the sailor holding the lantern and he leaned down, the light catching a toothless grin in a round moon face, "Say ye ain't a working, eh? Well, just where bouts do you think ye'll be sleeping and eatin'? Tis a long way to Boston and too far too swim back to California. Ye'll work or die. You make the choice."

The cowboy muttered something Joel couldn't hear and Abe issued a quick kick to the man's groin, doubling him up. "Ye sees what's good fer ye now. The rest of ye who's awake, follow the light to the foc'l, that'll be where you eat and sleep from now on. A good bowl of gruel and bread will settle that belly of yors. Sal's paradise punch does have its lingering effects."

Jessica tied the scarf that draped her hat and pulled it over as much of her face as it would cover. A merciless sun beat down on her and her backside felt callused, but she never complained. She was leaving San Diego and Sally's Palace behind and that was enough for her.

When her mother died, her drunken father abandoned her at twelve years old. Hungry and penniless, she had made her way to San Diego which was little more than a few saloons and a brothel. The first door she knocked on was Sally's. Sal had needed a dishwasher and someone to get the cook stove burning in the mornings so she took in the undernourished waif. She gave Jessica a bed by the stove in the kitchen so she would be near her chores along with three good meals a day. It was the first time in months that the young girl slept warm and free from hunger.

Soon the nourishing meals and regular baths began to have their affect on her. By the time she was thirteen her body had the roundness of a woman full grown and Sal graduated her from kitchen to parlor. The old proprietress perceived in her budding beauty a rare quality that reflected a certain refinement somewhere in her bloodline and knew she had a potential gold mine in the young girl. Dressing Jessica in fine silks, the older woman taught her to walk with grace and bearing. The aging madam taught her young innocent pupil the unlikely art of being a lady. When she had learned that, she taught her the art of seduction.

Sal kept her on display until her fourteenth birthday and then she sent her upstairs to an elegantly prepared room, which showcased her beauty. It was there, within those four walls that Jessica, little more than a child, learned the harsh reality of a demanding world. With her lost innocence went any misplaced gratitude toward Sal for taking her in.

When she resisted Sal's plans, she found that her benefactor's only concern was the return she could receive on her investment. At fourteen and no where to turn, the young girl's only option was to fulfill her employer's expectations. She closed her mind to the things her body had to do and locked her heart against any emotions that might intrude. Meanwhile she bided her time until she could escape.

Now her time had come. The ticket away from her past stood in the stirrups of his mighty horse on the hill just above her, his hands shielding his eyes. He stared toward the horizon and their destiny.

The hot breeze parched her lips, her eyes burned from the glare but she squinted, looking up at her husband. She pulled her shawl tightly around her shoulders and shivered. She knew he had shortcomings--- that marriage was not something he relished. Perhaps he even had a mean streak in him. Her eyes softened as they feasted on the man in whom she had placed all her hopes. Perhaps it would take time but she'd tame that stallion to be content with the joys of home and hearth. A smile parted her full mouth, now dry from the unremitting wind. Suddenly hope stirred a strange tenderness in a heart that she had thought securely garrisoned against any such sentiment.

Jessica kicked her little buckskin mare and rode up beside Aaron. "How much further do you think it will be?"

"Not as many miles as it has been. I think we'll hole up tonight on the other side of that draw. If my memory serves me right, there's a river and a nice watering hole for the horses."

"Maybe I could take a bath?"

Aaron looked at her and chuckled, "You could use a bath."

She laughed, "Speak for yourself, mister."

"Yeah, guess we all could do with a little of this grime off us. Perhaps we'll relax tomorrow, take it easy and such." He looked at her knowingly.

"I thought this was purely a business arrangement for you." Jessica responded, a sly smile turning one side of her mouth upwards.

"What's wrong with mixing a little business and pleasure?"

"Is there some reason you don't relish getting back to your Pa?" She asked as an afterthought. "I thought once we took care of Joel you would be anxious to get home. That is what you told me anyway."

Angry sparks danced in Aaron's eyes and he clenched his jaw, "The delay was merely to show you some consideration. This is a tough trip for a woman."

A half-smile played around Jessica's lips, her eyes not believing him, "Forgive me dear, for being so suspicious."

Aaron nodded his head and grunted something unintelligible just as Ben rode up.

"Why we dallying, Aaron? You know Pa's worried about us."

Jessica giggled and Aaron frowned like a thundercloud

"Well, he'll just have to worry. He'll understand plenty when he sees my little lady."

"But what if'n he's done gone and died whilst we've been gone?" Jim piped up beside Ben.

"Then there's nothing we can do to bring him back to life, now is there? Might as well take our time." Aaron drawled.

"Yea, we can see why you want to take some time, Aaron." Simeon teased as he ogled Jessica.

"A man's got a right to a little time with his wife."

"Why you sound like an old married man already." Jim observed with a snicker.

"You know. No woman's going to dictate to me or change the way I live."

"I bet if she has anything to do with it you'll have a bit and bridle on you before you can say jack rabbit." Jim laughed.

Ben, recognizing the dangerous glitter in Aaron's eye, intervened smoothly, "Lot of benefits to having a wife and ain't nothing wrong with settlin' down. Pa'll be proud you did."

"Yeah, that's why I did it." Aaron responded, his anger diffused.

Jessica's green eyes flashed but she held her tongue.

"Time you boys found you a wife." Ben said.

"Us? What about you?" Jim and Simeon croaked

in unison

"I'm a little young yet, but soon's I find one as pretty as Jessica, I will." Ben smiled encouragingly to Jessica who returned his smile.

Jim opened his mouth to comment, then looked at Aaron's thunderous face and thought better of it.

"Come on. We're wasting time, jawing like this." Simeon observed as he dug his heels in his mount and galloped off.

The small river that cascaded down the mountain proved a perfect oasis for them. Before long Simeon had the campfire burning and Jessica prepared a pot of coffee. When Ben brought in some fish he had caught from the stream, Jim offered to roast them and supper proved both delicious and festive. The earlier tension had dissipated in the cool of the evening. When Aaron and Jessica slipped away for a bath in the pool downstream, not one ribald remark was heard. Ben hiked upstream while Jim and Simeon rolled out their bedrolls.

Aaron reclined in the soft grass beside the stream; his head propped in his hand and watched his wife through half-closed, lazy eyes. Jessica bent forward and twisted her hair, wringing the excess water from it. She took a wide tooth comb from the pocket of her skirt and sat down next to Aaron. She smiled and leaned back against him, snuggling into the curve of his body. She began to comb her long red tresses and Aaron reached for her. His hand moved in a gentle caress up her back until it reached her wet cascading locks. Looping her damp curls one by one around his fingers, he smoothed each before he captured another. A sense of satisfaction spread over her like a warm blanket.

After a moment his hand moved to the base of her head and his fingers tightened in her hair. He pulled her head back across his chest, her face turned toward his. He sat up, holding her tightly against him. Their eyes locked and Jessica lifted her arms and pulled her husband's head down to her.

Twilight was falling and the clear gurgling stream sang a sweet refrain. Wood smoke from their supper fire drifted down stream, teasing Jessica's nostrils as she lay nestled in the curve of her husband's arms. She turned toward him and traced his lips with her fingertips. He roused from the gentle sleep that had claimed him and looked at her, a question in his eyes.

"Tell me about your Pa, Aaron. And the ranch."

"Pa? I guess he's just like most pas. He's getting old and worries about his kids."

Jessica murmured under her breath. "Not like my pa."

"Your Pa?" Aaron asked, a puzzled frown on his face.

"Yeah, my good for nothing Pa. He never worried

about anybody but himself." Jessica explained, then sat up and leaned against the tree, pulling a shawl around her and crossing her arms. Her face tensed as unpleasant memories intruded.

"Pa's all the time thinking about his kids." Aaron explained.

"That must be wonderful." Her lips parted in a smile that didn't reach her eyes as she struggled to push the pictures of her drunken father from her mind.

"Wish he wouldn't get so all fired up worrying about us," Jessica's husband remarked, a faraway look in his eyes.

"Why?"

"Cause he interferes with the way I want to live my life." Aaron sat up and pulled her back into the circle of his arms.

"That's just because he cares about you." She smiled up at him, and lifted a hand to caress his cheek.

"Well, maybe. All the same it can be a nuisance.

"What will he think about me?"

Aaron looked down at her. "He'll think you're pretty."

"Not that, I mean 'bout your taking a wife. Did he really want you to get married?" She pressed.

"In the worst sort of way."

"What about you?"

Wariness crept over Aaron's countenance, his blue eyes hooded in the lingering light of the day. "It's gonna take some getting used to."

Jessica chuckled, "For us both."

A wicked grin parted his face, as he leaned down to capture her lips, "Some aspects of married life seem mighty appealing already."

A surly voice spoke from the shadows, "Sorry to interrupt this tender scene, but Sal needs you back at the Palace, Jessica. Business just ain't the same since you left."

Aaron's head jerked up, his hand moved to his side. The stranger laughed. "Sorry old man. Is this what you're looking for?" He held up a stained holster while holding Aaron's Paterson colt in his right hand.

Jessica bolted upright, one hand clutching her blouse while the other pulled at her skirt. The intruder laughed at her, taking in her frantic gestures, "Don't worry about getting formal with me, Miss Jessica. You look quite fetching."

Jessica felt Aaron stiffen by her side and she said, her voice syrupy, "Why thank you for the compliment. Now why don't you let us go back to our campsite where I can get my things?"

"You're going nowhere, Jessica." Aaron shouted, rage in his voice.

"Just a minute, cowboy. She'll do anything I tell her. You're not in control here." The tall stranger with brooding, dark eyes spoke quietly, as the long blue barrel pointed at the them reflected the last light of day. The click of its hammer cut through the twilight and even nature seemed to hush.

Jessica's heart thudded, and fear gripped her. Aaron's hand tightened on her arm, his nails digging into her flesh. She winced and then felt more than saw his hand move toward his boot. In one liquid motion he cast her away from him and hurled a knife toward their captor.

Fingers of fire parted the deepening shadows as Aaron's gun exploded. When it had settled, Aaron's blood soaked the ground where Jessica had experienced hope and happiness just moments before.

Like a mystical banshee, she screamed and clutched the body of her husband to her. With each beat of his powerful heart, his life drained away and with it the hopes and dreams of all her tomorrows. Jessica buried her face in his hair sobbing, "Oh, Aaron, I could have loved you, I could have loved you."

The intruder pursed his thin lips and shook his head as he observed Jessica's anguish. "He ain't worth grieving over, Jessica. You'd have nothing but a life of hard work and a hurtin' heart with that one. Sal's is the best place for you. Now get your things, we've got a long ride back."

Jessica raised her tear stained face, her eyes blazing, and whispered through clinched teeth with only her lips moving, "I will never go back to Sal's so you might as well kill me, too."

An evil light fired the man's eyes extinguishing

any brief compassion that might have touched them. Now they slid up and down Jessica, taking in her open bodice, her skirt pulled tight around her hips, the shapely leg stretched behind her. "Mess up all that beauty with a six gun? Not a chance, Sugar. But I do aim to enjoy it before I take you back." And with one swift movement he reached across the motionless body of Aaron and grasped Jessica's arm, jerking her across the few feet that separated them.

She landed with a thud on the ground beside him. A slow malevolent grin spread over his face, then he leaned over her. His hand moved up her arm in a slow caress until it reached her shoulder where his grip tightened. He pushed her to the ground, impounding one of her arms painfully beneath her. He held her down and unfolded his long legs on her skirt. Stretching out on his side, he pressed his barreled chest against her. A mixture of sweat, horse and tobacco assaulted her nostrils. His heavy breath invaded her ears and she felt his heart pounding against her.

One of his hands still clutched Aaron's gun while the other moved from her shoulder to her throat, pinning her to the ground Her eyes widened, she coughed, her breath cut off for a moment. Then he loosened his grip and caressed her throat, crooning, "All it would take is a flick of these fingers and you'd join that cowpoke in hell."

"Then flick 'em, I told you I'd rather die than go

back to Sal's." Jessica whispered, her throat aching.

"Ay, my pretty, but you wouldn't want to choke to death. You'll do my bidding, and I'll get the pleasure that Sal denied us 'common' folk. Not a very nice thing you and her did to us. Parading you around and givin' us a hunger we couldn't satisfy."

"That was all Sal's doings. I got no pleasure from those games she played with me." Jessica protested.

His hand tightened on her throat as he rolled over on top of her, pressing the breath out of her. She closed her eyes, realizing to resist would do no good and knowing she didn't want to choke. A low triumphant laugh rolled from his throat when he felt her relax beneath him. He released her throat and placed his weapon on the ground above her head. "I guess I won't be needing this for a while."

River gravel cut into the back of Jessica's legs and the arm beneath her grew numb. She flexed her fingers, stretching them out and they touched the cold steel of the knife Aaron had hurled at the intruder. Arching her back against the man's weight, she gingerly moved the blade until her hand gripped the handle.

Her captor placed one of his hands in the dirt on the side of her head and with the other unbuckled his own holster and flung it to the side. A knowing chuckle rumbled from him, as he explained "Don't want it to get in my way, it might hurt the little lady."

"Thoughtful of you," Jessica responded, sarcasm

lacing her voice.

He shifted his body so that he could stare down into her face and a lurid smile parted his mouth. When he blew his putrid breath on her face nausea boiled in her throat, and she turned her head just as he leaned over to capture a kiss.

He cursed and grasped her shoulders. "You'll not be playing the high and mighty with me, missy."

"You're hurting me." She moaned.

He laughed, "Be good for you. I always did think you needed a little taming."

"Why do you keep talking as if I should know you?"

"Oh I was around. Had to watch you from the shadows. You were too uppity to know I existed, but not tonight."

"What's your name? At least tell me your name." Jessica stalled, grasping at straws to delay the inevitable.

"They call me Tex. But you can call me 'darling' like I heard you call that cowpoke over there." He laughed in her ear. "Let me hear some of that sweet talk you were giving him."

"What sweet talk? I don't know what you're talking about." Jessica objected. Her hand tightened on the blade beneath her wondering how and where she could thrust it into her body and end the torment he planned for her.

Suddenly four shots split the newly fallen night

and she remembered Aaron's brothers for the first time. Tex swore under his breath and looked through the darkness toward the campsite. "What are those boys up to? Looks like they could take care of two cowpokes all tied up."

Lifting up to reach for the gun belt he had cast aside, he failed to see the flash of moonlight reflected on the razor sharp dagger that Jessica buried in his back. Surprise contorted his features as she pulled her legs from beneath him and kicked him in the chest with both feet. He fell backwards pushing the knife through his heart as Jessica rolled clear and out into the darkness.

Slipping and sliding on the rocks in the stream she crawled along the bank her feet in the water. Her heart pounded, her breath came in short gasps and tears streamed down her cheeks. She had to get away. But where? How many other men were there? And what about Ben, Simeon and Jim? Had they killed them, too? Then Tex's words came back to her. He'd said two cowpokes. What about Ben? He'd gone upriver to bathe. Could it be? Dare she hope?

Through the trees Ben's voice called her name and hope became reality.

"Ben!" She screamed and she heard feet crashing through the brush before the moonlight outlined the tall lanky body of Ben Isaacs.

She climbed out of the stream and suddenly he cradled her trembling body in his strong arms, "Are you all right? Where's Aaron?"

And relief was swallowed up in sorrow. She keened, "He's back there on the riverbank. He's dead, Ben."

Ben stepped back, his face silver in the moonlight, his eyes large and dark, disbelief frozen on his features, "Aaron's dead?"

"That man shot him."

"How did you get away?"

"I killed him."

"You?" Ben's voice denied what he'd heard.

Before she could answer, Jim and Simeon's shouts thundered through the night drowning out the sounds of water cascading over boulders. They had found Aaron's body and Ben believed.

"We'll just leave 'em out for the coyotes to have." Jim motioned toward the two dead cowboys, answering Ben's question.

"I still say it's a shame that we can't take Aaron's body back to Pa." Ben shook his head, a dread in his eyes.

"If'n we did how's we gonna explain we didn't bring Joel's, too?" Simeon asked.

Jessica's eyes widened in the darkness, "What do you mean? I thought your Pa was trying to get Aaron away from Joel."

Ben looked down at the ground; he ground his

heel uncomfortably in the ground, the firelight dancing on his frowning features.

Silence reigned for a few long moments with only the sounds of the night intruding. Then Jim chuckled, "Aaron just made up that story."

Jessica's heart sank. "Why would he do a thing like that?"

"To talk you into helping him get rid of Joel." Ben explained quietly, raising his head to look at her.

"And you went along with them, Ben?" Jessica's eyes impaled Ben's, an unspoken accusation rang in her voice

"Only because they wanted to kill him. I thought your idea was better." Ben responded, misery in his eyes.

Suddenly Joel's warm brown eyes and tall muscular frame, invaded Jessica's memory and she shuddered.

"What's any difference between us and you? Gettin rid of Joel was the ticket to what you wanted, jest like us. Don't get all high and mighty on us, Miz Jessica." Simeon spate out.

Jessica dropped her head, misery flooding her being as she accepted the truth of Jim's statement.

Jim rummaged through his saddle bag and drug out a jacket. "This here is Joel's jacket. We need to shoot a hole in it and rub some of them varmit's blood on it, so's we can tell Pa that both Aaron and Joel got killed, and we barely escaped."

"Too bad about Aaron but it shore does make

our story more believable." Simeon drawled, his face parting in a cruel smile as he took in Jessica's misery. "It even solves the problem about our little friend here."

"What are you talking about, Simm?" Ben demanded, his eyes widened in alarm.

Simeon grinned, "We don't need her anymore. Fact is, we need to be rid of her. She's the only one 'sides the three of us who knows what really happened to Joel. And I ain't a risking her telling Pa what really happened."

Jessica backed up against a small cottonwood sapling, her knees suddenly weak.

Jim gave his brother a hard look, "I ain't in favor of killin' a woman."

Simeon laughed, "Don't have to. Just leave her here and let her go back to Sal's."

Jessica's heart sank. Why hadn't Tex killed her when he shot Aaron? Better that than die of thirst or Indians in the wilderness between here and San Diego. Anyway to go back was no option."

Ben interrupted, "She'd never make it back by herself and you know it."

"Way I see it. That ain't our problem."

Frantically Jessica looked from one man to the other, trying to discern their intent. In Ben's face she read determination, but feared he had little influence with his brothers.

Jim leaned over and poked at the last embers of their campfire with a long stick. The glow illumined his face, touching his eyes and pursed lips, "Would be easier traveling without her."

Ben turned toward him and took a step toward the fire, his eyes like flint, "She is coming with us, whether you or Simm like it or not."

Simeon drawled, "Now who says so, lil brother?"

"I do." Ben words parted the air. The tone of his voice offered no compromise as he slid his Paterson revolver from his holster, adding quietly, "and this says she'll go."

"Now, Ben, do you think I believe you'd use that on your brothers?"

"Try me." Ben challenged, his eyes unwavering.

"Ben may have a point, Simm." Jim agreed. "How else will we be able to explain why we're so late 'cept we have Aaron's wife with us? Besides won't she be a comfort to our Pa, losing Aaron and Joel. He always did want a woman around the house. Maybe he'll quit staying after us about gettin' married."

Anger strutted the veins in Simeon's neck as he blustered, "Yeah and what's gonna keep her from tellin' Pa what really happened to Joel?"

A sly smile parted Jim's mouth, "Because she's the one who got rid of him. It's her guilt she'd be admitting, not ours. That's a secret she'll have to live with the rest of her life."

The truth of Jim's words stung Jessica and guilt, like a weight of cold steel, settled in her innermost being.

CHAPTER 4

The night's breeze proved a welcome relief from the relentless sun and the ocean's stillness of the previous day. Now a west wind had picked up, and after a half-day's delay, filled the sail above Joel's head moving the ship forward.

This was the fourth week at sea for the Sea Sprite and Joel had settled into the routine of sailing life. He'd learned right away that survival depended on his working hard and keeping his mouth shut. But that had proved no problem for him. He had relished the demanding tasks that drained his body of energy, for it left him little time to brood about the betrayal that had put him here. Now and then in the brief moment after his head hit his pillow a vision of sparkling green eyes and scarlet lips beneath a cloud of flaming hair taunted his memory. But he closed his eyes and she was gone, lost in the gentle respite of sleep that claimed him.

Joel sighed in the moonlight that bathed the ship in silver, hiding her imperfections. As a member of the first mate's larboard watch, he had pulled the morning watch from four until eight. His favorite duty. A little solitude, space and sometimes a glorious dawn proved his rewards. He glanced downward into the white foam startling against the black water as the Sea Sprite cut through the sea, then he looked up into the billowing sails. The brig heeled slightly to starboard and the wind whipped his face.

He had to agree with old Jim; a ship under sail rivaled the beauty of any woman he had ever seen. Then once more the specter with emerald eyes and pouting lips intruded and he had to amend his thoughts. Still, there were some aspects of being a sailor that might appeal to him, given another time and other circumstances.

But it was not another time and the circumstances were grim.

Thoughts of his father, always in the back of his mind, surfaced. Questions of what had happened to him; how had Aaron explained away Joel's absence or, worse yet, had Aaron even returned to him? These thoughts always lurked ready to torment Joel. He pushed them aside, knowing that to consider them would only frustrate him. A captive here, he knew that it would be more than a year before he'd have any hope of returning. Until then he had to survive.

And he had learned the skill of survival quickly. On a ship of mostly criminals and misfits his powerful and agile body, paired with a quick mind, captured the attention of the officers. No task was too dangerous or menial for him to tackle. If the blow was stiff, he was first to go aloft to reef the topsails. Yet he did all his feats with such an attitude of cooperation that he won the grudging respect of the motley crew. The cook had taken him under his wing and often times, he'd save out an extra portion and slip it to him when no one was looking.

Along with the cook Joel had gained the friendship of the crippled sailor, Jim. On their brief moments of rest on alternate Sundays, the older sailor had relayed the sad tale of his life touching Joel's heart with the tragedies he had experienced.

While Joel had made the best he could of a bad situation, he waited with certain trepidation. Somewhere out there, according to what he had overheard, a vessel stalked them, seeking what was rightfully theirs. What would happen when the confrontation occurred if the other ship proved successful? Would Joel be held responsible for a crime in which he innocent? He shuddered at the thought.

A sense of helplessness washed over him and dimmed the shimmering beauty of the moonlit night. He stepped down to walk the watch. Suddenly a cold blast of wind hit his face, startling him. How could the wind be so cold, when the day had been so hot? He chuckled, remembering the lessons old Jim had tried to teach him during their short time together. 'Twas not only in beauty was sailing the seas like a woman," Jim had observed, but in temperament as well. Joel knew very little about the temperament of a woman, but he'd take Jim's word for it. His mother had died when he was very young, and riding the range left little time for socializing with the local girls. His dad determined to protect him from the life style of his brothers and barred him from going with them to the cow-town saloons.

He turned the corner just as the fore and aft sails popped ominously on the gaffs that secured them. The Sea Sprite heeled sharply and the first mate called out the alarm for all hands to come on deck to take in sail.

Soon the deck buzzed as the crew arrived on deck, wrested from their hammocks, to deal with the sudden turn of the weather. Joel hurled himself aloft at the first mate's command to trim the topsail. He gingerly pushed himself out the yard, the timber now wet and slippery from the sudden squall. Now icy pellets struck his face stinging it. His hands clung to the wet massive beam trying to maintain his balance as the little ship buffeted to and fro. Excitement stirred within him, wiping away the thoughts troubling him only moments before. A smile curved his generous mouth as he thought how accurate Old Jim had been when he likened the sea to a woman, unpredictable, and calm one moment while in a rage the next. And with the thought, a vision of red pouting lips and fiery green eyes intruded between him and the rigging. He lost his grip and the world turned upside down. His legs slipped and the gale blew him backward into the halyard. Would that beauty with flaming hair be the end of him? Anger boiled in him as he fought to stabilize himself with his powerful legs. He willed his body to reach up to grasp the broad timber, but the wind battled his every move. A movement above him caught his eye and he saw his wiry friend sliding out the yard toward him.

"Hold on, mate, I'll anchor you." Jim shouted as he threw his body across Joel's legs grasping the slick timber with both hands and hanging on with his legs.

Suddenly the ferocious wind lulled as if to take a breath. With the weight of Jim's body on his legs stabilizing him, Joel lunged upward and to the side reaching for the yard with one hand. His fingers touched the wet wood and he grasped it.

"Move off me, Jim, I might dislodge you." Joel shouted as he swung suspended in space by one arm and his legs.

Slowly Jim sat upright and slid away from Joel as the younger man pulled himself to safety beside the old sailor. A chorus of cheers went up on the deck far below as young sailor and old formed a bond that only the threat of death could seal.

Joel perched in the forecastle bucking and rolling from the screaming gale topside. His harrowing experience had earned him a brief respite from his duties. Shaking from the cold and his brush with death, he grasped a warm mug in his hands and rotated it with icy fingers. He took a deep breath to quiet his pounding heart and inhaled the full rich aroma of the coffee as steam from it drifted up to caress his cold cheeks. The dark brown beverage was a luxury that his near death encounter had earned for both him and the aging sailor who sat beside him. Joel took a sip, letting its tepidity soothe his insides while his mind still rioted with what might have been.

He looked toward the wizened old man his face still pinched from the icy wind on deck. Feelings of gratitude and curiosity battled inside him as he considered this man who had been little more than a congenial stranger to him. Curiosity winning out, he blurted, "What ever possessed you to climb up there, Jim? You know the first mate excuses you from that duty."

"I don't know, Joel. Just felt in my gut that I needed to go up there and try it one more time." Old Jim dropped his eyes, giving too much attention to his coffee as if Joel had brought him to a place in himself he'd rather avoid.

"And a good thing it was for me that you were there. But why take such a risk?" Joel insisted, needing to know why a stranger cared and he was alive, when his very family members had only wanted to be rid of him. He shook his head trying to put his past out of the equation, seizing on the comfort that Old Jim had offered him high above the rolling deck and snapping sheets, a comfort he had not acknowledged he needed. But it was no use. When a man stares the icy jaws of death in the face, he's forced to look inward and what he found was questions wanting answers.

"Hard to say, boy. But sometimes a man has to prove to himself he still has worth, gimpy leg and all." Jim confessed.

Joel flushed in the flickering lamp, startled and a little uncomfortable by Jim's revelation, as one man is when another offers a glimpse into his soul. He responded choosing his words carefully. "Well, Jim, my pa always taught me that a real man's worth is not in the strength of his body, but in the depths of his soul. There's nobody could make me believe that as a man you don't tower head and shoulders above the rest, gimpy leg and all."

Jim dropped his head before Joel could read the pleasure in his eyes, and muttered, "Yore pa must've been a fine man. He's taught you something I'd plumb forgot." He took a deep swig of the warm beverage rolling it around his mouth, savoring it.

Joel nodded, "Both he and my ma. When my ma taught me to read and write from the Bible, she poured more than just the words into me, she explained the meaning, teaching me what she called principles of living. Now with Pa it was a little different." A sad chuckle rumbled in his throat as he remembered. "Although he shared her notions, he had a different way of teachin' 'em. Sometimes he' pounded them into me behind the woodshed, other times it was riding the range learning to finish an unpleasant job, or maybe it was just watching him give his word to someone and know he'd live up to whatever he promised."

"In other words, ye larned it by watching the way he lived his life."

Joel nodded, suddenly battling a lump in his throat that threatened his composure.

Jim fixed an intense gaze on him and cautioned, "Joel, me boy, don't let working around this riff raff steal the worth of your papa's truth from yer mind."

Joel's mouth parted in a sad smile, remembering. "I could hardly do that, Jim."

"Somehow when a young un gets away from home, he kinda leaves his teaching behind." Jim reminded, an urgency in his eyes

"You're forgetting I didn't leave mine behind by choice." Joel's soft-spoken voice took on an edge as he recalled what had put him where he was.

Old Jim's eyes narrowed, the crows feet on each side of them deepening, "I been wondering about that, boy. How come you wuz in the kind of place to get shanghaied? You don't seem to be the kind to loll around sech places."

A bitter chuckle cut the air. "I wasn't "lolling"

anywhere. As a matter of fact I was at my brother's wedding and the last thing I remember was toasting the bride."

"Ye don't say now." Jim's faded blue eyes brightened with interest, knowing he was about to find the answer to the mystery that had plagued him since Joel landed in his care.

Joel sighed, suddenly needing to sort out the conflicting emotions that were ready to assail him, almost compelled to tell someone his tale of betrayal.

Old Jim bowed over, shaking his head in disbelief. "How could brothers treat another in sech a way?"

Joel shrugged, old hurts, things he had never understood threatened to boil over. "I guess you'd have to ask them."

"Didn't you have the same Pa and Ma? The ones who taught you from the Good Book?"

Joel leaned back in his chair, his hands laced behind his head, "Not the same Ma."

"The same Pa, then?" Old Jim encouraged, bewildered at this tale of family betrayal.

"Yea. Their ma died soon after Ben was born and Pa didn't marry until ten years later. He told me my ma was the best thing that ever happened to him, settled him down. I guess when the other boys were young, he sowed a few too many wild oats, maybe they didn't grow up seeing the same Pa I saw. He seemed to regret his past deeds and tried to make it up to the boys, but like he said he couldn't call the years back."

"Then your ma couldn't influence your brothers?"

"They resented her. She was an----." Joel hesitated, suddenly fearful of Jim's reaction.

"What son?" His leathery face turned toward Joel, his eyes encouraging.

Joel whispered, "An Indian. They never forgave Pa for marrying her."

"What a pity. I learnt a long time ago, 'tis not the color of the skin that determines a lady's worth."

A knowing smile tugged at one corner of Joel's mouth, "Kinda like the strength of a man's body-----."

Jim dropped his head, his eyes falling on his crippled leg, "I guess you could say it's the same principle."

"Believe me, Jim. My mother was a lady in every respect. She was educated and cultured, thanks to a small mission school just outside her village. She had a thirst for learning and goodness."

"Then what was the problem?"

"Jealousy, I reckon. My brothers thought Pa disgraced the memory of their mother by marrying an Indian. They refused all her efforts to be a mother to them, although Pa demanded they respect her, she never could win their approval or affection. When I came along in his old age, they resented me. I guess he did make a difference between us. But he had changed, had settled down and was ready to be a proper parent.

By that time it was too late with them."

"Are you telling me yore brothers had this done to you?"

"It had to be them. I guess I should be thankful they didn't have me killed."

"But you said something about a bride. Maybe it was this woman and your brothers had nothing to do with it." Jim said, his eyes refusing to believe a brother could condemn another brother to a life of practical slavery.

"I wish I could believe they hadn't had a hand in it. It would be easier to blame her. Less painful you know." Joel fixed his eyes on Jim, pleading for understanding, his heart hammering inside him as he finally faced the truth he had refused to believe.

Jim nodded in response, his fingers drumming on the table, trying to make sense out of what Joel had told him. "Why would she or they do such a cruel deed?"

"I don't know. Pa sent me after them 'cause they had been gone so long and he was worried."

"Why were they in San Diego?"

"Trail drive. Pa got sick and sent them on ahead. We needed the money so we wouldn't lose the ranch. Sometime when they had money in their pocket they weren't as careful as they ought to be."

"In other words your Pa was afraid they'd come home without the money." Jim interjected, understanding dawning.

"He couldn't risk any of it; he needed it all just to buy that little ranch he had his eye on. He knew the boys didn't share his dream. They were after him to move on to greener pastures."

"But what about the girl? How come she would go along with it, if she did?"

"Oh, she did. She's the one who gave me the punch. All it took was one slug and I was out cold."

"That don't explain why she did it."

"Maybe it was the money. They do get money for it, don't they?"

"We get most of our men from Sal's, I know cap'n has an arrangement with her, but as for yore brother's wife, I can't understand how she'd get mixed up in it."

"Even if she worked for Sal?" Joel asked quietly.

Old Jim slapped his bony knee. "You don't mean it, boy. Your brother married one of Sal's girls?"

Joel nodded, not trusting his voice, the memory of her taunting eyes burned in his mind.

"Which one were it?" Jim's curiosity winning the upper hand.

"Jessica."

"That don't mean nothing to me, boy. Wha' she look like?"

"Flaming red hair and----."

"Green eyes with the fire of emeralds?"

"You know her?"

Jim nodded, "I seen her around. Heard about

her too. Seems she was Sal's favorite. I can't believe she'd let that money maker slip away and get married."

"Well she did. Sal was at the wedding reception."

"But why would your brother's wife sell you like that?"

Joel's heart twisted as the old sailor forced him to face a truth that he wanted to deny.

"Simple as wanting the money?" Joel asked, even as he asked, his heart knew it was more involved than a simple business transaction.

Jim placed a gnarled hand on his young friend's shoulder, understanding and sorrow in his sunken eyes, "Tis easier by far to accept the betrayal of a stranger than one we love. But the sooner you face it the better, son. The question now is what are you gonna do about it?"

Joel inhaled deeply, more shudder than breath, then shut his eyes and shook his head, willing the pain away that clung like a leech deep within him. He shook his head, clinching and unclenching his fists as he faced squarely the betrayal. Gradually a lilting voice from the past whispered in his memory that forgiveness given is forgiveness received. He remembered his mother, her wretched existence with his siblings and marveled, suddenly understanding.

A tortured smile parted his face even while his eyes burned like glowing embers, "I'll go on with life, Jim. Though what they thought to do was evil, they'll not destroy me. I'll not dwell on their deed and let bitterness be the victor, but wring out the opportunities I find no matter how scarce and be the stronger man for it."

"Aye, my boy. Bitterness eats away at the soul and it's good you discovered that secret so early in life. You're a fine one, Joel, to make a heartache into a stepping stone instead of a millstone and I'm right here to help see you through it, anyway I can." Jim held out his hand clasping Joel's in commitment.

Suddenly the heavy weight that had bound Joel's mind and spirit lifted and for the first time since awaking in the fetid hole of the rolling contraband ship he felt free and confident that he had a future.

CHAPTER 5

Joel gazed across the azure sea. A welcome sun warmed his face and chased away the chill that had seeped into his bones. A light wind filled the billowing sails above him as the brig cut her way northward through gentle swells, leaving the terrors of Cape Horn behind them.

The warning Jim had given Joel about the Cape proved inadequate to describe the experience. For four days and nights the small vessel fought the southwesterly winds that pushed them through heavy slate-colored clouds that clung to the sea engulfing them in darkness only to come out of the fog into vicious gales mixed with both hail and snow. The over burdened ship, with its contraband cargo making it sluggish in the water, groaned and threatened to break apart from the force of the sea and wind.

Not a man aboard, including the captain, had enjoyed a thread of dry clothes from the first squall onward. Their only thought was survival; their only relief was a nap and a cup of hot tea grabbed during intermittent lulls. Now the men were enjoying a brief, well earned respite that even the captain acknowledged they needed thus avoiding the risk having a mutinous crew on his hands.

Joel's heart stirred as a series of islands stretching from east to west rose on the horizon like a mystical land. But they were not the wishful mirage of a homesick sailor, he knew they were the Falklands. Comprising two main islands, East and West Falkland, and some 700 smaller ones, they stretched for some one hundred forty-eight miles from east to west. Combine their indented coastline and deep harbors along with their sparse population, they offered the perfect place for the ship to pull in for much needed provisions and to repair the rigging.

Although the captain felt confident that there were no witnesses to his crime of thievery who could identify his ship, he was taking no chances. The fact is, if he were not forced to drop anchor, he would continue on. Needed repairs and depletion of provisions, both his and the crew's, made the decision for him. He had to stop, but the where was up to him. He chose this lonely outpost with few inquisitive eyes and wagging tongues to note his ship's whereabouts and activities.

Joel caught the crew's exuberance as they sailed into port, excited at the thought that his sea legs would feel the firm earth after so many days of experiencing only the roll and pitch of the unsteady vessel. A bath and a whole meal of fresh food sounded like paradise to him.

The deep, South Atlantic harbor the captain chose allowed the ship to approach near the shore and Joel had a full view of the few low roofs facing the ship. Soon the small boats were lowered and the crew gathered to go ashore. To Joel's dismay, he learned that all the men forced into the voyage would remain on board along with one officer and old Jim. The captain chose to take only the officers and crew who had served him on earlier voyages.

Leaving behind Joel, old Jim and a disgruntled crew, the captain headed for shore just after morning watch. All day a short-handed crew unloaded the small boats as they ferried back and forth from land to ship with much needed provisions. The captain remained in town for the night and the crew grumbled, feeling deprived that he was taking his pleasures at their expense.

When supplies arrived for repairing the rigging, the officer onboard shut himself away with a bottle of rum, leaving Jim in charge of the repairs. Although the rag tag band of men complained, they respected Jim and worked hard. Jim, believing that a little bit of sugar makes any medicine more palatable, took the liberty of providing them with extra rations. With their dispositions sweetened, they finished the task in half the time the captain had expected. So the ship rested, ready and waiting in the quiet swells for a delinquent captain and crew.

Midnight fell in a thick curtain of darkness as a heavy blanket of clouds blanketed the sliver of new moon that had peeked out earlier in the evening. The stars, usually so bright, retreated behind the ominous cover. Only the light from a few distant lanterns bobbing along the harbor parted the darkness. On shore occasional sounds of revelry from the small village broke the quietness of the night. On board an exhausted skeleton watch napped at their posts while down below sailors swung in their hammocks their snores beating against the hard timbers. The drunken officer lay sprawled in his quarters, past caring about the duties he had abandoned.

Under the cover of darkness, four longboats from a ship anchored in a cove between them and the sea, stealthily glided toward the quiet ship at anchor. As soon as they pulled up beside the vessel they dropped their oars and mutely climbed the ladders left hanging for the captain and crew who had failed to return.

Joel took a turn around the deck, unable to sleep for some reason though his exhausted body ached from the heavy workload of the past days. He paused and watched the village lights as they went out one by one. Obviously the captain nor his men would be returning this night either.

He looked around him at the men sleeping on

their watch. Even a cowboy turned sailor understood the potential danger; yet Jim seemed to think they had escaped unscathed, that they had evaded retribution for their activities. But had they? The sweet voice of his mom whispered in his memory, that there was always a day of reckoning, a harvest time where one reaped what one sowed. All seemed so peaceful, so far from recompense; yet, uneasiness swept over him.

The hairs on the back of his neck stood up just before he felt hard, cold steel press into the base of his skull as an arm encircled his neck, almost choking him. A hoarse voice quietly demanded in his ear, "Take me to your captain if you want to see the next sunrise."

Joel's eyes quickly surveyed the sleeping men before him and determined there would be no help from the sleeping men. Who was this voice? And how many more men had crept aboard?

"The captain is not on board, sir." Joel answered politely when the man loosened his grip and he could get his breath. His heart thudded in his chest as the man whirled Joel around to face him, the gun now pressed beneath his chin.

A cynical smile curled the stranger's lips, revealing white teeth beneath a closely trimmed mustache, "This is even better than I expected. When will he return and what is he doing?"

"Who are you and what do you want with the captain?" Joel inquired, his heart calming down. "I'm asking the questions here." The man growled. "Who is in charge in the captain's absence?"

A derisive smile parted Joel's face when he thought of the first mate down below. "He's incapacitated at the moment."

The gun jammed tighter into Joel's chin and he could see shadowy figures bounding quietly on deck then blending in the darkness behind his captor.

"Since you find this amusing, let me assure you, you are in a most precarious situation."

"I have no doubt about that. I'm not amused, sir. As you can see, there's no one in charge." Joel made a sweeping gesture toward the sleeping men.

"Surely your captain left an officer on board."

"Of course he did."

"Take me to him."

"He's drunk and passed out in his hammock."

"Take me to him anyway."

"It'll do no good."

"Let me be the judge of that."

"Perhaps you'd rather see Jim Ryan."

"Crippled guy?"

Joel nodded, bewildered that the man knew Jim.

"Why would I want to see him instead of the officer?"

"He's kind of been in charge with the officer, er incapacitated."

"Take me to Jim."

Joel turned on his heel, "Follow me." He felt the cold steel of the weapon pushed between his ribs.

"Don't try anything funny. I won't hesitate to use this. In fact I relish using it. However, I'd prefer using it on your captain. Too bad he's not on board."

"Jim," Joel nudged his friend asleep in his hammock. Lighting a small lantern to open up the inky darkness he explainsed, "This man wants to talk to the captain."

"Talk is not exactly what I had in mind. My men have taken control of this ship and all the criminals on it." He stranger said, his countenance hidden behind the flickering lantern he held in Jim's face.

"All of us are not criminals, sir." Joel objected.

"As far as I'm concerned you all are. This ship is filled with contraband hides, hides that my company bought and paid for and that you have stolen. You are guilty of piracy and theft. Every man jack on this ship will be held accountable for this crime, from your illustrious captain down to the lowest sailor."

"The boy's right. The captain shanghaied him in San Diego. He is on board against his will. In fact most of the men left on ship are here against their will. The captain wouldn't risk taking them ashore. I think you'll find the crew most cooperative."

In the darkness a cold smile parted the intruder's face, a triumphant chuckle rumbled from him, "This will be easier than I expected. What bout you old man?

Were you shanghaied, too?"

"No, but I give you my word I had no idea that our cargo would be stolen goods, or I would have never signed on."

"But you stayed on board." The stranger reminded.

"Once aboard with this captain, the only way to leave is burial at sea. When I found out what our mission was, it was too late to turn back. That's why I'm on the ship instead of shore. He knew I didn't go along with what he's doing."

"I see. Well what did you plan to do about it when you arrived in Boston? I assume that's where you're headed."

"I wish I could say I planned to do the right thing and turn him in, but I'm afraid I would just do the easy thing. Take my wages and disappear."

"Least you're honest."

Jim chuckled in the semi darkness, "After a fashion."

"The Jim Ryan I knew wasn't honest "after a fashion", his word was his bond. What happened to him?" The stranger lowered the lantern until it illuminated both faces.

Jim gasped, shame written in his eyes as they met his captor's probing ones, "Captain Bob Dundee, I never dreamed it was your cargo we carried."

"Would it have made a difference, Jim?"

Jim dropped his head, "Who knows? Maybe when I got to Boston I would have done the right thing."

"The Jim I knew would have whether it was my cargo or someone else's."

"What are you going to do about it? I deserve whatever punishment you have in mind, but this boy here is a good kid. Give him clemency. I beg you on the strength of the man I used to be."

Bob Dundee shook his head, and lowering his weapon, looked at Joel, "I don't know, kid. Jim seems to think I can trust you, but since he's not as honest as he used to be, can I take his evaluation? I guess it'll depend on what happens between here and Boston."

"Boston?" Jim and Joel said in unison, their eyes widened in the dim light.

Dundee chuckled, "Yes, Boston. I think by now my men will have taken control of this vessel. It should have been a fairly easy task considering the shape of your crew. Now I need to talk to your first mate."

"He's drunk."

"He'll sober up soon enough for my purposes." Bob drawled, then shouted, "Archie, get that first mate in here."

"Aye, Aye, sir. Here he is now." Archie affirmed as he pushed a disheveled bearded man with blood shot eyes through the narrow opening.

"Are you the first mate?" Dundee asked, unbelieving.

"Yeah, and what is it to you." The man mumbled, weaving to and fro.

"As the officer in charge, I demand that you officially surrender this ship to me."

"I can't ----do that." The man's slurred refusal came between hiccups. "Cause my captain would have my hide."

"He won't take near as much of it as the authorities in Boston will when you arrive to face charges of theft and piracy, if my men don't extract their own brand of justice before we arrive." The tall captain threatened.

Another hiccup, "Whatever you say, Captain. Your wish is my command." He giggled and lurched forward. Joel caught him before he hit the floor.

The captain's patience ended abruptly, "I am sending you ashore to inform your captain that I have commandeered this ship and my men will sail her to port where I will collect my hides and hand her over to the authorities there. His ship will be awaiting him in Boston minus its cargo along with charges of theft and piracy that I shall file when I arrive. Now be on your way."

At the tall stranger's command, two neat and muscular sailors appeared out of the darkness and grabbed the weaving first mate by the arms and dragged him out.

Dundee turned to Jim and Joel and shook his head, "Now what to do with you two?"

"Cap'n sir, do as you will with me, but spare this young man as you've great need for him. He is intelligent and educated far above a common sailor. Even though he's never been to sea, he has quickly caught on as if the salt ran in his veins. And then there's this rag tag crew of men, forced into a service they had no stomach for----He's won their respect and they follow him gladly knowing his fate was same as theirs."

"And you, Jim? I can remember a time when the same could have been said of you."

Jim dropped his head, unwilling to meet his former captain's gaze, "Aye, sir, he reminds me a lot of meself so many years ago, 'cept he's got the education I lacked."

"And the character?" Dundee probed.

Jim squirmed, his head still down, "I hope his convictions will stand the test of adversity better than mine have."

"Adversity?"

Jim nodded, "My gimpy leg. The sea was my life. With a little more learning, I could have been a captain some day; but then I fell, and who wants a sailor slow on his feet?"

"The worth of a man is not measured in his fleetness of foot, old friend. If you'd only come to me-- ---."

"And a man's pride can be his worst enemy. But this boy, he's got the makings of greatness. I just know it, feel it in my bones."

Dundee turned to Joel, "Well, young man, you have a real advocate in this old man. He almost persuades me to give you a chance. What say you?"

"Sir, my pa always taught me that while another man can verify the truth, the proof is in the action. I welcome the opportunity to prove my worth to you. As God is my witness, I have been held captive on this vessel and had nothing to do with the theft of your hides."

Dundee's eyes narrowed as he held Joel's. Connecting with something in Joel's steady gaze, the light in his hard brown eyes softened and he responded, "Alright sailor, you have your chance. Jim's recommendation has given you the opportunity, but it is up to you to prove him right."

A slow grin spread across Joel's face, "You won't be sorry, Sir."

Dundee nodded, replying brusquely, "I hope not. As for you, Jim, I've got a good idea that this young man-----"

"Joel Isaacs, sir." Joel interrupted.

"Yes, Isaacs here, is not the only one to whom the men respond. Remembering how you used to be, the men always followed you willingly."

Joel spoke before Jim could respond, "True, sir. We did the work in half the time with the first mate drunk and Jim in charge. You need him on this voyage."

Dundee chuckled, "You two got a mutual

admiration society going?"

"When you faced the cold fingers of death together and come through, there is a bond that ties, no denying that. Jim risked his life to save mine, gimpy leg and all. When the men saw that, he won their respect and admiration."

Dundee looked at Jim, "Well, Jim, some of the old Jim must be left. Maybe beneath the barnacles, the ship is still sound"

"I'd give the hope of a long life and great riches to find that so, sir."

"Well suppose we scrape the barnacles off this trip and see what we have underneath?"

"The chance to win my self-respect back is more than I could hope for."

Dundee nodded his head, "Alright, we'll see how things go on this voyage. And just to make sure, I've decided that rather than let my man sail her to Boston, I'll stay on board. It's a tricky sailing with an overloaded ship and an inexperienced crew, more of a challenge than I'd anticipated. I'll say one thing for that thieving captain of yours, he must be a good sailor to get this tub around the Horn in one piece."

"There's nothing wrong with his sailing abilities, the problem lies in his character. Money and pleasure drives him and he takes it wherever he finds it at anybody's expense."

CHAPTER 6

Joel took a brief respite from his duty at the wheel and stood aft watching the foaming white wake of the Sea Sprite as it made its way back to Boston. In the distance he could see the billowing sails of the Santa Rosa as she followed closely enough to keep a wary eye over their ship and crew, ever ready to lend a helping hand to their captain, if he encountered trouble.

It had been an arduous fifteen days since Captain Dundee had commandeered the Sea Sprite and retrieved his stolen cargo. Joel had never worked so hard, but it had proved productive and exhilarating to take a skeleton crew and accomplish the work a full crew had done before.

Surprisingly there had been more cooperation than grumbling from crew. Perhaps it was Joel's persuasive argument that cooperation would garner them a better chance of leniency once they arrived in Boston. Or maybe it was Captain Dundee's belief that hard work required proper fuel and unlike their former captain was generous with provisions for all the men.

Joel's duties extended from the tallest mast to the hold overloaded with cargo, from fore to aft, no duty too menial or too dangerous for him to accomplish. He even took his turn in the galley; albeit the men found his culinary talents to be far behind his sailing abilities, and were quick to tell him so.

At first Joel found himself under constant scrutiny by Captain Dundee. But as several days passed, he seemed to accept that the commendation that Jim had given concerning Joel was true. Soon the captain began turning more and more responsibility over to Joel and when old Jim came down with a fever, the job of first mate fell to Joel. Like a well oiled machine, the men fell into line under Joel's leadership and doubled their efforts so much so that the Sea Sprite sailed into Boston Harbor well ahead of their expected arrival.

As soon as they were docked, before they could unload the hides, Captain Dundee called the crew deck side. "Men, it was brought to my attention when we commandeered this vessel that those of you on board were here against your will and that you did not take part in the theft of my goods. Even when I knew your predicament, I was disinclined to grant you any leniency. However, because of your efforts, we have made a safe and speedy journey and I have decided not to press charges against any of the crew."

A roar of approval rumbled through the motley crew on deck, as a broad grin parted the faces of Joel and his older friend.

The captain held up his hand to silence the crew. "Not only am I granting you leniency, but you will be paid a proper seaman's wages for the days you sailed for me. Now it's not my responsibility to neither judge you nor lecture you on why you placed yourself in a position that permitted this unfortunate set of circumstances. I hope the Good Lord has allowed this situation in your life to give you better judgment in the future."

One sailor, berry brown with sun bleached hair and two missing front teeth raised his brawny arm, "Good Cap'n, Sir. Could you be telling us why you're treating us with such good regard?"

The men murmured, "Briny, man, shush lest he changes his mind."

The captain chuckled, "I'll not change my mind. Once it's made up, unless given good reason, I'll do what I determined. The truth is you gave me good reason to change my mind. But as far as the wages go, the Good Book admonishes a man to pay his debts, and I am indebted to you for your services. I also offer you the opportunity for a free passage back to California if you'll sign on to sail for me a year."

"Does that mean we'll be sailing under Joel and ole' Jim again? It seems as if we make a pretty good crew by your own admission, if you please, Sir."

"Now, sailor, you know you can't dictate your working arrangements. The offer stands, take it or leave it no matter whom you sail under. Now it's time to finish the job. Let's get this vessel unloaded."

Joel's heart sank when he heard the captain's response. Did that mean he and Jim would stand charges for theft and piracy? Did an undeserved gallows hang at the end of this journey?

The captain turned on his heel and left the deck, motioning to Jim and Joel to follow him to his quarters.

"Close the door behind you, boys. I've additional matters to discuss with you."

Jim eyes held Joel's, encouragement meeting the concern mirrored in the younger man's .

The captain sat down and placed elbows on his chart table, placing his chin in his hand. Silent for a long moment, he finally addressed the two pale men standing before him.

"Men as the leaders of this motley crew, you two would quite naturally hold more accountability than the men under you. However, by Jim's account, he alone was on board that ship by choice. Therefore he has requested that he bear any and all penalties, however severe, that arise from this situation."

Joel's head jerked toward Jim, "No, sir. I beg of you don't punish Jim for what you might feel that I or any of the other men deserve. Judge us on our own honor or dishonor."

The captain leaned back in this chair, carefully pressing his fingertips together. "So you're ready to take your own punishment, eh?"

"Aye, I am, sir." Joel's answer came swift and sure, the language of a cowpoke turned sailor.

"Even to the gallows?"

"Even to the gallows, if that is the judgment of a proper and fair trial."

The captain chuckled, never taking his penetrating blue eyes from Joel's. "Then stand or fall on your own, you will."

Joel's jaws clenched, but he stood straight and tall, determined to take his punishment, no matter how undeserved, like a man.

Captain Dundee watched Joel intently as the boy made final passage into manhood. His countenance softened, "Joel there will be no gallows for you. I've watched you carefully on this voyage and I believe that Jim has told me the truth about you. Not just concerning your innocence, but your possibilities. I would like to assist you in reaching that potential. I want to take you to meet my partner, Mr. Nate Wilkins. You have the makings of a true sailor. One I would be proud to sail with, but I concur with ole' Jim. Much as I hate to admit it, you have far more potential than planting your feet on the planks of a rolling ship for the rest of your life.

"Sir?"

"That's right no punishment and a job offer."

"I'm overwhelmed."

"Joel, I have to admit, when I found my hides

taken, I was angry enough to offer mercy to no one. My only goal was to recover my goods and to get retribution on all those involved, whether I had to take the law into my own hands or to bring them to justice in a court of law. But after retrieving my cargo without loss of life and the voyage giving me time to cool off, I saw things a bit differently, especially when I noted the crew's cooperation under the leadership of you and Jim. Not only did my thirst for revenge abate, but I felt a strong urgency to assist you."

"But, Sir. Why would you want to help a complete stranger? You know nothing of my background, who I am."

"You're wrong about that. Your friend and staunchest supporter has told me something about how you came to be in this predicament."

Joel looked at Jim who dropped his head with a sheepish grin. "I didn't think you would feel I had betrayed a confidence, 'specially since my motive was to gain you clemency."

Dundee shook his head, "I didn't accept what he said at face value, for I feared he might have embellished your character in trying to save you. However, observing you, your actions and reactions these weeks have convinced me that what he told me was true."

"I don't know what he told you ---------."

"A sad story of a brother's betrayal."

"Then, Cap'n, Sir, you know I have a sick and

ailing father that I must get back to see about. If my brothers had so little consideration for his property, will they not have less for his physical well being? I could not advance my own future at the expense of my father. That's what my brothers did."

"I understand, but what kind of future do you and your father have there?"

"Sir, I have given little consideration to the future, only to finding my father safe and well. That is my prayer."

Gently Dundee pressed, "But, son, how do you propose to find him? Even when I pay you your wages, they will be scarce enough to get you back to California, much less stake you while you search."

"Could I sign on board for your next voyage?"

"You could, but my ship will be going to England, which will not be any help to you. My trips around the 'Horn' are over. In fact, if these hides bring what I think they will, there'll be only a few more trips for me, then I'll settle down with my missus and live to enjoy my grandchildren."

"Then I'll just have to find another ship."

Dundee shook his head sadly, "Tis a hard time you'll find getting a one-way job. A good captain only wants someone who will sign on for the entire duty, and you want no part of the other kind of captain."

"I'll have to take my chances, sir."

"Joel, be reasonable. You risk life and limb with

a good captain, a bad captain only makes the risk not worth taking."

"What other choice do I have, sir?"

"Let me take you to Mr. Wilkins. At least meet him. Have you ever thought, lad, that our Good Lord may have brought you thus far, because he had something more for you than hot sun and a hard saddle? You know sometimes He goes to extreme measures to place us in His will."

"You think he'd have me abandon my pa?"

The sea captain shook his head slowly as if pondering the question, "But there is the possibility that he didn't survive or that your brothers did their duty as sons."

"And I would anguish over the not knowing."

"Aye, you would."

"Suppose you go with me to meet Mr. Wilkins, maybe he would have an answer to this dilemma. He is a kind and generous man, even though he is in the cream of society and wealthy to boot. I respect his judgment and so can you."

"Well seeing I have neither money nor a way to return home, I will go with you to meet Mr. Wilkins." Joel turned toward Jim. "What about Jim?"

Dundee chuckled as he looked at the older man, "I don't think a gallows would fit that scrawny old neck, do you?"

A broad smile parted Joel's face, his shoulders

relaxing, "No sir, it wouldn't fit at all."

"I think the only thing that fits this old salty is the rolling deck of a ship."

"For sure, he fits that. From what I saw, he's tailor made for the salt sea air."

"Used to be, Laddie. With this gimpy leg, I'm hard pressed to be the man I was." Jim interjected.

"Perhaps an older and wiser man, but I'm convinced you're no less than the man you used to be." The captain responded

"No, sir, only the shadow of the man I used to be. This leg is proof of that."

"You know, Jim, tis the heart of a man that dictates his measure, not his limbs."

"Are ye forgetting, Sir, where you found me?"

"No, but I'm knowing the frailty of man and acknowledge there are moments of weakness and temptation for each of us, lest our Savior wouldn't have need to die for us. Your signing on with that bunch of thieves was done in ignorance, I'm believing when you got to Boston, you would have done the right thing."

"You don't know that, Captain."

"No, I don't know that, but that's what I believe. That's why I'm giving you a second chance. I want you as my first mate on my next voyage."

"With a crippled leg? Now how would I be able to be what you need?"

"It's not your physical prowess that I need,

although from what Joel tells me you do pretty well with that "gimpy" leg of yours. What I want from you is your wisdom of life and your knowledge of the sea to train this young crew we'll be taking with us."

"But my education, it's sadly lacking." He murmured, eyes dropped, unwilling to look his captain in the eye.

"Jim, yours is the education that life and experience have taught you, nothing these young men can learn in a text book. You will teach them skills with your words, but the strength and integrity of your character will prove a guide they need for their lives."

"How do you know that your confidence in me is not misplaced?"

"Because you were willing to accept the consequences of your own choices, and beyond that you wanted to take Joel's punishment so that he could go free. 'Tis something our Savior did for us so many years ago."

"Ah, but, Sir, young Joel here was innocent of any wrong doing in this case, but we were guilty ones when our Savior died in our stead."

"Right you are, Jim. I shall never stop praising Him for so great a love."

"You really think I can do the job, Sir?"

"Without a doubt."

Jim stretched out his hand, "Tis not only the Savior who rescues the perishing, but you, Captain

Dundee. However, me thinks my Lord had His hand in this for the heart of a righteous man is in the hand of the Lord. I thank ye kindly for so great an opportunity. With God's help, I will not fail you, if it takes my dying breath."

"I know, Jim, I know." Captain Dundee replied, his voice husky as he shook Jim's hand. "A handshake and the deal is made. We will be in port two weeks then we sail to Savannah for our cargo and on to England. I expect you to hire on the crew. Perhaps some of the same ones that were aboard the Sea Sprite might be willing sailors this time. Wherever you get the men, I trust your judgment. Now I have to report to the authorities that I have commandeered a ship that was not mine. I may need your and Joel's testimonies."

"You have it, Sir." Joel responded crisply.

"Then carry on. We have a cargo to unload and a voyage to prepare for."

CHAPTER 7

The ground felt strange beneath Joel's feet as he walked down the teeming wharf. The crew had unloaded the Sea Sprite and the Santa Rosa, and with the jingle of wages in their pockets were on firm earth for the first time in two months and anxious to take in the sights and sounds of Boston.

Captain Dundee had asked Joel and Jim to accompany him as witnesses to the offices of the port authority to turn over the Sea Sprite and to press charges against her captain. As they strolled along the dock, Captain Dundee pointed out several ships that were part of Mr. Wilkins' successful fleet. Busy seaman unloaded ships' cargos from not only the west coast and Caribbean islands, but from around the world.

Some of these ships Wilkins' firm owned while other ships were owned by a select few captains like Captain Dundee. These voyages primarily went to the West Coast for the acquisition of hides for his tannery to turn into leather. It seemed that Mr. Wilkins had multiple business interests in Boston and the country beyond.

Joel was amazed at the activity going on around him and marveled that Dundee thought his wealthy partner would be interested in the likes of a simple cowpoke like him.

The business at the offices of the port authority took little time. They only required a brief statement from Jim and Joel. It was obvious that Captain Dundee's as well as Mr. Wilkins reputation was above reproach and that their testimonies were little more than a legality. It was equally evident that the skipper of the Sea Sprite had an infamous reputation and that the authorities were glad at long last to have tangible evidence against him. When or if he ever dared show his face in Boston, justice awaited him.

Surprisingly this knowledge gave Joel little pleasure. It saddened him that a capable sea captain would let the lure of ill gotten gain abort what could have been an honorable and profitable career. He was glad, however, that the captain's days of shanghaiing unsuspecting men were over. How many of these men found themselves, like Joel, on what seemed a foreign shore without the faintest notion of what they were to do. He supposed that many of them would take the Captain's good offer of signing on for his voyage to England. But what of those whose wife and children awaited them at home, not knowing what happened to them?

Remembering under what conditions most were shanghaied, Joel could not help but ponder what his mother had said so long ago. "Son, the devil's greatest lie is that you can sin and get away with it. Sin not only hurts the guilty, but the innocent as well. Lives of responsibility take into account how our actions will impact the lives of others, for good or for bad."

Captain Dundee bade the two seaman goodbye, explaining where Joel was to meet him the next day and advising them of suitable lodgings and a place to purchase some clean clothes.

He told Jim to meet him the day after in order to make plans for the next voyage, then eager for a reunion with his wife and family left them to be on his way.

Joel was glad to have old Jim by his side to lead the way as he found himself in a strange environment. How different the metropolitan Boston was from the cattle towns to which he was accustomed.

The reception area with its fine mahogany furnishings bespoke of wealth and success. As Joel waited, this time without the ever present Jim at his side, he felt uneasiness in the opulent surroundings. His stiff collar and store bought coat which strained across his broad, muscular shoulders added to his discomfort and he struggled with the temptation to leave before his meeting. How could this man in these surroundings have any interest in him? All that he knew how to do was drive cattle and do seaman's duty on a ship. His experience had been altogether manual labor out in the open air of sand, wind and sea. He rose as if to leave, then thought of Captain Dundee and his kindness toward him and sat down again, reluctant to disappoint the man who had shown such confidence in him.

He had faced the dangers of the prairie, the mountains, the desert and the sea with confidence, he had faced death on an icy lanyard without fear, yet the office and the man beyond those closed ornately carved doors caused dread to gnaw at his insides.

He asked himself why and he knew. It was the unknown and he had no control over that.

He smiled and relaxed as he remembered that the Good Lord has brought him safely thus far and his future was in His hands. As he relinquished his future the door opened and a young man, dapper in his suit motioned for him to come in.

The large mahogany desk dwarfed Mr. Wilkins. A man of small frame and immaculate dress, he appeared lost behind the behemoth piece of furniture. His head was down intent in the document before him. His thinning sandy hair that had once been a rich red gold now was washed in strands of silver.

Joel stood quietly waiting for him to finish his task.

When Nat Wilkins looked up, Joel forgot his opulent surroundings, his uncomfortable clothes and the apparent frailty of the man before him. The kindness and the twinkle in the eyes that greeted him brought the whole room to life and vanquished any self-doubts or fears that Joel had entertained.

"Hello, Joel. I'm Nat Wilkins and I've heard some very good things about you." He said as he reached an outstretched hand to Joel. "Please have a seat, as I want to learn even more."

Joel shook Mr. Wilkins' hand and chuckled, "Mr. Wilkins, I don't know how you heard any great things about me. I'm just a cowboy, recently turned sailor and I'm wondering what in the world I'm doing in an office like this."

Wilkins' laugh, deep and mellow, belied his delicate frame. "Joel, you're here because I believe that our Lord directs a man's steps in good times and in bad. I understand you are in pretty desperate situation right now. You need a job, you have a little money but not enough to last or to get you back to California. That you are concerned about your family and that you don't know what happened to them and would like to find out. Is that pretty accurate?"

"Yes, sir. That about sums it up."

"I'm also told that you are diligent, intelligent, a man of high integrity and a believer. Is that right?"

"I cannot speak to the scope of my intelligence, sir. I am a believer in the Lord Jesus Christ and because of that anything I do should be done whole heartedly. I hope that I prove diligent in every endeavor. As far as integrity goes, my dad taught me that a man is only as good as his word and that the measure of his worth is his character, not his ability or his riches."

"A good, Biblical principal-----a good name is rather to be chosen than great riches." Wilkins responded, nodding his head.

"It appears that God has granted you great riches along with a good name. I have also heard about you. I know your reputation is of the highest caliber and I thank you for taking the time to encourage me. I know you must be a busy man."

"I have not always been a rich man, Joel. How old are you, Joel?"

"I just turned nineteen, Sir."

Wilkins chuckled, "When I was nineteen I had no prospects for a prosperous future. You are the same age as I when I came to this strange and intimidating land."

"Land, Sir?"

"Yes, my boy. America was not my home. I shipped out from England when my parents died. There was no future for me there and I had heard that this was the land of opportunity."

"Seems it has been for you, Mr. Wilkins." Joel nodded toward his surroundings.

"Aye, it has been that. But not without a lot of hard work, sacrifice and hardship."

"A man's willingness to work is fundamental to his character, my pa told me."

"From what I hear you've learned that lesson well. According to Dundee you labored far beyond your responsibility."

"I had much to prove to Captain Dundee, but beyond that he needed each of us to do the work of two men as he was short handed."

Wilkins nodded his head, "Sorry bit of circumstances all around.   But maybe you'll be instrumental in apprehending that thief and renegade."

"I hope that somehow his evil practices can be stopped."

"Undoubtedly he has ruined the lives of countless men who have been shanghaied like you."

Joel nodded his head in agreement.

Wilkins continued, "Joel, I would like to see this experience become a stepping stone rather than a millstone for you."

"I don't intend it should be a millstone, sir, but I can tell you truly right now the future looks dim and opportunities slim."

"There is opportunity here for the right person. I'm not getting any younger and I'm looking for bright, young men to train in areas of management. They have to be hard working, men of integrity and leadership ability who want to learn. I have a broad section of business and investments. I'm sure you could find a place where your interest and expertise would fit."

"Mr. Wilkins, I'm flattered but I'm just a wrangler forced into sailing.   Look at my hands; they're not the hands of a gentleman.   And these clothes----this stiff collar is chaffing my neck and these britches are scratching my legs. I'm used to chaps and homespun. I've never been to school and I need to go home."

The older man smiled, "I know you want to go home, son. But where is home? From what I hear, the only home you have is a saddle and the prairie and you may not have a family. Here you have opportunity. As for the clothes, the proper tailor can alleviate your discomfort and as for an education, you may not have been to the university but you've proved you are a quick study by your actions on board ship and your vocabulary and manners tell me that someone has taken great pains in giving you an education. Am I correct?"

"My ma. She taught me to read, write and do sums when I was a little fellow."

"She taught you more than that, I'll wager."

"I learned lessons in how to live from the Bible and she gave me a thirst for knowledge that I learned to satisfy with books."

"Books out on the prairie?"

"She brought some from the mission where she went to school and then my pa ordered books for me after she died."

"And your brothers?"

"My half brothers." Joel corrected. "They were never interested in book learning. But they were good cattle men. They taught me a lot about how to herd cattle."

Wilkins chuckled again, "I'll wager they did it by experience."

Joel nodded, his eyes met the older man's and understanding passed between them.

"I, too, had some half brothers. That's the reason I'm here instead of England. There was no opportunity left for me. I'll wager that there is none waiting for you back out west if your father is not alive."

Joel dropped his head, knowing what the older man said was true. Then responded after a pause, "But I have to see about my pa."

"I understand, Joel. Suppose you work for me while you earn your passage back to California and meanwhile I'll do what I can to find out what I can about your family?"

"But how? We are all the way across the country from where I left my pa. I've questioned how in the world I could find out anything with me here and who knows where he is. Or if he is."

Wilkins chuckled, "I will make some inquiries, post a letter to my business interest in California."

"That will take a mighty long time to get an answer."

"There might very well be some news from other packets coming into port later this month. News has a way of boarding ship, you know."

Joel shook his head, "That would be a mighty fine thing to know something one way or the other. Until then I don't know how to get on with my life."

"I understand, Joel. But I've always believed that we do what we know we should do at the moment and the Lord will reveal our next step if we but ask Him and are willing to obey."

"You have a point there, Mr. Wilkins."

"Your first step is to get a job that will pay you enough to earn your fare back home, if that is what you decide is the right thing for you."

"You wouldn't happen to have a ranch and some cattle in this city that needed a cow hand would you?"

"No, Boston isn't conducive to ranching, but I do have a shipping and ship building firm as well as tannery and other interests."

"Well, don't reckon I know much about tanning hides, but I do have a strong back and could work down on the docks."

The older man pursed his lips as if in deep thought. "You may be right, Joel. The docks might be a good place for you to start. However, my intentions go way beyond loading and unloading cargo."

"Like I said, Mr. Wilkins, I'm not equipped to do anything but manual labor."

"Don't sell yourself short. By Dundee's evaluation, you have leadership skills and a keen intelligence that needs cultivating and channeling in the right direction."

"Would your efforts be worthwhile since I'll be here only temporarily?"

"Investing in lives is always worthwhile. And someone needs to show you your potential. You've been looking at the ground too much wrangling cattle, you need to look up, Joel. You have a future beyond that."

"Where and when do you want me to start? The sooner the better. I surely don't have anything else to do in this strange city."

"I remember that lonely feeling."

"Work will take care of that. Besides the sooner I began earning a paycheck the sooner I can check on my pa." Joel reminded, not wanting Wilkins to feel he had changed his mind about going back home, wherever that was now.

"All work makes for an imbalanced life. When old Jim ships out, you'll be strictly on your own."

"I'll miss Jim, but I'll do just fine, Sir."

"I have a daughter just about your age. When she comes home from school, I'll have her introduce you to some of her friends. Can't have you alone and working all the time."

"That is mighty kind of you, but I hardly think I would fit in."

Mr. Wilkins paused for a moment, and then a broad smile parted his thin face, "You don't know my daughter! When she comes home, we'll just see if you're comfortable with her and her friends. I think you'll be quite surprised."

The older man paused, then smiled. "Tell you

what, why don't you come home with me for dinner? I'd like my wife to meet you."

"That's mighty kind of you, but I couldn't put your missus to that trouble. An unexpected guest and all that." Joel objected.

"Won't be a bit of trouble. I'm bringing home guests all the time. I really feel like it's a ministry. People arrive here alone and disoriented. It helps to have a warm meal and friendly conversation to anchor them. I'm able to give them a little direction about how to navigate their lives here in Boston and in this country. Sometimes they become close friends, and sometimes I never see them again, but each leaves knowing that there is someone they can call on in a crisis."

"Have you ever been taken advantage of?" Joel inquired.

"Very rarely. But those few times can't be compared to the sense of satisfaction knowing that I had a part in encouraging someone in a better future."

Joel chuckled, "And for sure I'm another project needing encouragement."

"Not this time, Joel. From all I've heard about you I see mutual benefits for the both of us. I can help you meet your need, but I think you're going to help me as well."

"I don't understand how I can help you on such a temporary basis." Joel reminded softly.

"We will take this a step at a time. Your coming

to work for me is the first step, God has the rest of our steps all planned out. We just don't know what they are yet. In His proper time He will reveal them to you as well as to me, if I'm to have a part in your future."

"When you put it like that, it gives me great encouragement. I'll do what I know to do and let God lead the way."

"You can't go wrong like that." Wilkins agreed. "Suppose you meet me back here around three in the afternoon and we'll go home to meet my wife."

Joel nodded his head, "I'll be honored to do that. I'm supposed to meet Jim after this meeting."

"Then old Jim can show you the ins and outs of Boston harbor. Ask him to show you my establishments so that you'll know where to meet me tomorrow. And by the way, Joel, don't do anything about your lodgings after tonight until you see me this afternoon."

"Very well, Sir." Joel reached to take the hand that was offered, puzzling over what Mr. Wilkins meant by his last remark.

CHAPTER 8

"He asked you to have dinner with him and the missus?" Old Jim asked, incredulity raising his voice to a squeak.

Joel nodded.

"He shore as shootin' got something big in store for you, boy. I'm sorry I'll be shipping out before I find out where this tale is leading."

"It's a big mystery to me why he has taken this interest. He seems to be a good and kindhearted man."

Jim stroked his chin for a few moments, "I've heard he is, but this goes beyond a simple kind act, I'd say."

"That's what worries me. I don't want to give him any expectations that I can't live up to, seeing I'm only here long enough to earn the money to go find my pa."

"Does he know that?"

"I kept reminding him that I was temporary, but he swept that aside as if it were not an issue."

"Strange business, I'd say."

"You think I misread him and he's not as

benevolent as he seems on the surface?"

"No, I've never heard anything but good about him. And believe me, you'd hear it on the docks. That rag tag crew rather complain than look for the benefits in anybody or anything. All I've heard from them is that Mr. Wilkins gives a fair wage for a good days work. Some of them even had some kind things to say about him. 'Specially when he and the missus lost their son."

"They had a son?"

"Yes, I saw him once. Fine, good looking, young man. He was just about your age when I saw him. His dad had him working on the docks for a while. Seems he wanted him to learn the business from the bottom up. The next thing I heard, he had shipped out on a packet to the islands. One of those fierce storms blew up. The ship and all that were on it perished. That would be about five or six years ago. It was said that it nearly killed his mother. Maybe that's why he wants to help you. Knowing how he'd want someone to treat his son if he were in your situation."

Joel sighed, "Maybe. But he said it would be a mutual benefit for the both of us. I'd say he's looking for me to stay on long term and that's what worries me."

The older man put a hand on Joel's shoulder, looking him in the eye, "Didn't you tell him you weren't here for the long haul?"

"Several times."

"Then you have to accept that it is the Lord

watching after you and receive His blessings with thanksgiving instead of so much doubt."

A broad grin parted Joel's face, "I declare, Jim, if you didn't have such a scraggly beard and a raspy voice, I'd think my ma was talking to me."

"The truth remains the same no matter who voices it."

"You're right. From now on the introspection is over-----"

"The intro---what?"

"You know overly examining every angle of something instead of accepting God's blessings for what they are."

"That's my boy." Jim puffed out his chest and smiled proudly as if Joel were his own son whom he had just rescued from a grievous mistake.

The clop, clop of the matched grays made a rhythmic sound as they rode through the cobblestone streets. Mr. Wilkins had left for home earlier than expected and had sent the carriage back for Joel. The trip gave Joel a chance to relax and enjoy the scenery along the way.

Soon they left the business district behind, making their way briskly through the residential hills where houses lined the street. Standing tall and regal, some narrow, some broad but all were many storied and some on taller knolls faced the sea.

The houses intrigued Joel. They were so different from the low adobe ones to which he was accustomed. He wondered how it would feel to walk the widow's walk and stand above the city with the wind blowing his face and hair. Something like standing on the deck of a ship in a brisk blow, he imagined. Many a wife must have watched and waited for the sight of the sails that would bring her captain safely home to her.

The carriage made an abrupt turn and started up a steep incline. Beacon Hill the street sign said. The houses now were further apart and palatial in appearance. Soon they turned and passed through elaborate wrought iron gates and a long winding driveway. The house came into view and he smiled. Large and imposing, it was in keeping with the other houses on the street; yet there was warmth about it that seemed to draw you in. Perhaps it was its sparkling windows, or maybe the warm tones of the muted golds and browns versus the cold charcoal and gray of the neighboring houses. Joel couldn't quite decide what created its ambience, but suddenly he looked with anticipation to dinner and meeting Mrs. Wilkins.

Mr. Wilkins met him at the door, taking his coat and handing it to a butler standing nearby. "No need for you to be uncomfortable during dinner, Joel. As you can see, I've discarded mine. Tonight we will dine quite informally since there will be only the three of us. Come

I want you to meet my wife."

Joel smiled, "She's not miffed with you for bringing in a stranger to her table?"

"On the contrary she is anxious to hear about the west and your voyage."

"All of it?"

"Most assuredly, at least what is in good taste."

The older man escorted Joel into a large dining room ablaze with glowing candelabras and crystal chandeliers. Seated at the far side of a long table was a slender, elegantly dressed lady with silver hair whose beauty seemed almost ethereal. She looked up as Joel entered and gave Joel a welcoming smile that would have melted any heart. She left no doubt he was welcome.

"Hannah, darling, this is-----."

"Joel. Welcome to our home." She said, holding out her hand to him.

"Joel, this is my wife, Hannah Wilkins. When you meet my daughter, it won't take you long before you see where she gets her exuberance as well as beauty." The look he lavished on his wife bespoke a man captivated by his love for her.

Something Joel did not miss, and briefly a fleeting pain tore at his heart as he remembered his own mother. Recovering he took her outstretched hand and turned a winsome smile on Hannah Wilkins, his dark eyes twinkling, "Thank you, ma'am. I appreciate the invitation and hope it hasn't inconvenienced you any."

Her laugh was lyrical, "Not at all. Nate told me all about you and I'm eager to hear about your adventure."

"Well ma'am I'll be glad to tell you all you want to hear. That's the very least I can do to repay such a welcome invitation. It's been a long time since I've been in refined company or had a home cooked meal and I'm looking forward to both."

"Good. Please have a seat. It's been a long time since we've had a healthy young appetite at this table." A fleeting pain touched her eyes, dimming the sparkle briefly.

Joel noticed and remembered the story old Jim had told him about losing their son. He took the seat offered as Nate Wilkins sat between the two at the head of the table.

A bountiful meal of pheasant and fresh vegetables followed by a rich desert of bread pudding left little time for conversation. As soon as Joel finished his last bite and the table was cleared, Hannah Wilkins placed her delicate chin in her hands and leaned toward Joel, eagerness firing her eyes. "Now tell us all about your adventure."

"My dear, Joel's was more a painful ordeal than adventure." Wilkins chuckled, "My wife is a hopeless romantic, Joel. She thinks that every voyage is an adventure."

"Mr. Wilkins is right, ma'am. It was a painful ordeal from start to finish. That is until Captain Dundee saw fit to trust me, but even then I had a day of reckoning hanging over my head. I didn't know my fate until I got to Boston and even now I don't know my future."

"Well surely Nate has already assisted you in that."

"In every way possible ma'am, but there are some things that are beyond your good husband's scope."

"Pshaw! There is nothing Nate can't accomplish when he sets his mind to it."

"Now, Dear, I appreciate your confidence, but you know I have limits." Wilkins blushed.

His wife turned a gentle gaze on him, "I was just obeying the Good Book that admonishes me to respect and admire my husband. Besides I really can't imagine what challenge Joel faces which you can't help him solve."

"Joel needs to find his father."

"See! I knew it. You can just pull in your contacts and find him."

"He is somewhere out west and it will take time."

"I think there is more to this story than you told me, Nate." Hannah replied, the exuberance draining from her voice as she noted the pain in Joel's eyes.

"There is, my dear. Even I don't know the whole story and what I do know, I didn't feel free to share without Joel's permission."

Mrs. Wilkins turned to Joel, gentleness softening her voice, "Joel, wouldn't you like to share your story with us? Perhaps we can help you. Sometimes just to share your burden with another lightens the load."

And so it was that Joel poured out his heart to a couple of strangers in palatial surroundings. Beginning with his childhood, he told them the heartbreaking tale of why and how he had arrived penniless and alone in Boston.

Tears rolled down Hannah Wilkins cheeks as Joel told of the betrayal that had brought him to their home and when he had finished even her husband's eyes were brightened by tears too manly to shed.

"What are you going to do, Joel?"

"Mr. Wilkins has kindly offered me a job until I can earn my passage back home. I have no formal training, but I do have a strong back and can hold my own on the docks."

"Nathaniel, are you sending him down to the docks?"

"What would you have me do?"

"Something that will earn him more money than that. He needs to be on his way to see about his father. Can't you get word, have your people in California search for information."

"Mrs. Wilkins, I am thankful for the opportunity to work at anything that's honest and your husband has already promised to gather information that might be helpful in locating my family."

"Very well. So you have made some progress. I

think I have an idea. Nate can't pay you more than the other workers, but if you didn't have to pay for your lodging and some of your meals you could save most of your wages."

Mr. Wilkins put his hand over his mouth, trying to hide a smile, "Did you have something in mind, Hannah?"

"We have a carriage house that is in good condition and unoccupied. He could even take some of his meals with us."

"No ma'am. I could not take advantage of your hospitality like that. I wouldn't feel right it would be like taking charity."

"Of course, what was I thinking!" Hannah exclaimed.

"Your generous nature and tender heart were thinking for you, my dear." Wilkins countered. "But you did bring a solution to my mind."

"Yes, dear?"

"I'm sure Joel is as proficient with horses as he is a seaman."

"I hope more so, sir."

"We have some mighty fine horseflesh in our stables that need looking after. It surely wouldn't take all your time. You could still do the work I have planned for you and take mornings and evenings to exercise and see to our horses. Lodging has always been part of the compensation for that position. It would keep you close to the horses in case of a crisis and like Hannah mentioned, the carriage house is available."

Joel sighed, "I can't think of anything I'd rather do."

"Then it is all settled. You use one of the mounts to ride to work and have a job and lodging waiting for you when you return from the docks."

"I'm overwhelmed, sir."

"I'm really not doing you a favor; I need someone who knows something about horses. I've recently expanded my stables and have too much invested in them to neglect their welfare and, as yet, we have found no one who has had the expertise to satisfy me."

"My pa said I cut my teeth on a bridle. I've been in the saddle since I was a little shaver and it will feel good to have one under me again. My pa taught me how to appreciate and care for our horses. Of course they were working mounts, but sharing my pa's love for horseflesh, I read all I could about the different breeds. I have no doubt that I can satisfy what you need as a stable hand."

"Actually I want you to oversee the stable hands that I have. I have several groomsmen, but no one to manage the stables."

Joel nodded, "I will be more than willing to do whatever is needed."

"It might mean some nights without sleep when you have a sick horse." Wilkins reminded.

"I can well remember many of those." Joel agreed.

"That settles it then. Why don't you come with me and I'll take you on a tour of the stables and your new lodgings. You will excuse us, Hannah?"

"Of course, Nate. I'm just thrilled you and Joel have found a solution to your problems that will benefit both."

Joel could hardly contain the excitement as the carriage wound its way through the streets of Boston. What would his friend think of this latest turn of affairs? He knew Jim would be as excited as he. He could hear him now, "The Good Lord is smiling on you, my boy.

And he knew it was true. How could such good fortune come his way except from God's benevolent hand? He remembered his mother telling him that every good and perfect gift came from above. And this was a gift beyond imagining. A job, a place to live and to be working with horses again. And not just any horses, but some of the finest bloodlines.

His tour of the stables had left him amazed. The wide expansive buildings of rock and brick were fine enough for human habitation and they housed the finest horseflesh he had ever seen.

It didn't take long for Joel to notice that Wilkins had not exaggerated when he said he needed an overseer. There were evidences of neglect both in the building and the horses' care. Joel made mental notes as he went from stall to stall of changes needing to be made. He pointed out some that were most obvious, thus pleasing Mr. Wilkins and affirming that the older man had made a wise proposal earlier. He was eager to begin, to show his benefactor what a well run stable could accomplish.

He was no less amazed at his future lodgings. The carriage house was nicer than any place he had ever lived. From the large windows of the parlor with a view of the gardens to its expansive fireplace with large bookcases on either side, it had a warm ambience that invited him in. He had a strange sensation that he was home, at last. He shook his head as if to clear it of these strange emotions and walked on into the galley.

Though small, it was plenty adequate enough in which to prepare his meals. The bedroom also faced the garden with a large four poster feather bed reigning center of the wall facing windows which would catch the first rays of the rising sun.

Jim was waiting up for him, eager to hear about his evening and to share news of his own.

"Tell you what, Joel. 'Tis no doubt that our Lord has his hand on you. How else can you account for the events of this night?"

Joel nodded his head, "Yes, but why? Why does

this opportunity come when my mind is set to find my pa?"

"Jest like I said, you take one step at a time and do it with a grateful heart. The Lord knows the future and He's got you and it in His hands."

"I'm going to like this step, for sure. But what about you, Jim? I hate to leave you here to shift for yourself. Can you afford this room if I leave?"

A broad grin parted Jim's face and his beady blue eyes danced, "Got some news of me own. I was dreading to tell you 'cause it meant leaving you here to fend for yourself and I knew that you'd never be able to afford this lodging and save enough to get back to California."

"What is it, man? Speak up! I want to hear all about it."

"Seems that Captain Dundee is going to take a few weeks off to be with his family. They're expecting a wee one soon. He wants me to move onboard ship and see to getting her ship shape and readying her for the voyages. That means I'll be in charge of outfitting her with supplies and men. He said he needed an honest man he could trust and one what could get it done."

"That's great news."

"Can you imagine it, Joel? He wanted me after that last voyage with those crooks I signed on with."

"You didn't know they were crooks."

"I should've. I'd heard of the man's reputation, and the truth be known, I don't know if I would have said anything to the authorities about his cargo if he'd made it back to Boston without being caught."

"I've got enough confidence in your goodness to believe you would have."

"I ain't good, Joel. The Bible says that none of us is. We are all like sheep who has gone astray, else why would we need the Savior? I'm just thankful that I've been given a second chance."

"It seems that we both have." Joel agreed softly, patting Jim on the back.

CHAPTER 9

Days turned into weeks and weeks into months as Joel labored on the docks and spent the early morning hours and evenings caring for the horses.

Soon the stables took on the appearance of a well run establishment. Each piece of gear in its proper place and all the harnesses, bridles and saddles cleaned and buffed. Joel dismissed the four stable boys when they refused to rectify the slovenly condition. He attended to the remaining duties working many nights past midnight and arising before five a.m.

Late one night when Wilkins couldn't sleep, he wandered down to the stables only to discover Joel busy cleaning out stalls.

"Joel, how long has this been going on?" Wilkins demanded.

"What, Sir?"

"You're working late into the night when you have to be at a hard days work on the docks from early in the morning?"

Joel chuckled, "Hard work never killed anyone,

Mr. Wilkins."

"No, but lack of sleep can. Is this an every night occurrence?"

Joel nodded, "If you take care of these fine horses properly, it takes some extra time."

"Why haven't you hired some help?"

"You have been so generous with me, I thought to repay the favor."

"It will be no favor to me if something happens to you from overwork."

"I'm healthy and love to work."

"That's an admirable attitude but you're too valuable for menial tasks that we can hire others to do. I have plans for you that go beyond the stable and docks."

"But, sir, I'm here for only a brief time. It wouldn't be proper for me to take a job that you had to train me for since I'll be leaving as soon as I have the funds."

"That's something that I was going to discuss with you in the morning. One of my ships, the last one for this year, arrived from California. Come to my office in the morning and I'll introduce you to the captain. Maybe he or some of his men have news of your family."

"Thank you for your help. I surely want any information that I can get."

Joel slept fitfully despite his late hours. Dreams of his father destitute and in need tormented him. After two hours of sleep he arose and tended the horses. Arriving at the dock before his shift, he sought out the foreman and told him he had to be off for a couple of hours.

The big, burly Irishmen grinned, "I wish I had a dozen men like you, Joel. Not many would show up two hours early to make up the time he would lose."

"I appreciate the job, besides you know I need the money."

"Yeah, I heard about your family. Maybe that new ship that came in will have some information for you."

"That's why I'm going to miss a couple of hours, Mr. Wilkins has arranged for me to meet the captain and talk with him."

"It won't be the captain that'll have some news for you. It would more'n likely one of the crew that frequented Sal's place. That's where you get the news east of the bay."

"Sounds like you've been there before. What are you doing on the docks if you're a sailor?"

"In my wilder, single days I'll have to admit I visited Sal's place a couple of times. But when I met my missus that was the end of that. I go home to her every night. That's why I'm here instead of on the deck of a ship."

"I thought once a sailor, always one."

"Guess I wasn't one at heart. Anyway that's not the life for a married man. Too many lonely hours for the wife and the man. Nope I like going home in the evenings. Anyway this job is steady and the pay's good."

"So you like married life." Joel teased.

"Tell you what it tamed this tiger. You ought to find you a little filly and settle down."

"I don't have time for that. Anyway I'm just here temporarily."

"Much to my regret, I'll have to say. You could really advance in Mr. Wilkins' organization, I believe. I know you wouldn't stay here for long. You're too smart to be breaking your back on the docks."

"I've enjoyed the work." Joel countered. "It's been just what I needed."

"You're right, hard work can help a man's mind when he is troubled. Sort of works the kinks out, you might say. We'd better get busy unloading these hides. This is the last shipment until next year."

Joel worked until mid-morning when most of the cargo had been off loaded. When he saw the captain leave, he gave him a few minutes and then followed.

When he arrived at Wilkins office, he was ushered right in.

"Ben, this is the young man I've been telling you about. Joel, this is Ben Chapman captain of the Windsong."

Ben Chapman rose from his seat and extended his hand to Joel, "I've heard a lot of good things about you, young man. I'd like to have you aboard my ship, but

Nate tells me you wouldn't be interested."

"Only if you were going back to California, Sir."

Captain Chapman shook his head. "No, I'm bound for home for a few days then off to the Caribbean, back here and then to Portsmouth, England. It'll be a couple of years before I return to the west coast."

"Well, sir, I suppose Mr. Wilkins has told you my plight."

"Yes, he has. That is a terrible practice, shanghaiing men. I understand you're looking for information about your family. I can't help you but perhaps some of my men can. There were a few I picked up in California. Some of them wanted to get back to the east coast; some of them claimed they were tired of wrangling cattle. I think they may have had second thoughts about that after going 'round the horn." Chapman chuckled.

"Will they be returning to California?" Joel asked, his heart skipping a beat.

"Not for two years. They signed on for that long."

"Joel, I've been thinking, if you'll work for me two years I'll send you back with Chapman at my expense and you can have enough saved by that time to stake you. How does that sound?"

"That's a mighty generous offer but I was hoping to get back sooner. No telling what could happen in two years."

"Perhaps you can find information from Chapman's crew that will assist in making your decision."

Wilkins suggested. "If you have lost your family, it seems a waste for you to go back where you no longer have any ties. There's no future for you there, the opportunities are here. Even if you find your father, why not bring him here where he could have an easier life?"

"Pa would die housed up in the city. He likes the wide open spaces."

"How about you, Joel?"

"I like Boston. As long as I could have a hand with some horses and a mount under my saddle, I could adjust. I wanted Pa to start raising horses instead of cattle anyway. We just never found the right set up and never had the money to buy good stock."

"You go with Ben and talk to his men. I'll see you later to find out what happened. It's my prayer that you will find some answers today, Joel." Wilkins urged, his voice gentle.

A gentle breeze wafted from the harbor, bringing in the smell of the sea. Joel paused for a moment and lifted his head toward the sun, his countenance thoughtful.

Captain Chapman cleared his throat, speaking hesitantly, "Joel, I hope you will find some information to help you make your decision. You know Wilkins is right, there is great opportunity for you here. He has taken quite a liking to you."

"He has been more than kind to me. Under different circumstances I would gladly take up his offer."

"You know you remind him greatly of the son he lost."

"No, sir, I didn't know that. "

"He told me so himself, and even I can see the resemblance. He was a fine young man and just about your age when they lost him."

"I am so sorry about their loss."

"Wilkins planned for his son to take over the business in his stead, that's why he was working in every aspect of it. Learning from the bottom up. Kind of like you are doing."

"Sir?"

"I believe his plans for you might be similar to those he had for his son."

"Oh, no, sir." Joel denied. "He has shown great kindness to me and given me opportunity equal to my abilities."

"Not according to what he said to me. He thinks you have great potential. Has he not told you that?"

"He has encouraged me, but until I find out the whereabouts of my family, I have no future to plan and I wouldn't want Mr. Wilkins spending the time to train me if I couldn't live up to his expectation."

"Come on then, we'll see what we can find out and then maybe you can get on with your life. It's a terrible handicap to live in limbo as you must have been doing."

"It is distressing not knowing about my family,

but hard work and a goal keeps me from looking forward with hope instead of dwelling on the past."

"Good for you, Joel. Here we are and I'll let you start with my first mate. I know that he doesn't frequent Sal's establishment, but he might be able to steer you to the men who do. May God bless you in your quest and in your future." Chapman said as he held out his hand. "If I can ever do something for you, just let me know. The offer still stands, you can sign on with me at any time."

"If you were returning to California, I'd sign on today."

Chapman chuckled, "I don't think I've ever met a young man so devoted to his family."

"My pa." Joel corrected. Unwanted feelings stirred within him as the image of his brothers flooded his mind. "I feel responsible for his welfare. He sent me to do a job, if he is alive, I mean to complete it."

"And if he isn't?"

"I haven't allowed my self to entertain such thoughts. Pa just has to be alive. I've a task to finish for him and as for my brothers---- that, too, is an unsettled issue that needs a resolution." Joel spoke, his voice deepening with determination, his warm brown eyes turning to flint.

"Revenge never solves anything, Joel. Though it would take a better man than me not to have those thoughts." Chapman admitted softly.

"Not revenge, Sir. Understanding."

"Good man." Chapman affirmed, his voice growing husky as he took in the struggle raging in Joel.

Joel's quest took longer than two hours. At first it looked as if the Windsong would offer little in the way of information that he could use. As the sun moved from directly overhead toward the mid afternoon, Joel questioned officers and regular crew to no avail. Finally as he was about to give up hope, a large burly sailor swaggered up to him, "You the kid looking for information from Sal's?"

"I'm looking for information concerning my family from wherever I can get it." Joel countered.

"What's it worth to you?"

"Quite a lot, but if you're talking money, I have very little."

"Enough for a pint of ale when I get a chance to get off this rocking piece of perdition."

Joel frowned, "I take it you don't like sailoring."

"No, but I'm stuck for two more years. Now what about that pint of ale?"

"I think I can manage that much." Joel agreed as he reached in his pocket and brought out a few coins.

The burly man put one of them between his teeth and bit down. "Reckon these are good."

"About the information you have?" Joel snapped.

"Jest be patient. I'll get to the point of my news in my own good time." The sailor's beady eyes took in the flurry of activity surrounding him.

"It's just that I don't want you missing work. The captain was kind enough to let me interrupt his crew."

"That captain, the way I see it, he's got his pound of flesh from me and now it won't hurt to let me rest a bit."

Joel urged, "But I have a job to return to. Now you have the money, give me the information."

"Are you the bloke that got hisself shanghaied?" The sailor grinned a toothless smile.

"I was shanghaied." Joel admitted softly, struggling to control his growing frustration.

"Yeah, I heard all about you. Those brothers of yours really put one over on you, but I guess you might have the last laugh after all, heh?"

"What do you mean by that?" Joel asked between clinched teeth. "You talked to my brothers?"

The older man paused, the derisive grin wiped from his face as he encountered the steel in Joel's eyes. "Not directly. The story was making its rounds at Sal's place before I got there."

"I thought you had some useful information for me."

"How could I be the judge of whether it's useful to you or no?."

"The question was, and is, do you have any current information about my family?"

"I'm just getting to that, if'n you'll show a little patience." The seaman's ruddy face reddened as his eyes locked with Joel's.

"I'm at the end of my patience. I want to know what you meant when you said that I might have the last laugh." Joel insisted.

"When I first arrived at Sal's the story of how your brothers had bamboozled you was making the rounds. One night jes' before I signed on with the cap'n this drover came up to the bar. He'd been riding hard and looked like he had a story to tell. He said that the week before he was on his way back from San Diego to join his drive, that's where he had to meet with a Mr. Smithwick about buying his cattle."

"And-----." Joel interrupted.

"He'd seen three men, a woman and what appeared to be an old man camped along the river."

"So they were alive and well?"

"Not so fast. That was on the way out to the cattle. When he drove the cattle to water on the way in, he found their bodies."

"Did one of the men have red hair and was the girl one of Sal's?"

"He was in a hurry on the way back to his herd and only saw them from a distance. They all had on hats. When he came back, well, I don't quite know how to put it, but they didn't seem to have any hair, if you know what I mean. And as for the girl, well you wouldn't have been able to tell if she was one of Sal's or not."

"Indians?" Joel's heart thundered

"Yup. That's what it looked like to him. I tell you, he said it was not a pretty sight."

"But he couldn't tell you definitely who they were." Joel urged, a glimmer of hope refusing to die.

"Everybody knew who they were. Even one of Sal's men came back and told her that she could just forget getting her property back because the Indians had taken care of that. Like I said, you've had the last laugh."

With one lightening swift movement, Joel grabbed the sailor and pinned him to the wall, his forearm locked beneath his chin. "Losing my family is no laughing matter."

Green eyes bulged, fear erasing all signs of levity. He sputtered as Joel pressed his arm tighter against his throat, "I meant you was lucky you were on a ship, else your fate would have been the same as your family's. Anyhow if I ever heard of anybody getting their just deserts, it was that woman and those brothers of yours."

"And who are you to decide what anyone deserves?" Joel suddenly released the man, despair flooding every ounce of his being.

The mariner, rubbed his throat gingerly and then fled back onto the deck of the Windsong and safety. Arriving back aboard, one of the crew met him. "Jeremy, I heard what you were telling that young blade."

"So? What's it to you, Jack?"

"Half of what you garnered from him to keep me

mouth shut."

"Why should I do that?"

"Because I know you never made it to Sal's place so how could you hear such a story? You were in the stockade from the time you got to town. Fact is that's why you signed on board the Windsong, to get out of jail."

"Maybe I heard it there. But anyhow what's a pint of ale without a friend to share it with? Come on with me soon as we finish our job."

"No, Jerry. I'll take my half now. I'll not want to be sharing a pint with the likes of you." Jack stretched out his hand, his one bloodshot eye spearing Jeremy as he dropped the coins in his hand.

Meanwhile, Joel, grief stricken, made his way down the docks, oblivious to his surroundings, forgetting the job to which he was supposed to return. Tentacles of guilt for his father's fate gripped his reasoning, bringing unbearable pain. If only he had been wiser, he could have made it back and his Pa's life would have been spared. He must have done something to provoke his brother's betrayal. But what? If only he could undo it!

An agonizing groan ripped from deep within him, causing passersby to look and then scurry away as they took in the grief on his twisted face. A brisk wind howled around the corner, but brought no answers with it. Its mournful wale only reinforced that his family was lost. His anguish wiped away Mr. Wilkins' promise of a bright tomorrow. Now only a lonely uncertain future stretched out before him.

CHAPTER 10

An insistent pounding resonated in Joel's head and awakened him from the fitful sleep he had fallen into sometime just before dawn. Sunlight streamed in his windows, hurting his eyes and the unrelenting hammering continued. Disoriented, it took him a moment before he realized the noise was not in his head, but at his front door.

Disheveled with a full day's growth of beard darkening his face, he turned away from the unwelcome noise. Today he only wanted to retreat from a world too harsh to face. Whatever the problem represented at his door, someone else could handle it. Tomorrow maybe he would get his bearings and head out. But to where? And to what? Life had lost its direction. His plan lay in shambles. There was no pa to rescue, no brothers with which to settle past grievances. There was no one left to explain to him why his brothers had treated him as they did and through it all heaven remained silent.

Once again it hit him full force, he was untethered, no family and no direction for his future. He groaned and piled more pillows over his head, trying to shut out the sun and the incessant pounding. Suddenly it quieted and he heard Nate Wilkins call his name.

There would be no escaping the world today. This man who had shown him such kindness deserved an answer as to why he had not returned to his duties at the dock. It was a first for Joel, not fulfilling an obligation. He had attended the horses when he arrived home; but not being able to face people he had not returned to work, instead he had walked the streets of Boston with tormenting questions, unanswered, screaming through his mind. Why? And where was the God of his mother in all of this? She had told him that the God she served would never leave or forsake. Then why was he so alone?

He stumbled to the door, grabbing a rumpled shirt he had heaved into a pile beside his bed in his exhaustion the night before. When he opened the door, his eyes met the worried eyes of his benefactor and he dropped his head in silence, ashamed that he had let him down.

Still mute he motioned the older man inside.

Wilkins scrutinized Joel's face, anguish still leaving its mark there. The droop of his usually erect shoulders relayed a message of despondency. The older man grasped the younger's shoulder and quietly asked, "My boy, what has happened? Your supervisor told me that you never returned to work yesterday."

"'Tis true, sir and I deeply regret not honoring my work and letting you down after all the help you have been to me."

"I've done nothing for you that you haven't earned many times over, Joel. But Nick was worried because he knew that you would have come back unless something untoward had happened to you."

"Nothing to me, Sir. Only my family."

"You had word of your family, then?"

"Aye," Joel slipping into a sailor's tongue.

"And?"

"They are all dead." Joel clinched his teeth, trying to control the emotions that threatened to take control again.

"Dead? How?"

"Apparently at the hands of a renegade band of Indians that plagued the area recently."

"How do you know?"

"A sailor told me."

"And how did he get his information? Did he see them?"

"No, sir, but his friend did. Or at least what was left of them." Involuntarily Joel shuddered and closed his eyes as the sight described to him played through his mind.

"Are you sure he had his facts straight?"

"The description of my family, especially of my --," Joel hesitated as vivid red hair and alluring green eyes and their treachery brought the past back, "sister-in-law and where they were located."

"But, if not much was left of them, then how could you be sure----?"

"His friend saw them alive on his way into town and again on his way back. I've accepted the truth of it. Now I just have to deal with it. That's why I didn't return to work. I was trying to deal with it, trying to understand the whys of it all. I wondered if I had been there would it have happened. What did I do to my brothers in the first place that caused us to get into this mess? That's what prevented me from being with my family when they needed me. Most of all I wonder where was God in all this?"

Wilkins shook his head, pain darkening his vivid blue eyes, but said nothing.

Joel continued, as if begging an answer, "My ma told me that her God would never forsake you or leave you. But where was He in the desert when my family needed Him? Where was He, when they threw me in the hole of that ship trussed us like some pig for market? Why couldn't I go home and settle this issue with my brothers and take care of my pa? That's all I wanted. To take care of Pa and to understand why my brothers hated me enough to do what they did. Now I'll never understand."

Tears brightened Wilkins eyes, "Oh, dear boy, what a load you carry. I won't give you any platitudes to try to make you feel better. This is an issue that calls for grief. Time will walk you through it, but grieve you must. Believe me I've been there."

Joel suddenly remembered about the older man's loss. Empathy mitigated his pain for a moment. He considered how his own tragedy might re-open old wounds for this kind man. "I'm sorry, Sir. I know you have had more than your share of sorrow and I don't intend to add to your grief by piling mine on you. These thoughts tumbling around in my mind just burst forth. Guess it's 'cause you are the first person that I have talked to since I heard the dreadful news."

"No, Joel, you told me because you know that I am your friend and I care what happens to you. As for adding to my grief by burdening me with yours, nothing could be further from the truth. Nothing can assuage my loss and I will grieve over it until the end of my days. However, at times God uses my sorrow to help others who are experiencing the pain of loss. I hope I can assist you when you get over this initial shock and the destruction of your dreams."

"I guess you don't ever question why God does what He does. I know my ma would be disappointed if she'd heard me just now."

Wilkins chuckled. "Question God? Oh, yes, I have had a lot of questions for Him."

"Did He answer them?"

"No, not all of them."

"Then what did you do?"

"I railed out at Him."

"And you're still on speaking terms with Him?"

"That's right."

"How come He didn't just send a lightning bolt down on you or something?"

"Because in all my questions and railings, He knew my heart was seeking Him. The pain that provoked the questions revealed to me the superficial faith that was in my heart. It was easy to trust Him when I could see my way clearly, but I discovered that really isn't faith. Faith takes place when we have unanswered questions that hang in the balance, when what happens in our life makes no sense to us and Heaven seems silent. It was through this experience, the greatest pain a parent can experience, that I learned to trust Him no matter what the circumstances might be. I finally came to the place in my life that if Heaven seemed silent, I knew that He was working in the silence—and working for my good."

"How could you think that?"

"Because I came to understand that He loves me even more than I loved my son."

"Then why did He take him away from you, and why has He destroyed my life?"

"He hasn't destroyed your life. If the information the sailor gave you was true, then He saved your life by sending you here. Consequently you were not at the mercy of those renegades."

"I wish I had been there."

"It would have cost you your life."

"What life?"

"The life that God has in store for you. The one He preserved by sending you away from danger. "

"How do I know that?"

"Look at His hand of protection on you. You asked where He was when you were on board ship. Your life was spared when you slipped on the icy yard arm, in every circumstance you found favor with crew and those in authority. You could be facing a rope around your neck for being on board that thieving ship, yet you were pardoned and offered opportunity for the future. Your life is not over, it is just beginning."

"It feels more like it's over."

"I know, son. That's the initial pain of loss. The pain of losing a loved one is excruciating. So is the death of a dream."

"What do you mean by that? Death of what dream?"

"Your plans and dreams were focused on your family, now they are gone and so is your dream. You have lost your life's direction."

"Can I ever find it again?"

"God will show you."

"Will He answer my questions?"

"Perhaps not, sometimes He does at other times we have to wait. I'm still waiting for some answers."

"I don't know how I can go on without some answers."

"What if He just wants you to trust Him?"

"I don't know if I can."

"Why, Joel?"

"Because it seems like what my Mother taught me about her God and reality don't add up in the light of what has happened in my life."

"I know, son. Sometimes in the light of human wisdom, life just doesn't seem to add up. It is hard for you right now when you are dealing with the emotional shock of loss."

"How can I ever find purpose or resolution if He won't answer my questions? How can I ever trust Him again?"

"Why did you trust Him in the first place, Joel?" Wilkins probed gently.

"I believed what my Mother told me."

"And that was----?"

"That God had a purpose and a plan for my life. He had my best interest at heart."

"And you don't believe that anymore?"

"In the light of what happened, how can I?"

"Did your mother's life always run smoothly?"

"Of course not."

"Were there dark times with her?"

"Seemed more were dark than bright. My brothers hated her because she was an Indian and hated her "preaching" as they called it. She never preached to them, she just read her Bible and tried to love them tenderly, but they rejected her. I could see the pain in her eyes, but she never said anything bad about them, just treated them with gentleness and kindness. I asked her why she let them treat her so and she smiled and said she hoped she could show them the gentle savior's love and win them to Him."

"What a legacy she left you."

"Maybe but now all this has left me wondering was she right?"

"Joel, when we have had a strong godly influence in our lives, sometimes our faith is based on their faith. And that's good up to a point. Their faith and witness lead us to knowledge of the Savior, but second hand faith can't get us through the trials in life."

"What do you mean by second hand faith?"

"You have referred several times to God as your mother's God."

"He was."

"He wants to become Joel's God. No matter how strong a faith your mother had and no matter how much she taught you about Him, until He becomes your God you've only heard about Him, you have not known Him or walked with Him

Joel stammered, "I don't know what you mean. I've always tried to live by the principles of the Bible, done the things my Mother taught--------."

"I know and admire the strong principled man

you are, Joel. But we aren't talking about character or actions here. I'm talking about a relationship. No one is good enough to earn that relationship nor can they receive it from anyone else. It is something only a step of faith can accomplish."

"What kind of step of faith?"

"God wants an intimate relationship with you, but neither your good character nor your mother's teachings, great though they may have been, can give it to you. That relationship can only come through putting your trust in Jesus Christ who is the only doorway to the Father and eternal life."

"But I did that many years ago. I accepted Jesus Christ as my savior when I was a young boy."

"Perhaps now that you have become a man, it's time to take a step further with Him."

"What do you mean by that?"

"He not only wants to be your Savior, but your Lord."

"Is there a difference?"

"Our Savior saves us from the wrath to come or the penalty due on our sins. Our Lord directs our lives and the decisions that we make."

"How does that happen?"

"By acknowledging that the life you live belongs to Him and that it is His right to direct it in any direction He chooses."

"He or something has certainly been redirecting

it lately. I'm a long way from the cow poke I planned to be." A hint of a smile touched Joel's eyes before the pain closed back in.

"Sometimes it takes the destruction of our plans before we can or are willing to admit that He has the right to direct our lives and submit to where He wants to lead us."

"Everything I've planned is in shambles. There is nothing left."

"Wouldn't you call that a good place for God to start rebuilding?"

"I can't see how even He can have any kind of future for me."

"That's what faith is. Believing when you cannot see, trusting when you don't know the answers."

"I guess you're talking about blind faith."

Wilkins chuckled, "What else is faith? If we can see and have all the answers why would we need faith?"

"I must be the optimum candidate-----I can't see a future for me and I have no answers."

"That's the position you're in. Believing or not believing is your choice to make. If you choose to believe, then you'll have faith."

"Must it be so painful?"

"Sometimes the greater the work God has planned, the deeper the pain. I only know that on the other side of the pain, is a life of purpose and joy. But first you have to get through this pain. I'm here to be of any help that I can."

"I've burdened you too much already. I don't know what I would have done without your assistance up to this point. As for the future, I don't have any answers. I only know that going back out West is not an option just now, not even anything I want to do."

"Joel, you know I told you that there would be great opportunity for you if you stayed here and learned my business. I hesitate to bring that up at this time because I don't want my desires for you to interfere with what God may have in mind for you."

"Right now, Sir, I would just like to continue with my job at the docks, that is if Nick wants me after what I did yesterday."

"Don't worry about Nick. He wants you back, he, like me, was worried as to what had happened to you. I'll tell him what happened and that you need a few days off to recuperate."

"Beg your pardon, sir, but I would like to return today. Hard work helps clear the mind."

"How about we compromise? You just stick around the stables and catch up here for the rest of the week and then see how you feel about going back down to the docks?"

"I don't want to let Nick down. He'll be needing my help."

"Not until next week. I'll borrow some hands from my competitor. We are on good terms and he was complaining yesterday that he had too many men for the cargo that he had coming in."

Joel gave Wilkins a long look, narrowed his eyes, before a half smile curled his lips, "I appreciate the opportunity to focus on the horses. I could use some extra time with them."

"Right, and I think they need some extensive exercising and I want your steady hand on them rather than the new stable boys you hired."

"Good as done, Mr. Wilkins. Nothing like a good ride to help clear the mind."

"Better than unloading cargo?"

Joel chuckled, "Far better for this cowboy and you know it. Thank you for your kindness and wisdom."

Wilkins voice grew husky, "What are we here for if it's not for helping others?"

"May God grant me the ability and the opportunity to do likewise."

"He will. He'll use your pain to bring others with like pain into your life in order that you can comfort them with the same comfort God provided for you."

"For sure He has sent you to me today. I've heard of the loss of your son. What a terrible tragedy."

"The worst pain of my life. All my hopes and dreams were wrapped up in that boy."

"So how did you go forward?"

"Slowly at first."

"But you seem to have overcome the pain."

"No, I've learned to live with it."

"And help others through theirs?"

"That's how I survive, day by day. Helping others to see God's love in the midst of their sorrow and assist them to find a reason to go on."

"And the hopes and dreams that you lost when you lost your son?"

"I came to realize it's wrong to plan another's future. That's in God's hands and His prerogative." Wilkins chuckled, "I've had to be very careful with you, Joel. I found myself tempted to invest dreams and hopes in you."

"Me, Sir?"

"You remind me so much of my son."

"Surely not this cowhand, sir. I've never had the advantages that____." Joel blushed.

"That money and an education bring?" Wilkins finished for him.

"That's what I meant."

"I was talking of character and intelligence. Those are qualities that neither money nor education can buy."

"But opportunity---."

"Perhaps opportunity." The older man nodded. "And, if God wills, that is what I would like to give you. But first you must grieve and then we both must be certain that whatever the future holds, it will be your God-given dream, not mine."

"I feel deeply honored that you would even consider giving me a chance to advance, and that you could compare me with your son, well, that's more than I can take in."

"Don't even try tonight, tomorrow or next week."

"Right, Sir. I'm going to do some hard riding and clear the cobwebs from my brain. Then I'm going to determine the direction my life is supposed to take."

"Joel, God has His hand on you. If you follow His direction, your life will have meaning and purpose."

"More than just mucking out stalls and exercising horses?"

Wilkins laughed aloud, the sorrow lifting in his eyes, "If that's what God has in mind for you, then it will have meaning and purpose, but I have a feeling that one of these days, you'll be owning the stables and have a crew doing that for you."

"I beg your pardon, Sir, but I can't see these hands doing anything but hard labor all my life."

"If you put your hand in God's hand, my boy, there is no limit to what you can do or what you can accomplish in this world."

"When you talk like that, Mr. Wilkins, it gives me hope."

"And from hope, comes belief and faith."

CHAPTER 11

Giggling, high pitched female voices warned Joel that someone had invaded his male domain. For weeks the stables had been his sanctuary with only the horses and stable help as his companions. Nate Wilkins had left on an extended trip so he had seen neither Mr. nor Mrs. Wilkins since his talk with his benefactor. He had sent a message that Joel was not to go back to the docks until his return. Complying with his employer's wishes, the young man threw himself into the task at hand. Long hours of hard work left a man less time to ponder over painful events.

Joel experienced mixed feelings about his orders, concerned that he had let his dock supervisor, Nick, down but felt more than content to work with the horses. He discovered that being free from his other duties, allowed him to pursue the goals that he had set earlier but had been unable to accomplish. He invested all his energy into improvements needed in the stables. Gradually the stables took on the appearance of an efficient establishment in keeping with Wilkin's fine estate. Pride and a sense of accomplishment began the healing Joel so needed. While the grief proved just as real, dreams of a productive future began to take shape in his mind, renewing hope in the midst of his sorrow.

He had hired the extra help that Wilkins had commanded him to do. The men that he hired found him a fair, but demanding manager. He expected a day's work for a day's wages and put up with no slackers. After dismissing a few, he garnered the men's respect by not only supervising them but working along side of them. He found that the sweat of hard physical exertion proved the solace that he needed. Exhausted at night, he fell into bed and a dreamless sleep renewed his vigor.

Dressed in common work attire with a homespun protective apron draped about his tall muscular frame, his appearance blended with the now eight other stable hands that worked under his supervision.

Puzzled, as the sounds came nearer, Joel stepped out of the stall of the stable's newest acquisition, only to collide with a vision dressed in garnet taffeta running full tilt down the cobbled stone hallway. Throwing out protective arms, trying to avert collision, he suddenly found them filled with a soft loveliness crowned with golden hair. He struggled to keep them both from falling. Joel made the mistake of looking down into a pair of sapphire eyes that radiated a zest for life. Captivated, Joel continued to hold her a moment longer than needed as a strange reluctance to let her go seemed to grip him.

An unsuspecting smile curved her full pink lips before she removed his arms and stepped back, exclaiming "You're new here!"

"Not so new, I've been here for ten weeks." He protested, his face flushed by the strange sensations coursing through him.

"You're new to me! I haven't been home for eleven weeks. Can you believe that? I don't know how I could stand staying away so long." She paused for breath, "Wow! Things have really changed in here!"

A slow smile started at one corner of Joel's mouth parting his face in a delighted grin, as some of his embarrassment eased. "For the better, I hope?"

"Looks like a different place. Father told me there would be a change when I came home and a new filly would be here to greet me."

"Father?" Joel questioned.

She held out a dainty gloved hand, "I'm Melody Wilkins, Nate Wilkins is my father."

"Glad to meet you, Miss Wilkins. I'm Joel Isaacs."

"Oh you're my father's new protégé!"

"I work for your father, if that is what you mean."

"And you're responsible for the changes around here."

"Not by myself."

"According to my father you are."

"Believe me, this was a joint effort."

"One you oversee and for which you are

ultimately responsible. Believe me, my father has told me all about you. And the way this place has changed he didn't exaggerate."

"If he is pleased then I'm grateful. He has given me great encouragement and I would like to repay his kindness."

"He loves his horses and so do I. Now show me that new filly he was so excited about. Oh, by the way, this is my roommate, Anna Castile." Melody belatedly introduced a young dark haired beauty that had trailed behind her at a more lady like pace.

Joel nodded his head, "Pleased to make your acquaintance ma'am."

Bold brown eyes met and held his. "So you're the miracle worker I've been hearing about."

"No ma'am, no miracle, just hard work." Joel corrected.

She chortled, her voice husky, "That's all I've heard about since Melody's father visited us at school. She couldn't wait until the holidays to come home to see the changes."

"I hope they met her expectations."

Anna paused looked from Melody to him, and then her lips curled in a half-smile that didn't reach her eyes, "I'd say they have more than met her expectations."

Joel's face flushed once again as she conveyed a meaning that went beyond the stable changes.

By this time Melody had turned her attention

to the tall, chestnut thoroughbred whinnying in the stall. "Is this the one? Oh, what a beauty. Saddle her up immediately. I've got to ride her."

"In those clothes, Melody? You haven't even gone in the house to see your mother yet." Anna protested.

"I guess you're right. Where horses are concerned I do get carried away!"

"That's an understatement."

"Very well. I'll go in to see mother, change my dress and then I'll be right down. Have her ready."

"I'm afraid I can't do that, Miss Wilkins."

"Why not? Are you going somewhere?"

"No, but this filly is a bit much for a young woman to handle."

"But Father said that he bought her for me."

"Perhaps he did, but I don't expect he meant for you to ride her. She is still high spirited and needs work before she is safe enough for you." Joel explained.

"You just don't know how well I can ride."

"Perhaps not, but I cannot let you ride her yet."

"Do you ride her?"

"That I do. Everyday. It's my job."

"If you can ride her, I can ride her." Melody challenged.

"I hardly think so. She is only green broken."

"Then why did Papa buy her for me if she's not ready to ride? And how is it you can ride her?"

"I advised your father to get her. Fine blood

line and a beauty. She'll be a valuable addition to your stable for future breeding purposes. And I can ride her because I've broken many horses."

"That's right papa told me something about your being a cowboy in your former life."

Joel chuckled, "I don't know about "former" life, handling horses is sort of like a sailor and the sea. Once a cowboy, it's a lifetime love."

"You don't have to be a cowboy to love horses and to be adept at riding. I have no fear that I can handle that filly. I can always try, and if it doesn't work, no harm done."

"Beg your pardon, ma'am, but much harm could come to you."

"Oh shaw! Do you think I haven't fallen off a horse before?"

"I'm sure that you have, but not one for which I'm responsible."

"I relieve you of that responsibility. I'll take full blame for it, if anything should happen to the horse."

"It's not the horse I'm concerned about, Miss Wilkins." Joel explained, his patience growing thin.

"In that case, we don't have a problem. I'm seventeen years old and responsible for myself, so there. Saddle her up for me." Melody set her soft pink lips in a firm line as if that settled the issue.

"Not until your father gives his blessing. Beg your pardon, ma'am, but your father left me in charge and I will not be responsible for your getting hurt." Joel insisted, determination firing his eyes.

"We'll just see about that." With a toss of her head she turned and flounced out of the stable, leaving Joel perplexed. This was strange territory; he had had little contact with females with the exception of his mother and a devil woman with flashing green eyes and flaming hair. Neither of which had prepared him for an encounter with the wealthy, beautiful Miss Wilkins. Add to that she was his employer's daughter; he sensed an unpleasant dilemma ahead of him.

He shook his head. Horses he knew, but he had a lot to learn about the weaker sex. The one thing he did know, he had better take care. He shuddered. He had an inkling that Mr. Wilkin's daughter equaled the high spirits of that little filly whinnying in the stall. He could put a bit in the horse's mouth, but how did you reign in a woman?

He expelled a deep sigh, causing one of the stable hands, who had seen the interchange, to look at him and grin. Well, reining her in was not his responsibility, but seeing to her safety in her father's absence was. And that started with standing his ground with the lovely Miss Wilkins. No riding that flashy thoroughbred until her father gave his permission.

A half-smile eased the scowl on his face as her cloud of golden hair and the sweet fragrance of her filled his mind. For sure she was a beauty to behold. Then he shook his head, reminding himself that she was the boss's daughter and no matter how lovely to look at, he had no right. He worked in the stables and she lived in the big house, and he'd be wise to keep that uppermost in his mind.

To Joel's relief, Melody Wilkins did not return that evening or night to challenge his decision. She invaded his dreams though, disturbing his sleep and he awoke the next morning with dread displacing his usual anticipation for work. His head ached from lack of sleep and he felt altogether out of sorts.

When he heard her animated voice at the end of the hallway, and the husky voice of her friend answering her, he steeled himself for the inevitable encounter, dreading the consequences.

He stepped outside the stall, shutting the stall door behind him and leaned against the wall, waiting for her.

Just then she spotted him and an enchanting smile beamed up at him as if they had parted the evening amicably. "I'm here to ride. Saddle that beauty up for me."

"Would you consider a compromise?" He drawled with a smile and a relaxed stance that disguised his pounding heart.

"I don't think so."

"Surely you don't want me to lose my job, Miss Wilkins. I need it you know."

"Then saddle my horse."

"And put you at risk? That would be a sure way to become unemployed."

"That's ridiculous. I'm an excellent rider."

"I have no doubt of that. But you don't know this horse. She needs work."

"Then I'll work her."

"Later."

"Really, Joel!" She stamped her foot.

Joel answered softly, "Suppose I saddle up two other mounts for you and Miss Castile until your father returns. I will make it my priority to work with your horse all day if need be, until I feel she is manageable."

She furrowed her brow, as if considering his request.

Anna spoke up, her dark eyes fastened on Joel, "Melody, you're crazy to want to get on that horse before she is fully broken. I won't ride with you if you insist on taking her. I have a better idea. Why doesn't Mr. Isaacs saddle up the filly and ride with us. Then you can see first hand how she handles and we can have our ride in safety. What say you, Joel?"

"I'm not sure Miss Wilkin's father would approve."

"Of course he would." Melody chimed in. "That's a perfect solution."

"I'm not properly attired to escort you ladies." Joel protested, suspect of Melody's sudden concession.

"I can remedy that, you wait here." And before he

could reply she was gone, leaving him standing with her raven haired friend.

"You owe me, Joel Isaacs." A smile curved her full lips and her eyes flashed.

"Owe you?"

"For redirecting Melody. She is very stubborn when she sets her mind. And she was determined to ride that horse. That's all she talked about last evening. I heard horses until I thought I was going to whinny."

"I'm not sure she is re-directed." He chuckled.

"Hmm, perhaps---- but I have a feeling that she has met her match in you." Her fiery eyes suggested admiration and something indefinable as they captured his.

"I don't know about being a match for her, that's not my intention."

"Really? Then what are your intentions, Sir?"

"To fulfill my responsibility to Mr. Wilkins by not letting his daughter or guest participate in anything that might get them hurt."

Anna Castile gave a low sultry chuckle, "Well, Joel Isaacs, I can't tell you how safe that makes me feel."

"I don't believe it was your safety that has been in question, Miss Castile." Joel reminded softly, his dark eyes holding hers, a smile dimpling his cheek.

"All the same, the thought of having your protection seems rather inviting."

The tight fitting doeskin riding breeches and fancy white shirt with lace on the sleeves, felt strange on Joel. He looked in the mirror and smoothed his hair, placing the broad brim hat on his head. He had seen other Boston gentlemen out riding in similar clothes, but he had never pictured himself in them. No sir, homespun and a hat to protect him from the sun was what he needed. But he had to admit, dressed as he was his attire seemed more in keeping to escort two young ladies.

And that was another thing. What in the world would Mr. Wilkins think, the groom escorting his daughter and her friend? He had noted that Boston society had strict class rules. He knew enough to know that the Wilkins family was considered one of the "blue bloods". They had earned their station in society many years before. In fact it was inherited. Mrs. Wilkins' family was one of the original families settling Boston. How Mr. Wilkins arrived on the scene and made himself acceptable might prove an interesting tale. Joel just intuitively knew that it was a long journey from cow poking to Boston society, not that he planned to make that trip, but for today he had to present an acceptable image as the ladies' escort.

Joel took one more look and nodded. His appearance would do, he appreciated Melody Wilkins loaning him her brother's clothes as he would never

want to do anything to embarrass the older Wilkins-----
-or the younger either for that matter. He was confident
that his horsemanship skills would stand him in good
for the day; he was dressed properly and now if only
his people skills could tame that little blond tigress.
He smiled, trepidation and anticipation battled inside
him. He couldn't deny that spending the afternoon with
two lovely ladies was more than equal to an afternoon
cleaning out stalls.

Joel found Anna waiting at the double doors
of the stable, surveying the view of Boston which lay
below the Wilkins estate. She turned when she heard
Joel's footsteps behind her, and caught her breath. An
approving smile parted her face as she scrutinized him
from head to foot. "What happened to our stable boy?"

Joel flushed, "He's still here, maybe disguised
by unaccustomed finery, but still here. Clothes don't
change the man; he's still the same person no matter
what he's wearing."

"Interesting thought, Joel."

"Don't you think that a man's measure is what's
on the inside, not in the way he is dressed or in the way
he looks."

She chuckled, her ebony eyes sparkling with
lights that disturbed Joel, "You may be right, cowboy, but
looking at you just now makes me forget you're a stable
boy. Perhaps I need to get to know the man inside?"

Joel flushed, "Believe me, I'm just a simple man

whom you would find boring."

"Hardly," She stepped nearer and the fragrance of lavender enveloped Joel.

"Not boring, intriguing." She whispered.

"Ma'am?" Joel stammered.

Her laughter tinkled through the hallway, "You intrigue me, Joel."

"I don't understand how that could be, Miss Castile."

"You're mysterious. And I dote on solving mysteries."

"There is no mystery to me. I'm just a misplaced cowboy who understands his place in the scheme of things."

"And that is?"

"A loyal employee of Mr. Wilkins, doing my best to take care of Miss Wilkins and her friend."

Anna threw back her head and laughed, "And so you are, Mr. Isaacs."

"Thank you, ma'am, I'm glad you understand." His eyes held hers, communicating a deeper message as Melody came bounding down the hallway.

"Taking care of whom, Joel?" Melody asked, catching the last wisp of Joel's conversation.

Joel turned toward her, relieved that the effervescent Miss Wilkins had rescued him from a conversation which was drifting toward uncharted waters for him. "Why you and Miss Castile, Miss Wilkins."

"Now, Joel, you must call me Melody."

"And me, Anna."

"Even a cowboy like me knows that isn't proper etiquette."

"Oh, who cares about etiquette? If we are going to have a fun afternoon we just can't be so formal."

"My sentiments exactly." Chortled Anna.

"Ladies, believe me when I say that my addressing you in a respectful and proper manner will in no way hinder your afternoon's pleasure. Shall we go?" Joel demurred as he indicated to two of the stable attendants to bring the two ladies' mounts, saddled and ready.

Soon the three were cantering beneath the broad expanses of oak trees leading to the countryside behind the elegant estates that lined the avenue.

The filly beneath Joel behaved as if she were docile and well trained, not the green broke thoroughbred that she was, belying what he had told Melody.

Shortly into their sedate ride, when they had exited the tree lined avenue, Melody cast a mischievous glance at Joel then dug a boot into the side of her horse and shouted, "Beat you to the creek."

An astonished Joel watched as she raced off in a flash of green velvet and cascading golden curls, losing her hat along the way.

He cast a questioning glance toward Anna, riding sedately beside him. She waved him on and he was off, giving the filly her head. It was the first time she had been free to run and she ran like the wind. It took them only moments to catch Melody on her slower mount. Soon he passed her and arrived at the creek. Sundance was unwilling to rein in. Having been given her head for the first time, Joel had his hands full bringing her to a halt. When he applied the reins she reared, then bucked and snorted not altogether unlike the green quarter horses he had broken for his pa.

Melody's eyes rounded in surprised, then fear as rider and horse leapt round and round for what seemed endless seconds. Finally Joel gained control and they cantered toward the creek and then back to Melody where they came to a docile stop.

"Whew." Melody let out a relieved sigh. "I guess I owe you an apology, Joel. That was quite a show Sundance put on. You're right, I would not have been up to handling her."

"I was beginning to wonder if I could." Joel chuckled. "At the least I thought I might ruin your brother's fine clothes."

Melody shuddered, the mischievous light in her eyes gone. "It was not the clothes that worried me, Joel."

Joel shrugged, "I've been tossed off many a time, Miss Wilkins."

"Melody, please." She corrected softly, turning the full force of her blue eyes on him.

Joel's heart thundered and everything around him receded except the tender radiance in them, holding him spellbound. "Then, Miss Melody, it will be if you please."

She shook her head slightly and protested barely above a whisper, her eyes never leaving his, "Only Melody will please."

"Bravo, that was quite a performance, Joel." Anna chirped as she rode up, breaking the spell.

Joel turned toward the intruder, and tipped his hat, "Anything to entertain the ladies, ma'am."

"Anna, that was no show, Joel could have been killed."

"Don't be a ninny, Melody. He's used to that kind of excitement. I would wager that he's been in that predicament a thousand times. And just look at him, not a hair on his head has been harmed."

"Is that true, Joel? This is what it takes to break a horse and you've never been hurt?"

"Yes, ma'am. That's what you run into when you break a horse. Some worse than others, but as far as getting hurt, I've had a few bones broken, but nothing that wouldn't mend. But you never can tell about a fall. That's why I didn't think you should ride Sundance."

"Do you think she will ever be ready for me to ride?"

Joel chuckled as he remembered their earlier

dispute. "Why, Miss Melody, I thought you could handle any horse."

"I've never seen one behave like that."

"That's because the ones in your stable have been trained and ready for riding."

"But I have ridden spirited ones. I don't enjoy plodders."

"There is a big difference between a spirited, broken horse and a green broken one. The broken horse has been trained to bring that spirit under the control of the rider in obedience. If your father is to have the type stables that he really wants, we will be adding stock that is young and untrained in order to get the best blood lines."

"And who will break them?"

"As long as I'm here, I will."

"As long as you are here?" Melody frowned.

"Yes, ma'am. I don't know what my future is. I only know that right now, I've made a commitment to assist your father anyway I can until the good Lord shows me what He has in mind for me."

"I hope it is here with us, Joel. But I shall worry about you."

"No need to worry about me, Miss Melody, I was practically born in the saddle. And as for you riding Sundance someday, probably that will be sooner than you think."

"You're sure?"

"Well, she is high strung and will need a firm but gentle hand which I have no doubt you can give her. But I can promise you that I will not turn her over to you until I deem her safe."

CHAPTER 12

Melody returned to school leaving lingering memories of golden hair and azure eyes to invade Joel's thoughts. The week she had spent at home had proved a diversion for him. When her father arrived home, he insisted that Joel accompany the girls on their many jaunts across the countryside.

They would take a picnic lunch out to a clear babbling brook at the edge of the Wilkins estate and then afterwards follow the meandering stream for miles. Joel found the two young woman delightful company. They never made him feel inferior, but treated him as if he were a good friend rather than an employee. It was obvious that the school they attended taught them more than just the art of being a lady and household skills for they were well versed on history, the classics and they even carried on a lively discourse on current events.

Joel held his own and even dared disagree on some of their interpretations of historical events but he proved an apt listener when they discussed the issues of the day that concerned Boston. He asked pertinent questions about the economy and industry in the area. In fact he quizzed them so intently one day that Anna exclaimed she felt as if she were still at school.

He laughed and asked their pardon explaining that this was a whole new world for him, so different from the one he grew up in. His eyes turned sad as painful, unwanted memories intruded.

Anna noticed and changed the subject, diverting his attention to a hawk flying overhead, "Joel, were you a hunter?"

"Hunter?"

"Fox hunter."

He chuckled, "No, ma'am. I was a meat hunter."

"Meat hunter?"

"Deer and antelope. That's what would feed us through the winter."

"Hmm. Did you enjoy hunting?"

"Mostly it was a necessity. But I reckon I enjoyed the challenge and there was a sense of accomplishment when I provided meat for our table."

"Goodness, Joel. I just never thought about how the food gets on our table. I guess it was different out west." Melody chimed in as she strolled back from the stream.

"Quite a bit different."

"What did you do for fun?"

"Read when I could. Mostly I worked."

"What about time with your friends?"

"Ma'am friends were few and far between."

"What did you do without people? I mean didn't you ever go to parties?"

"Parties? People?" Joel laughed.

"And what's so funny, Mr. Isaacs?" Melody asked, tossing her golden curls.

"The idea of my going to parties! The nearest thing to a party that I ever experienced was at the end of a round up when we brought the cows to market. In a sort of celebration, the cook would butcher one of the cows and all the hands ate 'til they nearly popped."

"A party was just eating? You call that a party?"

"Well, I guess some of the cowpokes did a little drinking with their eating, but I never participated in that. It just felt good to eat all I wanted and know that we had accomplished what we set out to do which was bringing the cattle safely to market." "No music, no dancing?"

"Sometimes one of the guys would whistle a tune or play something on the harmonica. Usually it was a mournful tune, nothing that would be festive. As for dancing, why or how in the world would a bunch of cow pokes dance."

"Oh, I guess you didn't have any ladies available?"

A flush tinged Joel's face, "No women on a cattle drive and what was available in town, I would not exactly call ladies. Some of them danced, but it was in the saloon. I steered clear of them, except when I had to round up my brothers."

A pink flushed Melody's cheeks, as she suddenly understood Joel's meaning, "So you were your brother's keeper?"

"More or less. Sometimes they didn't use the best judgment and Pa would send me after them."

Anna watched the exchange with interest and looped her arm in Joel's as the conversation reached an awkward lull. "I'd say we need to show Joel what a real party is, Melody! Poor boy's been deprived. When do you think we could have a party?"

Melody clapped her hands in delight, "What a wonderful idea! Papa is home so I'll talk to him tonight."

"Oh, no, Miss Melody. Fancy parties are not for me. I've told you all along, I'm just a simple wrangler, more at home on a horse than in a drawing room. I can't dance and I'm sure not one for small talk. It would prove nothing but an embarrassment for you and for me. Besides, you forget, I'm only an employee, not one of your college friends."

"Oh, Joel, you know more about everything than anyone I know."

"Only about life's experiences."

"No, you are educated, intelligent and articulate."

"Only about what I learned in a saddle, on a ship or in a book. I am woefully lacking in the social graces."

"But a quick and intelligent learner." Anna chimed in. "And Melody and I are going to be your teachers."

Joe lifted an inquisitive eyebrow.

"First we'll teach you how to dance, how to dress and everything you need to know to carry on a polite conversation in society."

"And manners?" Joel probed, uncomfortable with the way the conversation was progressing. "I don't think so. I told you from the beginning that it is a long way from the stables to the big house. Don't even think of mentioning this absurd plan to your father."

Melody's blue eyes darkened with determination as she thrust out her dainty chin in defiance. "You don't really know my father, if you think he would mind. He would encourage us in it."

"Nevertheless, I refuse to be a part of any such ridiculous scheme. I have been your caretaker and protector per Mr. Wilkins' instructions while you and Miss Anna were here on holiday."

Amusement sparked Anna's dark eyes, "Is that all, Joel? Can you really say that all Melody and I have been to you is a duty?"

Melody's eyes widened, "Is that all? I thought you enjoyed our company."

Joel stammered, immersed in those blue eyes turned full force on him, "It was a er, responsibility that I thoroughly enjoyed."

"There you see. It hasn't been all work. You did find some pleasure in it. So what's the difference if we want to take it a step further?" Anna asked.

"Because of who I am and who you and Miss Melody are. It wouldn't be proper."

"Oh fiddlesticks! You are a hard headed man, Joel Isaacs. There is nothing improper about our plan." Melody exclaimed.

"Tell that to Boston society."

"Who cares about what society thinks."

"What about your friends?"

Melody stamped her foot, impatience wrinkling her brow, "They will accept you or if they don't, I'll just forget them."

Anna chuckled, "Joel, I'm Melody's friend. Haven't I accepted you?"

Joel nodded, "Miss Anna, you have been a delight."

"Then what's the problem?"

"It isn't that I'm fearful of being snubbed. I just don't want to take advantage of your father's goodness to me. It is one thing to perform a service for him, but it is something altogether different to impose on his hospitality. The last thing I would want to do is put your family in an awkward position."

"What Melody is not telling you, is that her family sets the standards in this neighborhood. If they accept you, all of Boston will. No one wants to offend the powerful Mr. Wilkins." Anna explained.

"No matter what you think, Joel, I will have a talk about this to my father."

"Not on my behalf you won't."

A sly smile parted her full, pink lips. "No, not on your behalf, my behalf."

Anna and Melody left for school the next morning. Joel watched from the stable doors as the servants loaded their trunks into the carriage. A sense of regret dampened his usual buoyant mood. He had to admit he had enjoyed afternoons with the two beautiful girls. That he would miss them surprised him. No doubt their presence had disrupted his schedule and delayed his progress with the horses. Yet he had to admit regret far outweighed any relief he might have.

He knew that he would miss the lively discourse on history, current events and politics. At least that was all that he would allow himself to admit, but somewhere his heart whispered he would miss those large blue eyes staring up into his, curls of spun gold and a laughter that bubbled out like a clear mountain brook.

Joel reluctantly turned back into the stables, pushing aside the troubling thoughts that teased him. He strode down the corridor of the stable, head down and determination in each forceful stride. From the shadows came soft laughter as a dark haired beauty stepped out into his path. Once again he found his arms filled with feminine loveliness as he struggled to keep them both from falling. But this time it was Anna, not Melody, and the collision appeared contrived.

"Goodness, Miss Anna, you gave me a start." Joel commented lamely as he tried to disentangle himself from Anna who seemed in no hurry to rid herself of the strong arms that held her.

She smiled up into his eyes as the sweet fragrance of lilacs engulfed Joel weakening his resolve to let her go. They lingered thus a moment longer than necessary when a voice from the doorway destroyed the moment, bringing sanity back.

"Anna, Joel-------wha--?" Melody cried out, misunderstanding what she saw.

Joel dropped his hands to the side and mumbled, "It's not what you think, you see, Miss Anna was---."

"I saw very well."

"Oh, Melody, don't be so melodramatic. I came out here to tell Joel good bye and to thank him for all of his good care of us." Anna explained.

"Looked like you were doing more than thanking him." Melody exclaimed.

"He ran into me, just like you ran into him that first day. Remember? By the way why were you out here?" Anna smiled, dismissing Melody's outburst.

"I came to tell Joel goodbye and that I had talked to father about the party."

"There you see! That's all I was doing, telling Joel goodbye."

"I had been outside in the sunlight and, when I came in, I failed to see Miss Anna walk out of the shadows. It was all innocent, Miss Melody. I would never treat you or your friends in an improper manner.

Your father has trusted me with his dearest possession and I would never violate his trust."

Melody sighed and then smiled, her good humor restored. "I believe you, Joel. The good news is father has agreed with me. You need a party."

"Begging your pardon, ma'am, the last thing in the world I need is a party!!"

"Sometimes we don't know what we need, and other people have to tell us. So we're telling you. Don't worry, it won't be right away. Maybe at the end of the summer or early fall. When I come home, your lessons begin."

"Lessons? Who is going to teach me and what?"

"I'm going to teach you all you need to know in order to be introduced into Boston society."

"And, me, too? Can I help you teach him, Melody?" Anna interrupted.

Melody gave her a long look, her brow wrinkled, "We will have to see about that, Anna."

"Why in the world do I need to know anything about being introduced into Boston society? I am in charge of your father's stable, not a candidate for the drawing rooms of your fair city."

"Joel, you are not always going to be in the stables. God has plans for you. I know that He has and you need to prepare for them."

Joel shook his head, "Begging your pardon, Miss Melody, but I can't imagine a plan that would call for me to move in those circles. It's not something that appeals to me nor do I have time for it."

"Did you not tell me that your Mother taught you to take every opportunity to learn?"

"I don't think she had this kind of learning in mind."

"Trust me, if God gives you the chance to advance, you need to learn what I can teach you. Did your mother not teach you the manners and politeness that you have?"

Joel nodded his head.

"Look at it as an expansion of what she taught you. Just think of it as a lesson in Boston culture."

"What if staying in Boston is not God's plan for me?"

"I won't accept that. You are here now, so you need to learn how to succeed here. And I'm talking about life beyond the stables."

"You haven't convinced me." Joel warned.

"We will discuss it again when I return for summer break. Meanwhile, thank you for a lovely holiday, it has been the best ever! Now we must go if we are to make our train. Goodbye, sweet Joel." With those parting words she stood on tiptoe and brushed a whisper soft kiss on his cheek and leaving Joel with a riot of unfamiliar emotions.

Joel redoubled his efforts in the stable in an effort to quell the disturbing emotions that scurried through his mind when a vision of his employer's daughter teased his memory.

Soon the stables were running seamlessly and Wilkins called him to the big house where he met him in his study. Surrounded by volumes of bound leather housed in ornate mahogany bookcases, Joel stood in awe as he looked at books of every known subject. From theology, science, mathematics and art to all the classics both fiction and non fiction, it proved a treasure trove of learning. When his employer entered, he found Joel gazing at the books in wonder.

Wilkins chuckled and asked Joel if he liked to read. When he nodded his head his employer replied that the books were at his disposal, borrow all that he wanted.

"Thank you, sir. I love to read, but I've never had access to so much learning."

"That's one of the reasons I wanted to see you this morning. I've decided that I no longer need you on the docks."

"But, sir, you have several ships due in this week. Have I displeased you in some way?

"Displeased? Absolutely not."

"I know that I've divided up my time between the docks and the stables, but since the men are doing most of the work with little supervision----."

"Thanks to your wisdom in hiring the right men and properly training them." Wilkins interrupted.

"They have worked out quite well, sir. But as I was saying, I'm able to spend even more time at the dock if I'm needed."

"I need your help more in other areas. You've been with me almost a year now, some nine months since you received the tragic news concerning your family. What plans have you for your future?"

"Sir, I've made no plans. I've just been busy working in the here and now, waiting for what the Lord might show me."

"And?"

"He has shown me nothing beyond what I'm doing."

"Are you open now to considering a future here in Boston?"

"All I know is that I want to do what He wants me to do."

"Then perhaps He wants you here with us." Wilkins sighed.

"Well at least for now, He must, because I am content and He has shown me nothing else."

"The Good Book tells us to wait upon the Lord. It seems that we both have been doing that. I think it is time for us to move forward. I know that you have too much intelligence and ability to spend your life loading cargo. I want to take you off the docks and into the office."

Joel shook his head, "I know nothing about office procedures."

"A mere technicality. You will master those swiftly."

"Sitting behind a desk might not be something I'm suited for."

"I'm not talking about bean counting or accounting work."

"Then what do you have in mind for me?"

"I have extensive real estate and manufacturing interests, I need someone with the right values and ability to manage them. I want you to learn something about each one of my holdings. Because my interests have been so broad, some of them are not doing as well as they should due to my inability to spend enough time with each facet. That's where you come in. I have seen your people skills and your organizational prowess. Some of my interests are suffering from poor management and organization."

"I'm only twenty and know nothing about business." Joel reminded.

"That's what you'll be doing the next year or two. Learning. There will be traveling involved and some behind the desk time and some after hours study, but

I've watched you. You are a quick learner and it may not take you but a year. Anyway my goal for you is that you can get areas of my business running as smoothly as you have my stables running and the efficient manner of handling cargo on the docks."

Joel quirked a questioning eyebrow toward Wilkins.

The older man chuckled. "Oh, yes. Nick told me about your suggestions that they implemented and how much time and labor were saved."

"It seemed to me they just made common sense. Time and labor saved is money earned in my mind and is a responsibility any employee has to his employer."

"And that is exactly what I am looking for in a manager."

"I'm overwhelmed with your consideration, Mr. Wilkins. Since the Lord has not shown me any other path, seems I'd be foolish not to accept your offer, that is if you would make it right with Nick."

Mr. Wilkins laughed out loud, "Put that concern to rest. It was Nick who suggested strongly that I was wasting you on the docks."

"Nick?"

"Yes, Nick. That hard labor you were doing there and in the stables was a test. Nick has been giving me job evaluations. I would never offer anyone the opportunity that I just offered you without checking them out very carefully. You proved your industriousness by your hard work, your integrity when you reported that attempted bribe along with the times you chided the shore men for their lack of zeal. We've already discussed your organizational skills. I'm convinced that you are the man for whom I have been looking. I felt it from the beginning, but I never wanted to interfere with what God might have planned for you."

"Nor do I. But He has shown me nothing else and your proposal sounds exciting."

"By the way, you will be introduced to a social environment for which my daughter and her friend think you are ill prepared." He smiled, a mischievous light in his eyes.

"Oh, no." Joel groaned.

"Yes, dancing lessons, I'm afraid."

"You are teasing me, sir."

"Partly. What the girls meant for fun, I believe in the light of our new arrangement has merit."

"Merit?"

"You will be thrown into new social circumstances. You will be more confident if you know our customs here. Besides it should be a delightful distraction if my daughter has anything to do with it." Wilkins smiled, a tender light igniting his gray eyes.

Joel's heart beat a little faster as he anticipated all that his employer and benefactor had told him. The challenge of his new job excited him, while the thought of his social training left him with conflicting emotions.

At twenty years old, his exit from the teen years had come and gone with little notice, he had yet to learn the ins and outs of the social graces. Growing up as he had left little time for recreation of any sort or interaction with people his own age, especially females, until Melody Wilkins had entered his world. The distracting effect of the beauty and charm the two young women, especially Melody Wilkins, had on him troubled him. He had no one to explain to him that what he was feeling was a perfectly natural, if a somewhat delayed, reaction and a vital part of his maturing into manhood.

As the weeks and months passed, his new opportunities left little time to worry about the worrisome emotions he had experienced during Melody's school break. When he did find her invading his thoughts he found himself thinking less of those tender blue eyes and golden curls and more of the laughter and good conversation that they had shared.

With summer approaching, he found himself looking forward to seeing the two young women who had opened up new areas of learning and enjoyment. Even the perceived "lessons" they had planned for him seemed less odious. He conceded that perhaps his former life of all work and no play had left a void that he never knew existed until those giggling female voices entered the stables and turned his world askew.

CHAPTER 13

Life took on a new dimension for Joel as it moved more swiftly than he ever dreamed possible. His duties carried him from the Boston harbor, to a shipyard in Bath, Maine where sleek sea faring ships were built. Afterwards he traveled back to Massachusetts to visit Wilkin's tannery where hides brought from California were fashioned into saddles, bridles and other leather goods.

As he went from one enterprise to another that his employer either owned or partnered with, he felt humbled and a little overwhelmed that Mr. Wilkins could imagine he might be an asset in assisting with the vast holdings that he had visited. But after a brief period at each establishment, Joel's innate intelligence brought him an understanding of business principles that could be applied to each one. His keen observation of the procedures provided him a quick education in the differences in each and as he learned more, his confidence grew with each challenge until he finally came to the realization that Mr. Wilkins indeed needed some assistance and confident that he could provide that help.

For the first time since he found himself in the rolling bowels of a ship, Joel could see a future and he realized that it was God who had set before him what seemed unlimited possibilities. Each day his certainty grew and with it, his excitement. He recognized the challenges were great but he welcomed them.

After a brief visit with each one of Mr. Wilkins holdings, Joel returned to the shipping offices and his much anticipated meeting with his employer.

"Welcome back, Joel." Wilkins stood and gave his hand in a warm and firm handshake, a pleased smile lighting his face. "I've been anxious to meet with you face to face to learn first hand how your trip went. It seems you've been away a long time and the missus and I have missed you."

Joel shook his hand, "It has been two months, sir. I've missed being here, too. But I kept busy and I believe the trip will prove beneficial for the both of us."

"Great news! That's what I hoped. Have a seat and tell me all you have learned."

Joel settled down into the large, supple leather chair, crafted by one of Boston's finest furniture makers and upholstered from the leather from Wilkin's own tannery. The fragrance of lemon oil and leather permeated the room and a soft breeze wafted in from the harbor bringing Joel memories of the first time he had entered this office and how ill at ease he had felt in these strange surroundings. He smiled, remembering. Had it only been a little longer than a year? Life had taken on an entirely new direction for him and he felt eager for the challenge.

"You are smiling. That's a good sign." Wilkins chuckled.

"Yes, sir. I was thinking what a difference a year can make."

"That's right. Some of it good, I hope."

"Out of the ashes of one dream, it seems another is emerging."

"Then I take it you are going to accept my offer."

"With pleasure, sir. This trip has shown me two things. One was that you do need help. You need someone who has your best interest at heart, who can get the job done. I will always have your best interest at heart. With some training I know that I can do what you need. I am indebted to you far more than could ever be repaid. In some small way perhaps I can return something of what you have done for me."

"That's good and noble, Joel, but it cannot be the basis of our arrangement. I won't allow it. This job must be something that appeals to you, that you can enjoy and get fulfillment out of it."

"And one I am capable of doing."

"There's no doubt in my mind about that."

"Nor mine, sir."

The older man nodded his head, pleased with Joel's affirmation. "I've observed you keenly, plus I have received glowing reports of your ability and your demeanor from all the places you have been. But what I want to know is do you think you can be happy and fulfilled as my assistant?"

"Yes. I'm excited by the prospects of what lies ahead."

"And what about God's plan for you in all of this?"

"Perhaps He has put me here for such a time as this. Every venue that I visited excited me. And the thought of being able to consolidate the management of them into one efficient organization which will prove both beneficial and profitable to you, makes me eager to begin."

Wilkins chuckled, "I could hardly want for better news! I plan to send you to each main location for a year so that you can learn everything about the business from the ground up, so to speak. After your resident training, you will arrive back here to oversee the consolidation of interests that we talked about."

"I'm ready to begin. Where do I go first?"

"I think you will go to Bath for your first year since shipping is rather like the cog of my organization and each other endeavor the spokes. I want you to learn everything you can about ship building. Study any new advances that might prove a benefit to the expediting of the goods we manufacture and the other commodities that we trade both in the Caribbean and Europe. I'm especially interested in increasing cargo size and speed as well as increasing my trading routes."

"I can see that there will be a lot of study and research involved in that endeavor." Joel responded, his eyes shining with excitement.

"Nothing that you are adverse to doing?" Wilkins smiled knowingly.

Joel chuckled in response to his mentor, "You know I'll relish the learning. I'm ready to go tomorrow. As you know my bags are still packed and I have very little except a few clothes."

"I think we might be able to round you up a good horse to take with you."

"Sir?"

"I have a ship that needs to go back to the yard for retrofitting. I think it would accommodate a passenger and his mount."

"You are too kind, Mr. Wilkins." Joel protested.

"Not at all, the workman is worthy of his hire."

"When is the ship leaving?"

Mr. Wilkins laughed aloud. "Not for a couple of months."

"I thought you meant right away."

"No. You have forgotten, my daughter and her friend have great plans for you this summer."

Joel groaned. "No, I haven't forgotten, I just hoped

they had."

"On the contrary, Melody has been indignant that you were not here when she arrived home. She and Anna have been anxiously awaiting you for two weeks and planning not one party but a series that will last all summer."

"And there is no way of escape?" Joel asked.

"None. But cheer up, Joel. One could have a worse fate than two attractive females overseeing your successful leap into Boston society."

"I'd just as soon not make that hurdle."

"Seriously, with the plans that we have, social skills are a necessary evil. Each society has its own particular set of cultural values and Boston is stricter than most. When you arrive in Bath, Main you'll find that it has its own peculiar way of socializing. However, you will find that most is based on common courtesy and manners. You already have all the basics that you need in that area. Your dear mother did a fine job. Manners really for the most part are based on thoughtfulness of others. You are well blessed in the considerate treatment of others. All the girls plan for you is to put the final polish on the diamond they pride themselves on finding."

"Final polish?" Joel asked, his eyebrows rose.

"Yes. All the etiquette and apparel that will be proper in the ballrooms of Boston."

"Ballrooms?"

"Oh, yes. They can't wait to teach you how to dance."

"You think this is necessary?"

"Absolutely. You need it and I need it or else that daughter of mine will give me no peace."

As in all his endeavors, Joel proved an apt student of everything the two young women taught him. Much to his surprise he thoroughly enjoyed the venture and found out that dancing came as natural to him as horseback riding. In only two weeks, Anna and Melody declared him ready to grace the drawing room of any home in their elite neighborhood.

When he arrived at the first ball with one lovely young lady on each arm, he created quite a stir among the mothers' of eligible young debutantes and a flutter of hearts and eyelashes from their daughters. Tall and handsome with a winsome smile, he whisked many a hopeful young beauty around the dance floor as Anna and Melody watched with mixed emotions. Their project had been successful beyond their wildest expectations, but were they happy with the results?

The week following his successful venture into the halls of Boston society, Joel found himself deluged by invitations from young idle swains to while away the afternoon hours riding and gaming. An equal flurry of invitations to dinner parties and balls arrived. Had he not been introduced to Boston by the Wilkins family, his immediate acceptance would not have been forthcoming. But because they considered him a Wilkins protégé and worthy of escorting Melody, his reception proved warm and immediate. His charm and good looks proved an asset to any gathering, and it was whispered that the mysterious young man's future in the family's holdings seemed limitless.

With Melody's help Joel responded affirmatively to the evening invitations while declining the afternoon outings on the grounds his work would require too much time. Before long, the constant barrage of partying grew wearisome to him and he longed for a quiet evening to read and gather his thoughts.

The ever present Melody disturbed him more than a little. Her zest for life and her sweetness had grasped his heart and he was at a loss to define the emotions that she aroused in him. He was sure that, considering who she was and how young she was, he had best be about quelling the distracting thoughts that arose at the most inopportune moments. Even now thinking of her wide blue eyes dancing with merriment and focused on him made his heart beat faster.

In the weeks that followed, Joel dutifully attended to his social obligations, escorting Melody and Anna, but the relaxed camaraderie between the three had exited as he battled with what he felt was an unsuitable attraction to his employer's daughter.

With genuine relief Joel saw the date approaching for his departure to Maine and the girls back to school.

But before he could make a timely escape, one more hurdle loomed. The final party was to be held at the Wilkins mansion. To further complicate matters, Anna's parents had ordered her home to Philadelphia to spend the rest of her vacation with them. A pouting Anna left, leaving only Melody in Joel's care.

The night of the ball arrived and Joel dressed with trepidation, his mind on Melody. She informed him that he would be her dinner partner and she expected at least three waltzes from him. The thought of holding that lithe young body in his arms with her fragrance enveloping him while her vibrant blue eyes locked into his, weakened any resolve he had to put her out of his mind.

He arrived just as she was descending the stairway. Her sapphire blue silk gown dipped discreetly in the front and molded her body to accent her tiny waist before billowing out in yards of iridescent fabric . The color of her gown touched her eyes which sparkled brighter than the large blue gemstones surrounded by diamonds that nestled in the hollow of her throat. Joel held his breath as his eyes took in the vision floating down the stairs. Her hair was upswept revealing her slender perfectly formed neck and making her appear older than her eighteen years (she had celebrated her birthday at school just before leaving for summer vacation).

He shook his head, inwardly rebuking the

unwanted longings that threatened his resolve. He averted his eyes lest she see the turmoil going on inside him.

Melody saw and paused midway. Misinterpreting what she saw, pain darkened her cobalt eyes.

When she reached the last step, Joel reached out his hand and turning, placed it in the crook of his arm without comment.

A sad smile touched Melody's lips, "You have learned your lessons well, Joel. Perfect attire, perfect timing, and perfect maneuver. I fear your need for me is ending."

"I'm glad that you are gratified with my progress." Joel remarked, ignoring her silent plea.

"Gratified?" Melody whispered, the sparkle gone from her eyes.

"Maybe satisfied?" He gave her a cool impersonal smile.

"That's not quite the word for it." Melody muttered, anger flushing her face. "Shall we go in to dinner?"

Joel dutifully filled in the dance cards of many hopeful young beauties, putting off Melody's until last. When he finally approached her, dashing young blades surrounded her and his heart skipped. One gazed at her with sheer adoration, while another clamored for her attention. Her eyes sparkled as she laughed at them holding court with her admirers, that is, until her eyes fell on Joel. Pain touched them briefly once more and then it was gone as she lifted her determined little chin and held out her arm, her card attached to her wrist.

"I'm sorry but I have only one dance left, and that is the last waltz which I promised to Joel." She told the enclave as they parted letting Joel through.

Growls of good natured complaints greeted him, but he never heard them, he was lost in the cool, blue gaze that held his.

The haunting strains of the final dance had already begun when Joel took Melody in his arms. He swept her out on the floor and they floated to the music as if they were one. Halfway through the waltz, Melody's eyes met Joel's and held them, "what a graceful partner you are, Mr. Isaacs."

A wry smile curled one side of Joel's mouth, "I had a fine teacher, Miss Melody."

"Perhaps we did our job too well."

"What do you mean by that?"

"I'm tired of dancing, Joel. Let's go out on the porch."

"And risk ugly rumors?" Joel hedged, unwilling to be alone with her.

"Quite. As long as I behave in a proper manner, then let people imagine what they will."

"Do you think that is wise?"

"At this moment I don't care whether it is wise or not. I want to get out of this crowd."

"Very well." Joel replied as he swept her out the double doors leading to the broad side porch.

The air was heavy and the fragrance of a late blooming rose wafted in from the garden creating an intimate cocoon that surrounded them. He stood close enough to her to see the pulse beating rapidly in her neck. Fighting back the desire to take her in his arms, he spoke quietly and stood, aloof, by her side.

Melody turned to him and stepped closer, her eyes, bright with unshed tears, turned up to his. His heart thundered and he stepped back. She clinched a delicate fist and pounded him gently on the chest, tears welling up in her eyes and trailing down her cheeks, "Joel, what's wrong with you, with us? "

"Whatever do you mean, Miss Melody? There's nothing wrong with me." Joel lied.

Suddenly anger fired her eyes replacing the sadness, and she stomped her foot, "How many times do I have to tell you not to call me Miss Melody?"

"You know that wouldn't be proper."

"Who cares about proper?"

"You do. Haven't you been spending a summer teaching me what is and what is not proper."

"That was a social lesson. I'm not talking about us."

"And what is the difference?"

"I had hoped there was a difference between me and all the other young women that you have been mesmerizing."

"I've been mesmerizing no one, Miss Melody."

"Then what do you call it?"

"Polite attention."

"Ha!" Melody jerked her head to the side dislodging one of her golden curls.

"Now look what you've done. You've messed up your coiffure and now people will really talk."

"The only one I care about talking is you. And all I'm getting from you is evasion."

"Evasion?"

"The truth of the matter is you are not the same person that I met and had so much enjoyment with during my holidays. If I had known you would change this much, I should never have taught you to dance."

"You think teaching me to dance has changed me into another person?"

"Well something has, and that's when it started."

"What do you mean that I've changed."

"Toward me."

"How?"

"The way you look at me."

"How do I look at you and how should I look at you. The last thing in the world I would want to do is offend you." Joel replied, his heart galloping.

"You know good and well you have done nothing

to offend me. If anything, you are too polite."

"How can anyone be too polite?" Joel asked, trying to guide the conversation to safer ground.

Exasperated, Melody's voice cut through the night, "Joel Isaacs, you know exactly what I mean. My question is why has your feelings changed toward me?"

"Believe me, Melody, my feelings have not changed only deepened."

"You don't act like we're friends anymore."

"Is that what you want of me?" Joel smiled, his heart suddenly in his eyes as he took her hand and kissed it.

"Oh, yes, I need your friendship. I just couldn't bear it if I lost it." She said as she hurled herself into Joel's arms.

He held her thus, drinking in the touch and fragrance of her, his heart breaking, "Then I'll be the best friend you've ever had."

"Always?" She looked up into his eyes.

"Yes, little one, always." He vowed, his voice just above a whisper as he placed a chaste kiss on top of her cloud of golden hair.

CHAPTER 14

Autumn in Maine turned golden but the crisp days too soon gave way to harsh winter winds howling and hurling icy pellets. Joel scarcely noticed the weather except for the interruption of his brief rides into the countryside. The rides served two purposes, he surveyed Wilkins' real estate holdings and gave his fine gelding, Donovan, and himself some much needed exercise.

For the most part he stayed housed up in offices learning all he could about constructing procedures of the ships and the potential market for each. Most of what they turned out was contracted, but Joel felt that there was a broader market to be tapped. At night he stayed in his room studying ship construction. If they could find new innovations and add to their workforce, he knew that what was now a reasonably profitable enterprise could double or triple its success.

He wrote Wilkins that he had read about several new innovative designs for ships and would like to visit other shipyards to observe what they were doing. His employer gave his blessing but asked Joel to delay any trips until Spring when the weather was more conducive to travel, adding that he surmised from his letter that Joel was sinking back into the world of all work and no play. He urged him to enjoy some leisure time and expected him to return to Boston for the Christmas holidays.

The letter brought visions of golden curls and pleading indigo eyes turned up to his. He shook his head trying to dislodge the poignant memory of that sweet voice urging him to be her friend.

"Oh, Melody, I will be your friend to the death, only my heart wants more and that can never be." Joel sighed as he remembered the churning emotions that he had worked to suppress. How could he spend Christmas with her family when he felt as he did toward their daughter? How could he be near her with his heart so full and never tell her? Torture that's what it would be and the only anti-dote for that was work.

But Joel discovered work that had been so challenging had suddenly become burdensome. His nights were disturbed by dreams of Melody's pleading eyes which suddenly turned to flashing green ones beneath a cloud of titan hair. He would awaken only to fall back asleep to dream of the one who had betrayed him, beckoning him to follow her and all the heartaches he had thought he had resolved would surface.

For two weeks Joel fought his nocturnal demons

until Wilkins took advantage of a lull in the weather and arrived in Bath. The telltale circles beneath Joel's warm brown eyes alarmed him.

"Joel, what's the meaning of this?" He gestured at the piles of books on the desk and floor in the study adjacent to his bedroom.

A lopsided grin parted his face, "It is kind of a mess, sir. I'm not usually as untidy as this."

"I not referring to the disarray. I'm talking about the mounds of work you've brought home. Have you been getting any sleep?"

"Some." Joel flushed, not wanting to reveal the disturbing dreams that were stealing his sleep.

"Well, it's apparent from your appearance that you're not getting enough. I applaud you for all your industriousness, but without a proper balance in your life, your health and ultimately your work will suffer. What have you been doing for relaxation?"

"I was riding and exercising that fine piece of horseflesh you gave me until the weather curtailed that. Now mostly I read."

"You mean researching."

"Well, yes, mostly."

"How much social contact have you had since you came here?"

"The workers at the yard."

"You need more than that and I'm going to see that you get it." Wilkins declared, his tone non negotiable.

"I really don't have time-----------."

"You will take time." Wilkins' mouth drew into a tight line, his brow wrinkled.

Joel sighed, "Whatever you say, sir."

Wilkins eyes pierced him like icy darts, then softened, "Joel, I appreciate what you're trying to do, but it doesn't have to happen in a week or a month or even a year. And your health and state of mind is not worth the risk if it never happens. I want you to have a balanced life and that includes contact with other people, preferably your peers. Bath is not the size of Boston by any means, but I know there are young people here and tonight you will be introduced to some. My friend has invited us to a dinner party and you're going."

The meal proved a delightful diversion for Joel. All ages were represented at the table and the lively, stimulating conversation made Joel realize how isolated he had become. After dinner the young people left to go ice skating and urged Joel to accompany them. Protesting that he had never ice skated, he finally acquiesced.

A regaling time of laughter ensued as Joel managed to stay upright and maneuver around the small lake. Lanterns on poles surrounded the small frozen body of water reflecting like so many diamonds on the silver ice rimmed by a blanket of snow.

Soon Joel sailed around the pond as if he had been

skating all his life and that evening proved the first of many outings with the young people of Bath. He forged friendships during the following months and into the spring. For the first time Joel experienced friendships with young men his own age and relished the time spent sharing dreams, goals and times of recreation. It opened a whole new world that he had only glimpsed in Boston. His affect on the young women proved equal to the sensation that he had created in Boston. However in Bath, he reciprocated by escorting various young women to the many invitations that he accepted, hoping that one of them might subdue the image of golden hair and lovely form that haunted his memory. It proved a futile effort. While he enjoyed the Bath beauties' company, none quelled the longing to drown himself in those azure eyes. He decided that going to Boston for the holidays was not an option for him.

When spring arrived Joel left for an extensive visit to the many shipyards up and down the New England coast. Some he found ran more efficiently than Wilkins, but most were years behind the clean facility at Bath.

Joel shared plans with his mentor concerning streamlining certain procedures at the yard and requested that he remain another year to see them through. Disappointed that he was reluctant to return to Boston but seeing the wisdom of his suggestion, Wilkins agreed.

What was to have been one year of training in Bath turned into two and then three. He made brief visits to Boston but he always managed to arrive when Melody was at school or on her extended tour of Europe. His memory of her remained vivid in his imagination for she still managed to write him at least monthly. Each time he opened one and the fragrance of her filled the room, he was transported back to that summer evening when he held her in his arms and promised to be her friend forever.

He could tell from her letters that her interests were maturing and finally she wrote him the letter he knew would come one day and had dreaded in the depths of his soul. She had accepted the suit of one of the young swains who had been pursuing her relentlessly. Their wedding would be the following June. She wanted to know if he would be there to kiss the bride?

How could he not? But how could he bear it, her belonging to another man?

When a crisis in the shipping company occurred, Wilkins requested Joel's immediate return to Boston. Bidding farewell to his friends and companions, Joel boarded the first vessel sailing to Boston that could accommodate his horse and his belongings. The owner had communicated in no uncertain terms that his presence would be required in Boston on a permanent basis.

Puzzling over what crisis in Boston would require

him there permanently pushed the thought of seeing
Melody to the back of his mind. Anyway he remembered
that she wrote to him of a trip to Italy that she had
planned with her maternal aunt. Relieved that he would
not have a divided mind in dealing with whatever issue
Wilkins had encountered, he approached Boston with
little anxiety.

In the three years that Joel had been away, he had
not only learned all he could about the ship building
business, but had studied all of the interests that
Wilkins had. Of special interest to him was the shipping
business and potential commercial trade that had
been overlooked. After the crisis subsided, he looked
forward to sharing with his mentor some expansion
ideas that seemed reasonable and timely. But he would
bide his time. First things first, he would make himself
available in anyway his employer needed him. Perhaps
if he stayed focused on the issues at hand, his emotions
and heart would not betray him.

Boston harbor proved a beehive of activity as
he hailed a carriage to haul his luggage home. Making
his way down the dock leading Donovan, Joel heard a
familiar voice herald him.

Turning he saw the friendly face of the dock
manager and his former boss, Nick.

Grasping   Nick's   outstretched   hand,   Joel

exclaimed, "What a sight you are, Nick. Looks as if you are busier than ever."

"That I am, mate. The mister has bought out two more shipping firms and 'tis my duty to get these men working together for the common cause. My! You're a healthy sight for these aging eyes. I almost didn't recognize you. The boy has become a man, and sporting a nice beard you are. I really only recognized your mount, then I realized it was you. You've made a handsome fellow with an aristocrat carriage, if you don't mind me saying so."

"Guess no one minds a compliment, Nick. But I'm still the same fellow that unloaded cargo for you almost four years ago."

"I knew then that your destiny went far above the docks. The boss man has been telling me what a fine job you're doing up there in Bath. We never have had so many ships delivered ahead of time, but we're going to need twice as many with the new companies. I heard you'll be staying with us. Hope it want cause a slowdown on the other end."

"I think not. We've recently hired some new personnel and a capable new manager. When I left things were ahead of schedule and running smoothly. Our main concern is our suppliers, getting the raw materials timely. In business too often you are dependent on circumstances beyond your control."

"I heard you were an expert at getting what we

needed, when you needed it. I'm surprised knowing your gentle nature, but then I remember how you got the dock workers to turn out."

"Sometimes logical persuasion properly communicated can do the job quicker than an irate conversation. If you attack a man you only get his defenses up. If you can persuade him that to cooperate is to his advantage then you've usually won him over. Right?"

"I'd say so, mate. Anyhow that's what I observed with these two orbs of mine and I know it worked down here. Actually that's what I've been trying since you left and things are running smoother than I expected."

"Let a man feel that what he can contribute makes a difference and pride will dictate his response. I just believe a man does better if he's led than if he's driven" Joel explained

"That's for sure. Every man deep down inside wants to know that somehow what he has done has value."

"Good to talk to you, Nick. Do you know if the boss is in his office?"

"Sure is and anxious to see you."

The familiar fragrance of oil and lemon greeted Joel as Wilkins' assistant waved him on into the older man's office.

Wilkins faced the window, his eyes closed, and his hands on his chest. Joel waited a moment before he spoke, evaluating this man who had become almost surrogate father to him. Love and appreciation for the man threatened to overcome him. He had aged and Joel realized a frailness with almost an ethereal quality radiated from him and fear griped Joel. Was he ill? Was that why he called him home?

Just as these questions assaulted Joel, Wilkins stirred and opened his eyes. A broad smile beamed from his generous mouth and his blue eyes sparkled at the sight of his protégé. "Welcome home, my boy. It has been too long."

"Yes, too long." Joel said, his voice husky with emotion. No matter how his heart hurt for the woman he could not have, he could no longer deny himself the company of this man who meant so much to him. His apparent frailty brought to mind the fleetness of time that a youth too often ignored. He had neglected this man because he refused to deal with an errant heart. No longer would he act the cowardly fool. Melody belonged or shortly would belong to another. He would face that like a man, wish her well and get on with his life.

"I came as soon as I could, Mr. Wilkins. What kind of crisis do we have and how can I help?"

"That's what I like to hear. What kind of crisis do we have? Puts you fully on board, my boy." He hesitated, and then a wry smile twisted his mouth as he looked closely at Joel. "My mistake. The boy I sent to Bath to do a man's job has returned a man and a handsome one at that. Glad you are back and truly it's a man's job that I'm needing you for, but I've never ask any endeavor of you that you didn't more than accomplish."

"What's the problem?"

"One of more work than I can handle. I've just purchased two more shipping companies."

"Nick just told me. And busy he claims to be."

"He's got a job before him merging the work crews."

"He can handle it. Just give him a few weeks."

"I'm not concerned about that. With that purchase I have increased my shipping business fourfold, but I lack the ships to take full advantage of the new commerce. You know yourself that cargo arriving safely and timely is the key to remaining successful. That's where you come in. In your trips up the coast, did you find any good shipyards that might be for sale?"

"I did, but they were having the same problems as we faced. Inadequate raw materials, especially lumber and timbers tall enough for the new mast we are installing to make better speed."

"But I thought you managed to obtain an adequate supply of materials for our projects."

"Only a temporary solution. By the grace of God, I seemed to persuade our suppliers to meet our needs. To triple those needs would be doubtful. But I've been doing some studying on the matter."

Wilkins chuckled, "Why doesn't that surprise me?"

Joel shrugged, a good natured smile on his face, "In my spare time, of course."

"Of course and what did your study suggest to you?"

"It might be risky."

"Desperate times call for desperate measures."

"What if we invested in the logging industry? We would be our own supplier, ship builder and shipping firm. We would cut the middle man out and could realize a greater profit."

Disappointment darkened the older man's face, "I tried that, Joel. The loggers in the Northeast have the logging business monopolized, therefore they control the supply and price. You know the capitalistic way, supply and demand dictate the cost."

"I know about that, but how about oak from Georgia and fir from the west coast?"

Excitement fired Wilkins' eyes, "And we could use our older ships to ship them to the yards."

"Not only that, soon the railways will be traversing this country from east to west, making direct shipping lanes. It would be good to invest in the railroads against that day. You already have some real estate right along the proposed route."

"You have been doing your homework! How

would we implement all this?"

"First we need to firm up our supply source. I will go to Georgia to meet with loggers to see if we can buy their oak, then I'll go to California, Washington and Oregon and find loggers who are willing to sell their timber to us, but the main action I believe we need to take is to buy up forests and hire loggers to harvest the best and tallest trees."

"So you will leave us to return home?" Wilkins asked, his voice somber.

"This is my home. I only want to assist you in making your new endeavor a success. If I can lay some old ghost to rest with a trip out west, then so be it."

Wilkins nodded, "I agree. Sounds like this is what we should do and I've a proposition for you."

"Sir?"

"If you're successful in this venture then the new business will be half yours."

"But I have no capital to invest." Joel protested.

"I have the capital, you have the time and energy. A good combination for both of us."

"I can't accept so generous an offer. I owe you far more than I could ever repay you now." Joel shook his head.

"You've repaid me many times over. Your diligence has prospered my business and now I have the opportunity to help us both achieve."

"You know I don't have to have a vested interest

to do my best for you."

"I know that. I do have one regret."

"What is that?"

"I will miss you and my family, as well, has looked forward to having you near."

"Miss Melody and Mrs. Wilkins will be too busy with a wedding and such to miss me." Joel chuckled a mirthless laugh to cover his pain.

"I don't think so. Melody has been rampant in her demands that I return you to Boston. I can only imagine the war that this new plan will entail. But aside from that you know that you are more like a son to me than an employee."

"You've treated me as such."

"When you return, that is if you don't encounter ties so strong they will bid you stay, I will be turning much of the management of my business affairs over to you."

"The management of the business? Why would you do that? Are you ill?"

"Let's just say that I'm not getting any younger and it's come to my mind that I need to prepare for the future whatever that may entail. And also I want to spend more time with my wife."

"What about Melody's husband. Shouldn't he be the one?"

"Peter?" Wilkins rolled his eyes, "His wealth is inherited, he has spent his time as most of the wealthy young men do, playing. Besides his wealth came from agriculture, he knows nothing about my interests nor is he interested. I gave him the chance, he declined."

"Yet Melody loves him; therefore he must have value."

"Oh, yes, he is a good sort. Good character, handsome, socially prominent and totally smitten with my daughter; however, someday this will all be Melody's, I want it in capable hands, something to hand down to my grandchildren."

"Will that not cause a conflict in her marriage?"

"No. I've already told them my plans. Peter and Melody are both content with them. Peter because he needs none of Melody's wealth and Melody because she trusts my judgment. The only problem I can see is in the event the West lures you and you don't return."

"What an opportunity you and the Good Lord have laid before me. I can think of nothing that would entice me not to come back."

CHAPTER 15

Joel took longer to dress for dinner than usual. His emotions rioted within him at the thought of seeing Melody again. It had been four years since he had last seen her. Years that he had deliberately avoided any contact with her, hoping that time and space would eradicate or at least mitigate the feelings that he had for her. Work had helped push her lingering image to the back of his mind for brief respites, but then he would see someone with golden hair walking down the street and she would haunt his memory and he would remember the vow he had failed to keep. He had promised her his friendship and then abandoned her. But what else could he do when his heart cried out for more? Had he acted cowardly or was he protecting her? He sighed and acknowledged his cowardice. For the first time in his life Joel Isaacs had run from difficulty.

Tonight marked a new beginning. If Mr. Wilkins looked on him as a surrogate son then he would endeavor to be the brother that Melody had lost. He would be one who would protect her, comfort her, encourage her and offer counsel if she needed it, and keep what was in his heart to himself.

She opened the door on the first knock. The girl who haunted his memory had become a woman, the beauty hinted at in earlier years, now full blown. She took his breath away and with it his resolve to be a brother to her.

For a long moment they stood, unmoving gazing at each other as if transfixed by the changes. Then suddenly the girl beneath the womanly splendor burst forth and she hurled herself into his arms, weeping.

His heart ripped asunder and it was all he could do to refrain from pressing her to him with an embrace that would never let her go. Instead he gripped her shoulders and set her back a step and bent down to look into those amazing eyes, "Why these tears, my little one? Are you not happy to see me?"

"Not happy to see you? Not happy to see you? That's all I've dreamed about for the past four years. Why did you break your promise?"

"What promise?" He knew very well what she meant.

"That you'd be a friend forever. You abandoned me." She accused.

If his heart had ripped asunder before, now it tore into a million pieces, "Why little one, what are you talking about. I'm still your friend."

"Friends keep in touch with friends. You never came home and you rarely answered any of my letters."

"Sometimes friends have to be separated for a while. You were never here when I came back."

"And my letters?"

" I loved every one of them." He struggled to keep his tone light, not to let her see that each had proved a painful treasure that he had read and reread until the ink faded.

"And where were your replies?" The tears had stopped, anger flushed her face.

"Melody, you can't imagine how busy I was."

"No, I can't imagine one can be too busy for a friend."

"You're right, it was inexcusable of me but I thought the details of my life would bore you."

"Bore me? Letters from you letting me know if you were dead or alive."

"Come now, Melody, your father kept you abreast of my welfare."

"That's beside the point. A friend wants to know every thing about a friend's life. All about where you work, where you live, and, and who you see. Father told me that he had introduced you to some people your own age and that from the looks of things, you were enjoying them."

"Yes, he did. And I really had some nice times

with them."

"Was there any particular one that you enjoyed most?"

Joel's heart beat a little faster, "Of course I enjoyed some more than others."

"Why?"

"I guess it was similar interests."

"Male or female?" she pressed.

"Why you little imp. Are you suggesting that I might have a love interest up in Maine and not tell you about it" He chuckled and chucked her under her chin as if she were four.

"Why else would you not have time to write or want to come home?"

"I see. No I'm not the one with a love interest. How could anyone compete with you?" He quipped in a lame attempt to disguise the truth with levity.

"That's more like it." She smiled,

"I hear that it is rather you, my forever friend, who has abandoned me for a new love."

"Oh never, Joel."

"Then who is this Peter that your father has told me about?"

"Oh, Peter. I almost forgot." She grabbed his hand and pulled him with her into the hallway ablaze with light. "He is in the drawing room and is dying to meet you."

They entered the large ornate room hand in hand

and suddenly Joel faced a golden giant with puzzled blue eyes that took in his fiancé hand in hand with another. Nor did he miss the shining lights in her eyes.

"Peter, this is Joel." She declared as if announcing a king.

Peter stepped forward and offered his hand forcing Joel to relinquish Melody's. "Peter Smithwick, here, and I am finally glad to meet the man who can do anything."

Joel flushed and stammered, "Not quite. With horses I'm pretty proficient and that's actually all Melody knows about my abilities."

"It isn't only Melody, although she thinks you hung the moon."

"That's way beyond my expertise." Joel chuckled, embarrassed.

"Perhaps, but the entire family holds you in the very highest esteem."

"Thank you. I pray that I will live up to the confidence they have placed in me. I've also heard very positive comments about you." Joel countered, grasping for a way out of this disturbing conversation.

"Oh, really? I'm all ears." Peter laughed.

"I heard that you were a fine man of noble character and the most important thing is that you love our Melody with all your heart."

Peter's bantering grew serious and he moved to Melody's side and placed his arm around her as if staking his claim for all to see, "She is the epitome of all my dreams and my greatest desire is to serve her for the rest of my life."

A silence thick enough to cut filled the room before Joel found his voice and replied huskily, "A worthy ambition for a deserving lady. May the two of you experience happiness beyond your wildest imagination."

Dinner seemed to go on forever. In addition to Peter and the Wilkins family, Captains Dundee and Chapman and their wives dined with them. Mr. Wilkins wanted Joel to hear first hand some of the challenges they had faced the past year. Ordinarily Joel would have been eager to learn all that he could from the two best sea captains that sailed for the Wilkins line but not tonight.

During the conversation his eyes were drawn back to the beauty at the opposite end of the table and he would loose his train of thought. He struggled to keep his heart and mind under control, but it was no use. For the first time in his life, he understood what the word captivated meant as his eyes involuntarily returned to drink in her presence. His were not the only eyes that covertly watched his struggle. Three other pairs watched, one in horror the other two with hope. The object of his distraction appeared oblivious to the conflict as she made polite conversation with Captain Dundee's wife, leaving Peter to watch and wonder.

Joel threw himself into the business as if his life depended on it. But life in Boston was more than dollars and cents. It was social events during the week and worship on Sundays. It was a walk in the garden for a breath of fresh air or a brisk ride in the countryside to clear his mind. But everywhere he went, there was Melody. Melody with Peter, Melody alone. He didn't know which was more challenging, seeing her on the arm of her adoring fiancé or finding her in the early morning, reading in the garden, with sleep still on her as sweet as a just opened blossom. His only solace, a brisk ride across the countryside came to a halt when she clamored to go with him. Peter heard her and insisted that he accompany them. The look he gave Joel left little doubt that a jaunt with the two of them alone was not an option.

Joel agreed with Peter. The more he saw of him, the more he was convinced that the match between Peter and Melody was perfect. Had he not loved her, he would have applauded the match. They were cut from the same cloth. They shared the same background, the same faith, the same goals and aspirations and he adored her. There would be no cultural clashes. Whereas with him----he let himself go no farther. He knew all too well the answer to that. Besides Melody loved Peter. She must for she agreed to marry him.

He liked him. Under any other circumstances they would make jolly companions. But it was Peter who had Melody, the woman Joel loved and could not have. This made any friendship with him impossible. Instead he tolerated him and tried to hide his feelings.

He attempted to keep his relationship with Melody cool and impersonal. But she would have none of it. She sought him out asking his advice on everything from house plans and wedding gowns to how they should set up their stables. He had resolved to be a brother to her and she forced him into the role. If something needed fixing, she turned to him instead of Peter. When she had a cold, she asked him to read to her, when they went riding, she implored him to tell her of his sea adventures and the hard life out west.

As the weeks approached her wedding, Joel shrouded his emotions. When Melody sensed that he was shutting her out, she clamored for attention. Six weeks before the wedding, the Wilkins gave a great ball in Peter and Melody's honor. All the prominent people in Boston and the surrounding areas were expected. With the memory of the one four years ago so painfully etched in Joel's mind, he planned a trip that would keep him away for the days prior and following the event.

When Melody heard that he would not be attending, she marched up to the door of his cottage just as he was arising and banged on it demanding to be let in. Reluctantly he cracked the door, his hair tousled, his eyes heavy with sleep. She pushed the door open and stepped through.

Her eyes widened, her mission forgotten. She stood on tiptoe and brushed his hair away from his forehead, her hand trailing down his cheek. Sleepy and vulnerable, he grasp her hand and put it to his lips closing his eyes in a lingering kiss that said more than words could ever convey. When he released it, he opened his eyes, shaking his head as if to undo the deed. But it had been done and he stared into two wide blue pools, brimming with tears starring back at him. Without a word, she turned and fled.

Joel had to talk to someone. Had to have a release, some counsel. He had stepped over the self imposed boundary, the boundary of decency and he was angry with himself. He had kissed one who was promised to another and in that kiss revealed his deepest longing. That inappropriate longing had hounded him for four years, led him to envy another man's dream of happiness. His resolve to love her from afar, to care for her like a brother lay in ashes at his feet.

What was he to do? He wanted to fade away as if love had never come his way. To take his belongings and head west where the only complication would be the weather, Indians and livestock. But he couldn't do that. Mr. Wilkins placed too much trust in him for him to run away. He needed him and he would not let him down, add one betrayal to another. Yet how could he face the final loss of her? To see her often and know she belonged to another man? What kind of life would that be? Torture, pure torture.

Then he remembered Jim. Captain Dundee said that Jim was ailing and back in port. He remembered the wisdom of his old friend, how he had helped him after his brothers' betrayal.

"Well ain't you a sight for sore eyes, Joel. Come on in and set a spell. I've been hearing big things about you. Yes siree . Can't say I'm surprised. I knew you had it in you. Just didn't know you'd get there so fast. The cap'n tells me that Mr. Wilkins looks on you as a son and that you'll be a running his empire one of these days. Figured you'd forget old Jim, but I see you haven't."

"How could I forget you, Jim? You were my lifeline."

"No, twarn't me, twas our Good Lord."

"Well you were an instrument in His hand."

"Well praise be to Him if'n he can use an ole cripple like me."

"Maybe on the outside, but inside you're a giant of a man. I need some help. Will you help me?"

"Shore, son. But I cain't imagine you needing anything I've got to offer." Jim shook his old head as he bent to light a lantern in the darkened room.

"I need your wisdom, good friend." Joel's voice broke.

Jim looked up and straight into Joel's tortured eyes, "My word, Son, whatever has happened?"

"I have betrayed a trust."

"You have betrayed a trust? I don't believe that. I know you too well. Why don't you tell me about it? Start from the beginning."

So Joel told the story of hearing about his family's death and how Mr. Wilkins had provided opportunity and a future for him. How he had treated him as a son and trusted him with everything he had."

"How have you betrayed him, my boy? Did you take what was his?"

Joel sighed and waited to regain his composure. "I love his daughter."

"Does he object to that?"

"He doesn't know."

"Why would he object?"

"You know and I know that my background is too different from theirs."

"Yet he is going to let you manage his business?"

"Business and a daughter are two different issues. You know the problem when there is a conflict of cultures."

"How could there be a conflict of cultures?"

"The way I was raised, the fact that my mother was an Indian. Do you have any idea what would happen if Boston society found that out? They might even shun Melody. I couldn't live with that depriving her of the world she grew up in."

"What does Melody say about all this?"

"That's not the issue. She is betrothed to another."

"So she doesn't return your love."

"She looks on me as a brother. And I resolved to treat her with the care and the respect of a sibling."

"But you can't?"

"I can't and I didn't."

"Have you violated her?"

"In a way I have."

"Oh my son. I can't believe you would ever bring harm to another."

"Oh, it's not what you're thinking."

"I think you had better tell me, then."

"I succeeded in my outward actions toward her in keeping in the boundary of my resolve until this morning. I had just arisen from sleep, dreaming about her when she like a vision appeared at my door. I cracked the door and she pushed through, all upset because I had planned not to attend her betrothal ball. I had only put my clothes on and not attended to my toiletries."

Jim looked puzzled, "Go on, boy. What has that to do with anything?"

"That's the point, man. A lock of my hair had

fallen over my forehead and she stepped in close to me with the look of an angel on her face and reached up and brushed my hair away. She was so close the sweet smell of her engulfed me and I grabbed her hand and kissed it."

Old Jim looked stunned for a second, then a side splitting laugh rolled out until he could hardly sit.

Anger flushed Joel's cheeks, "I don't call betrayal a laughing matter. I came for help, not to be laughed at."

Finally Jim's laughter subsided and he spoke, his eyes still sparked with merriment, "I thought those society dudes were always kissing a lady's hand."

"Oh sure. But it was not that I kissed her hand, it was the way I kissed it. She knew. Now she knows I love her and not like a brother."

"How do you know that?"

"She ran away crying."

"I see. So now you have a dilemma. To face her everyday, to face her fiancé will prove awkward."

"Not only awkward, but painful for me. I covet what belongs to another man. That's a sin."

"She don't belong to him yet. It ain't a sin up till now, it will be after they are married."

"Which won't be long."

"Have you thought that maybe she might want you and not him. Could be you know."

Joel shook his head, "I know she loves me, but I told you it is more like a brother. You know, rather like the brother she lost. She has never given any indication that she looks on me any other way."

"You sure about that."

"As sure as a man can be."

"Well, then you do have a problem."

"What is your suggestion."

"The one thing I do know, Joel, is if this Melody is not for you then God has a better one in store for you."

"I cannot imagine anything on this earth better than having her by my side."

"This is the time to trust Him. But meanwhile you need some space from all this. Got any ideas?"

"My plans are to travel west in search of a new business venture for Mr. Wilkins. We had already made the decision that I would go after the wedding. Seems Melody was dead set that I should not miss her wedding."

"And the little miss always gets her way."

"Sort of."

"Uh hum. Well this time she shouldn't and after this morning she might see it differently."

"But what about Mr. Wilkins? He wants me to stay."

"You'll have to tell him."

"What?"

"That you love his daughter."

"I can't tell him that."

"You must. I've heard that he loves you as a son. If that's true, he would not want you to stay and suffer the torment her wedding will arise in you. Go on out west and work this thing out. Let God bring a healing and maybe a new love."

"It didn't happen in the four years I was gone. Just got worse."

"She wasn't married then. Somewhere in your heart you had hope."

"I don't think so."

"It was there, you just didn't allow it to surface. I know you, Joel. Once she is married that's final and you're too honorable a man not to trust God in this. It might prove awkward, but if you go away awhile, then things have a way of straightening themselves out. Go to Wilkins, tell him your dilemma and the good man will release you for what is best for all."

CHAPTER 16

A sea breeze caressed Joel's bearded face as he leaned forward to watch the San Diego shoreline approach. He was bronze from his hundred days at sea, golden highlights from weeks of exposure burnished his dark hair, and he was lean and strong from doing a seaman's duty. The youth who had left five years ago now returned a man.

The clipper, Windstar, which had brought him thus far, was a beauty to behold as she sailed through numerous gales, intent on a record breaking voyage to San Francisco. Having followed the new route charted by Lt. Maury of the observatory in Washington, the trip proved a glorious adventure. When the captain had need of an experienced crewman during turbulent seas, Joel had volunteered for the job. He welcomed the challenge and diversion of hard labor. When it became evident that they would fall short of the record of the hundred days that the Meteor had set from Boston to San Francisco, the captain opted to divert to San Diego in search of additional cargo before continuing on north.

The voyage had given him little time to think, that is until now. With San Diego looming in the distance, ghosts of his boyhood rose to haunt his soul and feelings that he had thought he had put to rest clamored to take control.

This was to be a journey of escape. But where was the sanctuary he sought? Certainly not here in San Diego where all his trouble began. Could this journey bring final closure to the nagging questions that he had learned to suppress yet threatened to overwhelm him today?

San Diego with its adobe huts shining in the noonday sun waited almost as if it beckoned him to come and solve the mysteries that plagued his mind. Yet how could a seaside village hold the answers to his past? His dreadful journey had begun here. Would it end here? He shook his head. His intended destination was San Francisco, and from there points north on a mission, sent by his friend and mentor to investigate new opportunities for his company. A sad smile curled his lips as he remembered his last encounter with the man whom he had grown to respect and love as a surrogate father.

Joel had taken old Joe's advice and gone to Melody's father, pouring out his heart, confessing how he had grown to love his daughter, how he had fought against it because of their different stations in life and, finally, what he thought was his unpardonable breach of trust. He dropped his head, unwilling to look his benefactor in the eye. He could not bear the disappointment and anger he knew must be in those gentle, but wise eyes.

When Joel finished, only the ticking of the tall case clock broke the heavy silence in the room. Finally a firm hand touched his shoulder and Wilkins softly commanded, "Look at me, Joel."

When he raised his head, he encountered not the anger or disappointment that he expected but instead only compassion and a sad smile.

"You are as honorable as I believed you to be. You came to me with what must be a humiliating experience for you."

"The most humiliating of my life, sir. To have to admit to you, who have been so kind and generous to me, that I have let you down and brought pain to your daughter seemed intolerable. I have to admit, sir, it was only at old Jim's insistence that I came to you. I just wanted to fade away."

"How glad I am that you took your friend's advice. Joel, you are agonizing over imagined failings."

"That I love your daughter as a man and not a brother is a truth that cannot be denied."

"I see no sin in that. One has little control over who captures our heart."

"But what one does with that event is a different story. I should have had better control over my emotions."

"From what you have told me, you went to every extreme to suppress those emotions."

"Until this morning."

"Yes, until this morning. But even then you did nothing to violate my daughter."

"Not physically, but emotionally. She recognized at once what I felt for her."

"Perhaps you were so disappointed by your reaction, you only thought she understood." Wilkins suggested.

"You didn't see her face. She knew and ran from me. There is no doubt she believes I have betrayed our friendship." Joel insisted

"I'm sure she was surprised, if you have never given her a hint of how you felt about her."

"Oh, sir, I never intended to. She is betrothed to another and she is your daughter. That's why I'm so distraught. I have betrayed your trust in me and her commitment to another." Joel moaned.

"If what you did would cause my daughter to reconsider her commitment, then it is better now than for her to enter into an unhappy marriage."

"From the look in her eye, it wasn't her commitment she doubted, but the friend she trusted." Joel protested.

"Now I have a confession of my own. Joel, you have not betrayed my trust, but rather I would have welcomed a suit from you for my daughter's hand."

"Me?" Joel's ebony eyes widened in disbelief.

Wilkins chuckled again, the heaviness in his eyes lifting somewhat, "The 'difference' in your station in life is in your own mind. I do not judge a man on his social standing but on his character. You have every quality that I would want my daughter's husband to possess. But the choice had to be hers."

"Aye, 'tis true. And it is another she loves." Joel agreed.

"I had hoped. She seemed very fond of you, Joel."

"As a brother and that's why I must be leaving. This morning showed me that a brother to her I cannot be. I have tried, but now she knows and that portends an awkward situation for all concerned."

"I understand how you feel. Perhaps a time of separation will ease the discomfort you feel."

"If I had known how you felt, I would have set out to win Melody's heart as a man and not as a brother. But I never dreamed you would consider me as a suitable prospect for your daughter."

"Had I let you know, then I would have manipulated your future and my daughter's. I had no idea that you felt as you did about her." Wilkins explained.

"And now it's too late for me. I know that Melody is fond of me, but she never considered me as a suitor."

Wilkins nodded his head and sighed, "My daughter has made her choice. I will love and support her in it and endeavor to treat her beloved as a son. But my heart is not in it."

"Then 'tis both our hearts," Joel agreed, sorrow bound his eyes.

"It goes without saying that what I have said must not go beyond these walls."

"You have my word on that, Mr. Wilkins."

Wilkins nodded his head sadly. "Now what are your plans?"

"I have no plan but to escape." Joel shrugged.

"Believe me, you have nothing from which to run."

"The potential embarrassment for Melody is very real. I would not want to bring any discomfort that might mar her enjoyment of her wedding and the festivities surrounding it." Joel explained.

"You have a point there, my boy. The very thought of sending you away again tears my heart out, but perhaps the timing is right for your west coast venture. It would provide a solution for you personally and the business as well."

"You still want me to represent you, to work for you?"

"More than ever. Get your things together. I have a brand new Clipper, the Windstar, waiting in the harbor bound for San Francisco." A smile parted Wilkins lips, hoping the news would encourage his protégé.

"I've seen her. She's splendid. I hear she is trying to break the 100 day record from Boston to San

Francisco. What an opportunity to take part in that!"

"Such an adventure might give you time to think and get a better perspective."

"You mean learn to love your daughter less?" Joel questioned.

Wilkins laughed, "Probably not possible."

Joel countered, "But perhaps get accustomed to the idea that she belongs to another?"

The older man nodded, "Something like that. Keep this in mind, Joel. If Melody is not the one God has for you, he has something far better in mind."

"Someone better than Melody? I can't imagine, but if that is true, I can't wait to see what He has in store for me."

"I can't guarantee you that your wait will be easy but it will be productive", Wilkins cautioned.

"You have been an encouragement in times past in reminding me of His way. Thank you for doing it once again."

"I'm sorry that both instances have proved so painful."

"I have read in the good book that with every temptation, God provides a way of escape and it seems that this time He has provided a glorious ship."

"I've a good captain aboard and if anyone can live up to the challenge of making it to California in less than 100 days, he can. I would like to make that voyage myself, but I scarcely think Melody would forgive me if

I were not here for her wedding. Maybe I will join you later. How long will it take you to be ready? I will have him hold the ship for you." Wilkins encouraged.

"I'm ready now, sir. I had planned to slip quietly away lest I cause Melody or you and Mrs. Wilkins any embarrassment."

"They will be so disappointed when I tell them you have gone."

"Perhaps not, after what happened. I upset Melody. There were tears in her eyes. She fled from me, as if she were in some kind of danger. I shall never forget that look in her eyes." Joel's voice grew husky. "I, the one who swore to protect her, to look after her as a brother, frightened and disappointed her. What was I thinking of?"

"You weren't thinking, for a moment your heart took precedence over your mind."

"And look what it has caused." Joel pointed out.

Even now thinking about those sapphire eyes wide and filled with tears brought all the pain and longing rushing back, pain that he had suppressed with the frenzied activity aboard ship. Did God have someone somewhere, better a more perfect match for him?

Joel shook his head. The Bible admonished one to "wait upon the Lord" and as nearly as he knew how, he committed his heart to do just that. Meanwhile he had a job to do for a trusted friend and employer, but first he would go ashore and face the old memories that taunted him.

The port of San Francisco bustled with activity. What had been a sleepy village of 800 shortly before gold was discovered at Sutter's mill had grown into a metropolis of thousands. Ships laden with food and lumber from the Northwest crowded the harbor. Some were there to supply eager prospectors with vital supplies for which they paid exorbitant prices. Others delivered their cargo of tea from China and swapped their cargo for lumber to transport to Australia.

Just as he anticipated, the visit to San Diego had proved a painful visit down memory lane. It did nothing to assuage the questions that rioted through his mind. He would have been better served if he had stayed on board the Windstar.

His arrival in the busy San Francisco harbor turned his thoughts to the business at hand and helped to quell the disturbing memories of times past, both recent and distant. He threw himself into researching trade and shipping in the harbor city. The more he talked to people, the more he became convinced that San Francisco was not the place to establish a new shipyard.

It was apparent that additional ships were needed, but land prices anywhere around the harbor had risen to ridiculous heights as well as building supplies. In short, what the east coast was experiencing in shortages was minor to what the west coast was experiencing.

Accommodations proved scarce, if not non existent and when he was about to give up, the captain of the Windstar introduced him to Andrew Brighton, a China tea trading captain who invited them to dinner. The captain and his wife were so taken with Joel they offered him a private room and meals in their home. Blessed with a comfortable room overlooking the harbor and tasty meals provided by the captain's missus, Joel made his inquiries all day and retreated to the comfort of the captain's home in the evening.

Frustrated with his research, he despaired that his idea of purchasing lumber for the eastern shipyards would prove more pipe dream than reality. One evening he returned to his lodging later than usual and discovered that the Brightons had a dinner guest, the captain's brother, Fred.

Arriving back from a trip taking supplies to the gold fields and further north, he regaled his audience with tales of adventure and misadventure along the way. When he heard of Joel's mission, he invited him to go with him on his next trip northward.

"You'll be wasting your time here, young man, trying to find an adequate shipment of lumber and sending it 'round the horn to the east coast. In the first place, the lumber is too expensive and in the second place, the shipping of it would prove prohibitive as well. I know that east coast timber made the thirteen thousand mile trip here, but there is no need for that. My advice to you is to go to the source and establish the whole operation here." Fred advised.

"And that would be?" Joel asked.

"I'm taking a packet that is making its first trip to Coos Bay, Oregon. I have heard that a settlement is developing around the bay right in the middle of lush Douglas fir forests. If a man could get a crew together, buy some timberland to harvest and then build a shipyard, he could send the finished product back east at a fraction of the cost." Fred Brighton's eyes brightened with anticipation as he encouraged Joel.

"You mean introduce ship building here?" Joel questioned. A new idea forming in the back of his mind.

"There are already some ship yards in San Francisco, some of them turning out a few lovely clippers, but most are producing lumber schooners for transporting the timber from the Oregon territory. Rather short sighted of them. Trade opportunity is so much broader than just up and down the west coast, this gold fever will wear off, but our natural resources far exceed the gold, but, for now, gold fever has ruined opportunity here. I believe that steam will be the wave of the future."

"Are you saying a yard should diversify and turn out beauty as well as utility?" Joel asked,

"That's exactly what I'm saying. You could have

eastern craftsman honing a beautiful clipper, while other technicians turning out utility schooners with an eye for the steam development later on." Fred exclaimed, his eyes alight.

"So what's your advice to me?" Joel's mind whirled with the concept. Could a shipyard build both and perhaps steam as well. He felt that in the not too distant future, steam would be the workhorse of trade. What a concept to take back home to Boston. Strange he was back out west yet in his mind Boston was home. Was it Boston or someone? Visions of her momentarily filled his mind distracting him. Suddenly Brighton's voice brought him back to the business at hand. He was here to do the best job he could for Melody's father, he best be giving Fred his full attention.

Fred was saying, "You need to move further north. Man power will be your problem. It's said that two thirds of the able bodied Oregon men have left for the gold fields. Soon enough some will be returning when they find themselves with little luck for making a fortune. No sir, the fortune to be made is in goods and services. San Francisco as you can see is a busy port. Trade with the east as well as Australia is booming. More ships and a diversity of them are needed here as well as on the east coast."

Joel's eye's brightened as he caught a vision of the potential opportunity that Fred Brighton described. For the first time in days, Joel felt his energy and enthusiasm returning. "What about the man power shortage?"

"Transport them from the east, if you have to. Import some of those New England craftsman to train these rough and tumble men; however, the first thing you need to do is find the place, buy the land and provide for workers. I'd advise you to not only transport workers but also make provisions for wives. The great northwest can be a lonely place and there is still danger from Indians."

"I grew up with that danger."

"How could a Bostonian like you know anything about Indians?"

Joel smiled, "Now do I really sound like a Bostonian?"

Fred laughed, "No, but you sure look like one."

"And how is that?" Joel asked, puzzled but amused.

"The way you are dressed, the cut of your hair and beard. Those are some fine duds you have on."

Now it was Joel's turn to laugh, "I'm just a cowboy gone to town."

"You don't say now. Maybe we'll get along after all." Fred chuckled.

"I fervently hope so, Fred, because I've got a lot to learn and you're just the man to teach me."

"Well, partner, how soon can you leave in the morning?"

"As soon as you want to go."

The ocean voyage in the small packet proved a rough ride. There was no sense of gliding through the surf, but rather pitch, roll, and fall. The baldheaded schooner, rigged without a topmast so that it could more easily tack into the strong westerly winds, was less than half as long as the Windstar and had a shallow draft for easing it across sand bars and into the narrow ports northward from San Francisco. The broad deck loaded beyond capacity, plowed through the rough Pacific surf, hoping to exchange the necessities it carried for lumber up and down the coast. Joel scarcely noticed the inconveniences the crude craft offered; excitement about his destination consumed him. He knew within himself that when he made land fall, he would find the opportunity for which he had been searching.

The craft pulled up to one of the rough hewn docks jutting into the harbor. Houses, little more than shacks, dotted the landscape here and there. Surrounding him were miles of untouched forests of Douglas fir. He had walked in the woodlands of the east, but nothing he had ever seen equaled this magnificence. Ships, houses and cities waited to be carved from this wilderness. He could almost hear them whisper his name. In his mind's eye he could see the graceful line of a ship cutting through the foam, houses warm and inviting, cities gleaming in the sunlight all cut from these forests.

He knew that his moment had come, his destiny had arrived. On this outer edge of civilization, he had discovered his place. He had no idea of how and when he would do it, but he knew he would.

"Joel?" Fred called his name, and he turned to find his new friend staring at him in a strange manner.

Joel shook himself and smiled, "Did you say something, Fred?"

"Only about three times. You sure were wool gathering. Must have been some little miss you were dreaming about."

"No, actually these forests overwhelmed me for a moment. I was day dreaming about what could be done with these trees."

Fred smiled and nodded his head, "You're catching the vision. But since we have to live in the present and plan for the future. We need a place to stay."

"Is there any place around here? I figured we might be camping out by a creek somewhere."

"Most of the fellows do, but I have a friend whose sister-in-law has a cabin outside of town. It's bigger than most, she lives there with her little boy. She is a widow and cares for her elderly, almost blind father-in-law."

"How did she get out here and how does she manage?"

"Her husband was killed in some altercation before their child was born and since she had no place else to go, she came with his brothers and father out here. They made a living trapping and lumbering until gold fever hit them, too. Now I understand she makes a living doing laundry and meals for the men that are left here. It's a hard way to earn a living, but she seems to have a good attitude and that little boy of hers is the cutest tike you'd ever want to meet."

"Seems a hard living for a woman up here without a husband." Joel mused.

"It is and she cares for that invalid father-in-law also. I send her all the business I can and if I know someone is trustworthy, then I send them out to her place for lodging and meals."

"Well lead on. I'm hungry as a bear."

"Yea, all that pitching and rolling could cause a fellow to part with what little he had eaten. First let's see if we can find us a decent horse anywhere. It's a good three miles out to her place." Fred explained.

Because of Fred's charm and knowledge of the settlement, before long the two men were mounted on fairly good horseflesh and heading east, which seemed a miracle in itself. The ride through the forest set Joel's imagination whirling once more and he plied Fred with questions.

"The best place to set up a saw mill is on a water source. Timber needs to be cut up above the mill and the logs floated down to the source. Once the timber is cut and milled, then it could be transported to the ship yard which should be located somewhere on Coos Bay.

Right now is the optimum time to find land on the bay. San Francisco bay property that was selling for a modest sum is now going for exorbitant prices, if you could find any available. But here, you have not only the bay, but the raw material as well. Perhaps the acreage behind the yard could be bought and harvested. A community for the workers would certainly be an enticement, especially for those who had endured the hardship of prospecting and return with empty pockets." Joel's new friend explained

"But first I must find the land." Joel murmured.

The trail turned sharply to the right and a log cabin perched on a hillside beside a stream tumbling down from the high knoll behind it. Smoke rose from the chimney and the smell of roasting meat caused Joel's stomach to rumble.

As they drew closer, they saw a little tyke with a mop of fiery red hair playing by the steps. He appeared to be about four or five. When he looked up Joel saw that he had a turned up nose sprinkled with freckles and wide, emerald green eyes. He ran toward them, talking as fast as his little tongue would allow and his eyes bright with delight. "Hey there, Uncle Fred. Who's your friend? I've never seen him before. We're having elk tonight. John Henry killed one and brought it to us. He's sweet on my ma, you know."

By this time Fred was off his horse and had swept the boy up in his burly arms. "Whoa, boy, you're talking so fast that I can't near bout make my brain take in all you're saying."

The little boy rolled his bright green eyes toward Joel, "What's he called?"

"This here is my friend, Joe."

Joel nodded and grinned. It was the first time anyone had ever called him Joe. And he knew that for the most part, last names weren't given unless necessary. Too many men were here with a past they wanted to forget. Truth of the matter, wasn't he?

"Do you think your ma would have enough of that meat for me and my friend?" Fred asked, a broad grin on his face.

"Sure 'nough. She always has enough for you, anyways it's a big elk. She's gonna cure some of it and smoke the rest, that's how much he gave her." The little boy exclaimed.

"Well is your ma sweet on John Henry?"

"Naw, he's too old. Besides she says he hardly ever bathes 'cause he smells like a pole cat most of the time."

"Picky, ain't she?" Fred laughed.

"She's gotta right to be. Pretty as she is, she's waiting for "her prince to come." That's the way she puts it anyway, whatever a prince is."

Both men laughed and Joel asked, "You know my name, but I don't know yours."

"I'm called Jay."

"Glad to make your acquaintance, Jay."

"That's not my real name."

"Really?"

"My real name is Jacob after my grand pap." He informed Joel proudly.

"Why my own pa was named Jacob. I've always liked that name."

"Yeah, it's a Bibli- uh Bibli-"

"Biblical name?" Joel assisted.

"Yeah, that's what I mean. My ma said Jacob was a special man in the Bible."

"I believe he had twelve sons."

"That's how many I'm gonna have when I grow up."

"That's a lot of children." Joel pointed out.

"Twelve sons could cut a lot of wood and then I would be rich. I wouldn't go hunting no gold, like my uncles. No sirree, me and my boys would just cut wood and hunt a little." Jay explained, his eyes round and serious.

"You've got that all figured out, have you?" Joel asked, trying to hide his amusement.

"I have. You know that Jacob in the Bible was not a nice man at first, but God changed his name and he became the kind of man God wanted. I hope God doesn't have to change my name. Ma said it's best to let Him have your heart from the beginning and then you won't have no regrets. Sometimes I think she might be talking about herself. But she ain't, I mean hasn't admitted that to me yet."

"Sounds like you have a very wise mother."

"And pretty, too. Do you have a wife, mister?" Jay asked.

"No, I haven't had that pleasure yet." Joel answered as visions of golden hair and sapphire eyes brought a sudden longing that for a moment blocked out the splendor surrounding him and the delightful conversation.

Jay looked at him for a long moment as if evaluating him. Then announced in a serious tone, "Could be that you're her prince. You don't smell bad at all and you look pretty clean."

The little boy garnered Joel's full attention with that suggestion and he could contain his laughter no longer. A big guffaw rolled from Fred. When he regained his composure he replied, "Jay, that's mighty flattering, but I think that's something your mom will have to decide."

"Yea, I s'pose so, but I keep bringing her candi-candi" He twisted his little mouth.

"You mean candidates?" Joel prompted.

"Yea, that's it."

"Have you had any success? Has she liked anyone yet?" Fred asked.

Jay shook his head, "Not yet, but Joe looks the best so far."

"You need to have more requirements than just

looks, Jay." Joel responded

"Oh I will. That's just the first step."

"Then what else are you looking for?"

"Someone who can work hard and take care of my ma and me. She works mighty hard."

Joel nodded, "And is that all?"

"Course not. He will have to love God. I think you might since you knew all about Jacob. Do you?"

By this time Fred had put Jay down and they were walking hand in hand toward the cabin door.

Joel leaned down and tousled his hair, "I do love God and I want to love Him more. Now are there any other requirements?"

"Yes, he must love my ma and make her smile."

"Is she sad?"

"She tells me she isn't. She says I'm all she needs that I make her smile. I try to, but you know someday I'm gonna marry and leave her and I don't want her to be lonely."

Joel felt his heart lurch as he encountered such tender love shining from the little boy's eyes as he spoke of his mother. Suddenly Joel had an overwhelming desire to meet this woman who had inspired such love.

CHAPTER 17

Jay broke loose from Fred and ran into the cabin, shouting, "Ma, ma, Guess who's here? It's Uncle Fred and he's got someone with him. You gotta see this one. He looks real good, smells ok, and he loves God."

A quiet voice inside the cabin admonished the little boy, "Hush, Jay, that's no way to welcome a stranger into our home. Now go wash your hands and then set two extra plates for supper while I get the biscuits out."

When Joel and Fred arrived at the open door, Jay's mother had her back to them as she stirred a pot in the big open fire place. Inviting aromas of stew and biscuits filled the air and a soft light from two lanterns staved off the fast approaching twilight.

Lustrous titan hair crowned the woman's head and a modest green calico dress molded a shapely slender body beneath it. She leaned over to reach into the fire, lifting the large simmering pot, and then turned to face the two men who had entered her cabin. Emerald eyes dancing with delight, and stunning beauty greeted the two as she exclaimed, "Fred, how glad I am to see you and you've brought a friend."

Fred smiled and turned toward Joel. "Yep, this is my friend, Joe and Joe, this is . . . . . . "

"Jessica." The titan haired beauty interrupted as she reached out a work worn hand to welcome the one whom she had betrayed five years before.

Speechless, Joel struggled to find his voice. Was this the same Jessica, this woman of the street who had sold him to a renegade captain? It was the same beautiful face and lovely form that had disturbed his dreams for years. But how could this possibly be the woman Fred had praised so highly, the mother of the little tyke who adored her, one who worked hard and cared for her invalid father-in-law,?

Sudden realization hit Joel, superseding the questions rioting in his mind. The father-in-law Fred spoke about was his pa. Pa was alive. What a glorious thought. Forget what the woman was or may still be. He would see his father again. What a miracle God had wrought.

Fred laughed. "Cat got your tongue, Joe? Bet you're surprised to find a beauty like this in the backwoods."

Joel's voice found footing, even while his mind tried to take in what had just happened. He replied softly, "Surprise couldn't begin to describe what I'm feeling."

Joel dropped his head slightly before she could notice the conflict going on inside him. When she turned toward Fred, Joel cocked his head and covertly appraised her. The five years that had brought manhood to him had brought a bloom of beauty to her that far exceeded that of her younger years. She wore plain calico with the grace of royal robes. Every line of her body, the contours of her face were exquisite; yet the secret of her surpassing beauty rested in her eyes and countenance. His mind returned to the provocative scene in the dusty streets of San Diego five years before. The memory of a golden dress and pouting lips, bold eyes and a whispered invitation raced across his mind. How could this be the same woman? Yet it was and while he had recognized her, she had failed to recognize the man he had become.

Fred continued, "Yes, sirree if I didn't have a missus of my own that I'm crazy about and was twenty years younger, I'd take this little girl back to San Diego with me."

"I like it here, Fred. I have no yearning for San Diego or San Francisco."

"Your life could be a lot easier somewhere else besides this wilderness."

"I don't mind the hard work," Jessica protested.

"What is it you like about this lonely country?" Fred pressed.

"Maybe I'm escaping from a sordid past." She laughed and tossed her head.

"Many of the people here are escaping, but I

would never believe that of you." Fred shook his head, affection and admiration shining in his eyes.

"Perhaps I feel like my life can make a small difference here."

"Like?" Fred probed as the conversation bandied about Joel, both of them unaware of the furor this beauty had erupted inside him.

"For one thing, I can care for Gramps."

"You could care for him nearer to civilization and have things a little more convenient." Fred argued.

Jessica looked at Joel and winked, "Here we go again. We have this discussion every time he comes. I can't get it through his head; I don't need to be rescued. I'm perfectly content here and with what I'm doing."

"You've got to be lonely." Fred insisted.

"I have Jay and Gramps." Jessica reminded with an indulgent smile.

"You need more than someone to look after; you need someone to care for you. Someone to love and to love you. I'm telling you, a good marriage is a little bit of heaven on earth."

"Perhaps that's not in the Good Lord's plan for me." Jessica's smile faded, the sparkle in her eyes dimmed.

"Now why in the world wouldn't that be in His plans for you?" Fred boomed, dismissing her reasoning.

"Could be I don't deserve it," She said her tone, wishful.

"Don't deserve it. That's hogwash. Next to my wife, you're the sweetest and most honorable gal I know."

"Then maybe you really don't know me." Jessica whispered as she turned from them to retrieve the biscuits. Joel watched fascinated as a tear trickled down her cheek.

Fred shook his head, unaware of the young woman's distress. "There's no figuring her out. I don't know of another woman that would have given an old codger like Jacob such tender loving care. And then there are those brothers, she has to wait on them hand and foot, practically a slave."

"Hush, Fred, Gramps might hear you. Besides you are exaggerating." Jessica murmured, her back to them.

"Do you scrub and iron their clothes?" Fred demanded.

"Well, yes."

"Do you cook their vittles?"

"Of course, what's wrong with that? Jay and I have to eat, too."

"What about the firewood, tending the stock and the vegetable garden?"

"That garden is one of my pleasures."

"Hmp! If that be true it must be the only one you have."

"You're being much too hard on Jay's uncles." She protested, still refusing to face Fred.

"If they'd take better care of you, I would have a better opinion of them."

"My life is no harder than thousands of other women on the frontier."

"That's my point. Let me take you back to civilization. My wife would be glad to introduce you around and with your seamstress skills, in no time at all you'd be making a good living and having some of the conveniences you deserve."

"I like it here and hard work never killed anyone. At least I can close my eyes at night and be proud of my day's work." Her voice grew husky, but the two men could not see the pain of a past remembered that dimmed the fire in her eyes.

Fred sighed, acknowledging defeat, "Joe, what do you do with a girl like her? "

"When you solve that mystery, Fred, please let me in on it." Joel shook his head as memories of titan hair and fiery eyes in another time and another place filled his mind.. The same eyes, the same hair, the same voice, the comely shape but a different spirit. Momentarily the years of suppressed pain engulfed him then his anger abated as an overwhelming curiosity pushed it aside. What had happened? It was a mystery he intended to solve, but meanwhile somewhere in the back of the cabin was his pa whom he had long since thought was dead.

Joy surged through him. Through one of those

doors awaited a reunion he thought was lost. But wait. He needed time to sort out his feelings, to understand what had transpired in this beautiful woman since he saw her last. She didn't recognize him. But then she had seen him only briefly and that was five years ago. His pa was a different matter. How could you not recognize your own son? What would it do to him for the son that he thought was dead to reappear? Fred said he was an invalid. Could his heart bear it? And then there was the matter of Jessica and his brothers, he was reluctant to reveal himself to them. He needed time to think, time to sort out his feelings.

Joel spoke, his lips in a tight line, as he tried to get control of his rioting emotions. "Miss Jessica, thank you for inviting us to supper. Can I be of any assistance?"

She turned back to them but not before she had wiped tell tale tears away with the homespun apron that accented her narrow waist. "Just wash up. Jay will show you where to put your things and then you can assist him in bringing Gramps to the table. His eyesight is nearly gone and he has a heart condition so he requires help finding his way to the table. But he always insists on joining us at meal time. Claims Jay and I need a man at the head of the table."

Joel's heart gave a leap. "Sure thing, Jay, just lead the way."

"Come on, Mr. Joe, this way. Gramps is waiting and he's a little impatient sometimes, especially when he hears we've got company."

They opened the door. Joel's galloping heart lurched as his eyes rested on a frail elderly man reclining on the bed covered with a colorful patchwork quilt.

"Is that you, Jay? Looks like you might have someone with you. Sorry I can't make out your face, but you look like a big man.

"You guessed right, Gramps. This here is Mr. Joe and he is big, I mean tall and strong. I bet he could take real good care of my ma."

Gramps chuckled, "Now Jay, me and you are doing ok, don't you think? I don't think your ma is interested in anyone right now."

"That 'cause she don't think her prince has come. This here Mr. Joe might be him."

"Really? That's mighty strong recommendation on such short acquaintance. I don't know what you said to the boy, Joe, but you've seemed to impress him."

"I can't imagine what he is talking about."

"Sure you do Mr. Joe. You look good, you don't smell bad and you love God."

"Well you make a mighty convincing argument, Jay. But don't you think your mama ought to have something to say about that?" Gramps chuckled. "Excuse my grandson, Joe. When he gets an idea in his head there is no getting him to release it. Ever since my three sons left for the gold fields he is convinced his ma needs a man around the house."

"But not just any man, Gramps. I'm real particular." Jay disputed

Joel spoke to Jay trying to divert him from his unsettling obsession, "Jay, you'll have to face it, you are not the one to make that decision. It would take your ma and the man to make that decision and it doesn't happen in an instant. Love has to have time to grow, or so I've been told."

"But don't she have to find the man first so as to let it grow. She ain't, I mean hasn't found anyone yet."

"You need to show a little patience, don't you think?" Joel admonished.

"I'll try to be patient soon as she finds somebody. But that's the problem. She's just too busy working and teaching me and--."

"Taking care of me." Gramps added

Jay shook his little head. "She don't mind that none, Gramps. But, Mr. Joe, the way I see it since Gramps can't see good and my uncles done up and left, it's up to me to find someone for ma. --"

"I think I understand, Jay. But don't be in too big a hurry, you might make a mistake. With matters of the heart, you just can't predict how that will play out." Joel tried to explain while his own mind filled with hair of spun gold, the voice of an angel and the pain of lost love remembered.

"I don't know about all that grown up stuff, I just know I'm looking for someone to look after my ma."

"I'm sure the right man will come along someday. Now what was this about your three sons, sir?" Joel asked, his heart racing.

Joel helped Gramps out of the bed and he slowly straightened up, sighing. "Yes, three sons. Two of my sons were killed by a band of renegades when they were on their way back from a cattle drive. My oldest son, Jay's father, and my youngest, son, Joel, were killed. Jessica and Aaron had been married in San Diego and they were on their way back home when they were attacked. Aaron was killed protecting his wife, but my son Benjamin had left the campsite for a bath and when he returned was able to rescue Jessica and the other two boys. It is just by the grace of God that I have any family left. Though I grieve everyday for the sons I lost, I thank Him for His mercy. And this Jay is the light of my life."

"I can well imagine that, Sir."

"Gramps tells me stories about his cowboy days, stories about my pa and other uncle. Did you know he was part Indian? My gramps had two wives and one of them was an Indian. Don't that beat all? He said she was pretty with long shiny black hair and big brown eyes. I wished I coulda knowed her." Jay interjected.

Pain once more gripped Joel's heart and he answered, his voice husky, "I bet she was very special."

"Gramps said it was her who taught him about God and now he teaches me and Ma. 'Course my ma don't need much teaching since she learned to read. She reads the Bible all the time and makes me memorize scripture verses. She says if I hide them in my heart, then I'll always know the right thing to do and won't get into trouble. She told me that is why lots of folks just don't know how to act because they never been taught the right way."

Joel shook his head as if to clear it. The thought of Jessica reading the Bible and teaching her child scripture was too much to take in. "How did your mother learn to read?"

"Gramps taught her before he lost his eyesight. He can't see to read now. It's like the middle is out of what he looks at. He can just see the outline of something so now Ma reads to him."

By this time they had assisted Jacob to the kitchen and he sat at his place at the head of the table. Jessica placed a large tureen of savory stew before them while biscuits as light as a cloud piled high in the middle of the table.

Despite the lump that had lodged in Joel's throat, his stomach rumbled at the inviting aroma and after the blessing, piled his plate high with biscuits and stew. He remained quiet during the meal and let Fred carry on the conversation which was an easy task for his gregarious friend.

That he was a trusted and valued friend of both Jacob and Jessica was obvious. He inquired about the whereabouts of Jacob's "boys" and found out that they had struck off for the California gold fields two years before and they only heard from them spasmodically. It seems that they had filed a claim in the previous year, but whether it would prove to be productive remained to be seen. Meanwhile Joel learned that Gramps and Jessica had been threatened with eviction because the men had used the cabin for collateral in order to finance their equipment and supplies.

"Can they do that?" Fred asked.

"Sure they can." Jacob replied, something between sadness and anger in his voice.

"Who is it that holds the note?" Fred probed

"Jack Kinsey."

"I've heard of the likes of him. Not a very reputable man. But what does he want with this cabin? I know it is a nice one, but he lives in a mansion in San Francisco."

"Oh, he could use the cabin, but it's the land he wants. When the boys were working and trapping they received three square miles of timber from the Oregon Donation Act. Trapping proved so profitable that they were able to build this cabin which sits right in the middle of all that acreage."

"That much land? Seems like a lot of timber." Joel mused.

"I told my boys. There is more gold towering above us than you can dig out of the ground. You see our land goes all the way to the Bay and a deep harbor."

"Which would enable transporting the logs to a mill."

"Yup. You got it, Mister. We're lucky to have several broad deep streams that feed from above where the timber is and empties into the harbor."

"I imagine that's why your boys chose this place."

"No, it was my doin'. I got them each to file a claim for a square mile that the government was offering, so they did that at my bidding. Seems they have a hard time seeing the opportunity available to them, it's always just over the next ridge." Jacob shook his head and sighed.

Jessica spoke up, "Gramps, I'm sure they have learned their lesson by now. When they come home, perhaps they will listen to you."

"Won't do much good if it belongs to Kinsey. And he's going to do all he can to get his hands on it. He wants the timber and the waterfront to expand his shipyard in San Francisco." Jacob explained.

"Gramps, you don't need to worry about any of that. Like you said the Good Lord will provide for us. If He intends for us to stay here, then He will make a way. He has seen us through Indian attacks, wild animals and Benjamin's injury. He'll see us through this." Jessica reminded.

Joel starred at her in disbelief. How could this be Jessica?

"You are right, Daughter. I just hate to see you work so hard and come up short. He is a demanding creditor."

Jessica blushed. "And I can handle him."

"What kind of demands is he making of you, Jess?" Fred asked, anger flushing his face.

"None that I haven't been able to circumvent yet."

"He's a mean and nasty man." Jay squealed.

"Now, hush, Jay." Jessica commanded.

"Well he is, ma. He comes around here smelling like a girl and follows ma around the kitchen telling her how pretty she is. Tries to pay me to go outside and play."

"Jay's right he is a mean and nasty man. He is up to no good. He has a wife and family back in San Francisco." Fred bristled.

"I can handle him, Fred."

"You know nothing about a low life like him, Jessica." Fred warned.

Pain creased Jessica's forehead and Joel noticed her eyes brighten with unshed tears, "You might be surprised, Fred, what I know about."

Jay's little voice piped up, diverting the awkward moment, "Gramps said I was never to leave when that varmint was here. That's why I'm looking for her a husband."

Joel chuckled, delight in his nephew overriding his conflicting emotions. "So that's the motive behind your plan. Seems you'd best be adding a good shot to your list of have to's."

Jessica shifted uneasily in her chair, "Jay, I want you to quit this nonsense. I have you and gramps to protect me."

"But you're working so hard and we can't make the payment this month. I heard him say that the month you don't pay up one way or the other this place is his."

"Then God will provide what we need, if my work falls short. So far it hasn't." Jessica reminded.

"Maybe I can send some more boarders your way, Jess. I've just been very careful in the past about whom I sent." Fred mused

"And I'm very appreciative of that fact, Fred." Jessica responded with a smile.

"No need to, Fred. If Miss Jessica and Gramps will allow me to make this my home base, I would like to lease this room and good meals for several months. What do you say, Miss Jess?"

"I'd say that would be heaven sent." She sighed, turning a heart stopping smile on Joel.

CHAPTER 18

Joel watched Fred's return to San Francisco and then on to San Diego with reluctance. The affable sea captain had become more than a casual acquaintance; he had become a treasured friend. His knowledge of the sparsely settled North Country and the vast forests it held amazed Joel. He had garnered information from the older man that saved him hours of fruitless searching.

Joel sent a packet by Fred to Mr. Wilkins with a full explanation of all that he had learned, his recommendations for the proposed expansion, and details of his plans for the next three months. It pleased him that at last he had positive information to send to his mentor and much of that success was due to the information that Fred had provided. The resources were there, the only element missing was manpower. Joel urged his employer to enlist men in the East to come and bring their families. Opportunity waited, the land needed workers, but the workers needed their families in order to settle the land and establish an ongoing community. What better person to equip ships and offer an affordable transport to bring families than Wilkins? He had the means and Joel had the dream.

His happiest news, however, was not the business potential, but that he had found his father alive as well as the knowledge that three of his brothers were also alive. For some reason, he omitted any mention of finding the woman who had betrayed him. He paused pondering why he would leave out this piece of information and realized that Jessica was a mystery he had yet to solve. She hardly seemed the same woman of his past so how could he explain her to anyone else when she still baffled him?

He knew that his employer would receive the news with mixed emotions, happy for Joel but disappointed that he would not be returning. Joel knew that his mentor harbored the hope that when his protégé's heartache healed, he would return to Boston to fulfill the plans they had made.

He had told him as much when he sent him on his way. "Give your heart a chance to heal. Explore our business potential out west and then come home, my boy. Your office will be waiting."

Visions of Melody on the arm of another man drove lumber, ships and anything else from his mind. Suddenly the raw pain that he had held at bay assaulted him. Would it ever get better? He shook his head. No, a return to Boston proved out of the question. He had fought his love for Melody for years and it still was no better. To drown in those glorious eyes, for his ears to hear her melodious voice on a regular basis, to long to touch her golden hair and never to claim her as his own would prove impossible.

He sighed and added a personal note for Wilkins eyes only, explaining the real reason why he wouldn't be returning. With a sad heart he sealed the letter, knowing the pain it would cause the man he had grown to love. But one thing he knew, Wilkins only wanted what was best for Joel even if it meant disappointment for himself. Joel had told him from the outset if his family had lived, he would have returned to the West and miracle of miracles, they were alive. So why did he feel torn between two worlds?

His prayer had been answered. All he thought that he wanted from life was to find his family. Not only had he found his family, but a world of opportunity here. He could carve out a thriving business on the west coast, to compliment Wilkins Boston enterprises. Trade with China and Australia would open up new routes for the company and with unlimited raw material for the building of ships, the sky was the limit. Yet there was a tug in his heart to return.

The only explanation rested in the woman with a cloud of golden hair who had unwittingly captured his heart, soul and mind by simply being herself. He groaned as the memories of her reopened the wounds still raw and unhealed. The unwanted if "onlys" intruded. If only he had known that he would have been considered an acceptable suitor, he would have pursued her. And if he had courted her, would she have chosen him? Or would she still have looked on him as a brother? Tormenting questions flooded his mind until the ache became almost unbearable.

He shook his head as if to clear it of the uninvited apparition and the futile self questioning. If God meant Melody was not the one for him, then He had a better plan, but Oh, dear Lord, how could that be? Someone better for him than Melody? It took a mammoth amount of faith to believe that.

Meanwhile, he needed to focus on the urgency of the present. The opportunities here and now, the ones God had presented to him. Determination set his countenance as he willed his mind to put the past in its proper place. He had learned a powerful if not painful lesson. One thing for sure, it had taught him that God's evaluation was not the same as society's. All men were equal in His sight, what mattered was character, not the genealogy of one's birth. Had he considered that, perhaps it would be his arms that now enfolded Melody and not another's. But then had things not come to pass as they had, would he have found his family? The voice of his mother whispered in his memory, "Son, the steps of a good man are directed by the Lord." He sighed acknowledging that God's ways were truly beyond his understanding.

Joel filled the weeks that followed his friend's departure with hard riding and long hours. He was up at daybreak and back after dark, his handsome face lined with exhaustion. Jessica observed him with quiet concern. She recognized the signs of one running from a painful past. Hadn't she run from her wicked past at the first opportunity? But hers was different, how could anything wicked pursue so fine a gentlemen? No, it was sorrow, not fear that she saw in his eyes. It must be a woman, perhaps rejected by the woman he loved. But then how could any woman in her right mind spurn him? Jessica marveled at the very idea.

In only a few weeks she sensed an affection growing for him. How could she not? The respect and consideration with which he treated her was something she had rarely encountered. No matter how tired he might be, he made sure that wood was cut, and the box filled inside. But the nearest thing to her heart was the gentle kindness he showed to Jacob and Jay.

In between his many exploration trips, he spent hours talking with Jacob. He never seemed to tire of listening to Jacob's tales from his past. He spent time with Jay instructing him in chores, reading to him and taking him hunting. He took him on one of his overnight trips and they camped out in the woods, much to Jay's delight.

Jessica watched with trepidation as Jay's attachment to Joel grew with each passing week. She knew that one day soon, Joe would be leaving them and she feared Jay's heart would be broken. In truth, his departure would leave a vacant spot in all three hearts.

She warned him of the dangers lurking in the forests and encouraged him to make his forages during daylight hours and to go properly armed. Agreeing with the wisdom of her advice, he sought an additional weapon to his sidearm. When he located a Kentucky rifle from a local, he bought it. Reminiscent of the weapon he had carried on that last fateful ride in search of his brothers, he caressed the cold steel and felt almost as if the past had come full circle. But he knew better. He yet had to solve the mystery of his brothers' and Jessica's betrayal.

Jessica watched him covertly from the rocker where she was mending Jacob's trousers. She noted the pain in his eyes as he stared out into the darkness outside her window. It was obvious that a painful scene from his past played out in his mind. Once more she longed for him to trust her with his story. But the time was not right. They had known each other for too short a time to share confidences. What a ridiculous thought, she chuckled to herself at the very idea. People came out here to forget, not to share. Would she want to reveal her past? No matter how well she knew him? But just the same where he was concerned, she couldn't help but wonder and wish.

For an instant her heart fluttered at something

in the way he grasped the rifle stirred her memory. There was something strangely familiar in the movement. It was almost as if she had seen those hands before, holding that same weapon. She shook her head. No man like this had ever been a part of her past. He was not one any woman could forget. Besides, he was not the kind that would frequent her past environs.

Jessica sighed as Joel finished oiling and cleaning his rifle. Perhaps it was a good thing his business kept him away so much, her heart had become too interested in solving his mystery. And that could lead to forbidden territory.

Joel's exploration of timber tracts revealed Captain Fred's wisdom when he had advised him to consider only the land which touched the bay with large fast moving streams capable of transporting logs. The more he explored the more he realized that his brothers' property proved the ideal location.

He found that other land owners adjoining their property were more than eager to sell in order to finance their own trips to the gold rush territory. Frustrated by the lack of physical labor, many were eager to abandon their dream of timber land and exchange it for the dream of riches in California. Before long, Joel had purchased thousands of acres along side and behind his brother's holdings. With the funds for purchasing the lands in a

San Francisco bank, the ready cash available made Joel's offer too enticing to turn down.

News of Joel's acquisitions reached San Francisco and the ears of Jack Kinsey. Kinsey had delayed in pursuing the adjacent land acquisitions because he had experienced a cash shortfall due to the palatial home he had just built and his excessive lifestyle. He had anticipated no problems acquiring their property once his cash situation improved.

Alarmed at the news, he arrived at the Isaacs' cabin middle of the afternoon, during one of Joel's trips. He had come prepared to call the loan and to force Jessica and Jacob out. What did he care that winter was already nipping at the heels of fall? It bothered him little that the vixen and the old man and boy could hardly survive a winter without a place to stay.

He chuckled as he thought, "They have no money for catching a packet out of there. Serve the high and mighty wench right. Who did she think she was anyway? On one of his trips to San Diego, he'd heard some tales of a titan haired beauty named Jessica. Now he had the goods on her and he'd have his pleasure. No need to have staved him off all these months as if she were some innocent."

Kinsey frowned, anger darkening his face as he considered her rejections. "She could have made it easier for them but she wouldn't. She would have to change her mind after all. He wouldn't let her keep the house and land, but to stay alive? To keep the old man and boy alive? She loved them and a mother would do any thing to protect her kid. Wouldn't she?"

A sly smile of satisfaction parted his face and he licked his lips at the prospect.

Loud sounds of shouting greeted Joel as he dismounted and led his horse to the lean-to. Puzzled, he heard a raucous laugh followed by a scream, then his father's shout and a loud thud. Dropping his horse's reins, he ran to the house, forgetting his rifle. Taking the steps two at a time, he charged into the cabin just in time to see Jessica tangled in the arms of a behemoth of a man and his father's motionless body lying in the corner behind the stove, a piece of stove wood clasped in his hands. He scanned the room in search of Jay, but the little boy was missing. Turning his eyes back to Jessica, he saw her ripped bodice as she squirmed to get free of the man who held both her hands behind her back. Her hair was a disheveled fiery cloud, her eyes icy daggers and blood trailed down her chin from a cut on her lip. The giant held her tight to him, placing both his boots on her small feet, to keep her from kicking him.

Jessica screamed, "Joe, help, Gramps----see about Gramps, he's hurt or----he hit Gramps."

The stranger turned his head toward Joel and gave him a cursory glance, then laughed, "Just wait your turn, boy. I've been waiting a long time to tame this one. And now that I've learned all about her life in San Diego------."

"Let her go." Joel commanded, his voice steady, his eyes cold steel.

The stranger snarled, "It would take several more like you to get her loose. You ain't even got a gun and I make three of you. See that old man over there? He thought he could help her. All I did was help him on his way to hell."

"Aren't you a brave man attacking old men and women. Turn her loose and see how brave you are with a real man."

The intruder laughed, "There ain't but one real man around here. Now you go on outside, you've been having your fun, now it's my turn."

Kinsey turned away from Joel, his face toward Jessica. Suddenly he crumpled as Joel crossed the room in three strides and landed two powerful chops to the back of his neck.

Jessica screamed, and then fell into Joel's arms, weeping. "He wouldn't take my money, said we had to leave. Oh! Gramps. Is he dead?"

"No, I ain't dead, but I shore have a powerful headache. How in the world did you do that, son?" Jacob said as he sat up and leaned against the wall rubbing his head.

Joel laughed, relief written in every line of his

face, "You might say, Gramps, it was a divinely aimed blow. I don't know how I did it, but whatever I hit sent him down."

Jessica stood over him, clutching her bodice, watching him in a dazed manner, she shuddered "Is he, is he---dead?"

Joel stooped and put his fingers on his neck, "No, his pulse is strong. He is just out for the moment. We had better secure him before he comes to. I don't know if I could repeat that performance and I would be hard pressed to win a fight with him. I came in so fast that my rifle and sidearm are still looped on my saddle."

"I, I have some twine. Would that hold him?" Jessica murmured as if in a trance.

"We could try it, but the main thing we need is to disarm him. Here, Gramps, you hold his pistol and knife. Keep it pointed straight at him until I get him tied up. Jessica, where is Jay?"

"Kinsey locked him in your room. I told him that if Kinsey ever caused a problem to run for help. Maybe he climbed out the window."

Relief flooded Joel when he realized that Jay was safe. The little tyke had captured his heart. Had he stayed, he might have been seriously hurt. Now what was to be done with Kinsey?

Voices wafted in from outside and Joel looked at Jessica. "Jay must have found help."

Joel nodded, then looked at Jessica, and replied

gently, "Jess, perhaps you'd better go to your room and attend to your dress."

Jessica looked down at the ripped fabric she grasped in her hands, then nodded and turned toward her bedroom just as five big brawny neighbors with shovels, pitchforks and weapons broke through the door.

Joel would carry to his grave the memory of Jessica's neighbors and the righteous anger etched on their faces. When they found Kinsey trussed up like a pig for market, anger turned to hilarity as each one of them shared a story of the culprit's misdeeds that stretched from California to Oregon. They told one tale after another of one man's riches at others' expense gained by defraud and deceit. They reveled in Kinsey's comeuppance and heralded Joel as a hero.

"I'm no hero. The good Lord is the one who aimed my blow. Now the big question is what are we going to do with him?"

"There is a packet coming in and we will take him all trussed up and put him on that boat and ship him home."

"First we need to take care of our business with him." Jessica's trembling voice said from the shadows.

"What business?" John Henry, Jessica's relentless and smelly suitor asked.

"The business of paying me what's owed me. And you good for nothing scoundrels better untie me and let me go before I have the law on you and this crazy man here for trying to kill me." Kinsey growled as he opened his eyes and pulled at the twine that held his hands behind him.

"We are the law around these parts and we know all about you and ain't nobody gonna hurt Miss Jess and little Jay. Yore going straight back to where you came from, mister, and don't you ever show your hide here again, unless you know what's good fer you." Henry informed, taking the role of spokesperson.

"I will get an eviction notice and bring the law back with me and you all will go to jail, especially this fancy easterner here who took it upon himself to try to kill me when I was trying to rightfully collect what was mine." Kinsey warned.

Henry and his entourage laughed boisterously, "Your law ain't no account in this place. It's what we say that goes."

"I've got a legal document that says this place is mine and I will take it."

"Only if I can't make the payments." Jessica protested, her voice stronger.

"Read the fine print, wench."

Henry kicked Kinsey's leg, "Watch your mouth and give Miss Jess respect!"

"Respect to the most famous harlot on the San Diego waterfront?" Kinsey sneered. "I think not."

Jessica's face turned ashen. Joel spoke quickly,

"What document are you talking about, Kinsey?"

"The one that says if I don't get my money, this place is mine."

"I tried to pay him. He refused it." Jessica whispered, her face still white.

"You tried to pay your payment. Read the fine print, you strumpet."

John Henry issued another swift kick to Kinsey's thigh and the giant howled with pain, "I'll get you for this, you lily livered stinking excuse for a man."

Henry kicked him again, a grin on his face, "It'll be my pleasure, mister. Now you show the proper respect to my friends."

"What does the fine print say, Kinsey?"

"That I can call the whole loan amount any time I please and I please to do it now." He smirked.

"And you would throw this family out in the cold with no place to go?" Henry marveled. "I heard you was a low down pole cat, but I didn't know even you would sink that low."

"I would have worked something out but she wouldn't cooperate."

"I saw how you tried to work something out. Look at Miss Jess's purty face, all bruised and cut up. That's why you are all trussed up and yore mighty lucky 'twarn't worse than that. If'n it had been me instead of Joe, you might never have seen the light of day agin."

"I won't be trussed up forever and when I get

loose he'll pay for this. You'll wish you had never left that fancy East. Too bad you'll never see your fine family and friends back home again." Kinsey sneered.

"That's mighty brave talk coming from someone who can't even stand up." Joel mused.

"When I get on the boat, we'll see who can't stand up. All those captains are my friends because they need my business. They'll see to it that justice is served and then it will be you all trussed up and this ungrateful strumpet will be out in the cold without the funds for her and that sniveling brat of hers to get back to civilization."

"So how much does she owe you?"

Jessica shuddered, "Too much to pay if what he says is true. I had this month's payment, but it is a small portion of what we owe."

"You mean what my sons owe." Jacob said. "They acted foolish and Jessica is the one who has tried to earn the money working her fingers to the bone."

"What do I care who owes it. It's a proper debt and one that is due. Pay up or get out." Kinsey gloated.

"And how much is that?" Joel demanded, his dark eyes cold.

"Too much even for you, pretty boy." Kinsey chided. "You'll not get to steal this land for a pittance like you have all the land around here. And without this land yours will be worthless."

"That ain't the story I heard." Henry drawled.

"Seems to me all them folks got a fair shake."

"Right here is where it stops. The payment is due, it ain't available, and the land is mine."

"I don't believe you told me what is due." Joel insisted.

"And I done told you, pretty boy, it's way too much for your fancy pockets."

"Perhaps. But humor me."

"How 'bout $10,000.00?".

The crowd of onlookers gasped. Kinsey looked around the room, gratified. Nobody had that much money

"You never gave my sons anywhere near that much money!" Jacob shouted.

"No, but you are forgettin' the interest and carrying charges." Kinsey grinned, enjoying himself despite his predicament.

"Why in the world did my sons do that?"

"Just face it, old man. Your good fer nuthin' sons just wanted to get away from you."

Anger burned Joel's eyes, blurring his vision. He leaned in to Kinsey and grabbed him by the collar, choking him until his eyes bulged, then dropped his hand brushing them off as if brushing filth off them, "Consider the debt paid."

"That won't do, Mister. They owe a debt they can't pay and I demand payment. The land is mine, just as soon as I get back to San Francisco."

"I will return with you and you will receive your money in a bank draft." Then looking at Jessica, "When is the money due, Jessica?"

Her green eyes widened, her face still pasty from humiliation, she mumbled, "Two weeks from now. He came early."

Kinsey's face paled, then he threatened, "Just wait until you board ship where there are no hooligans to protect you. I'll have your hide and then we'll see who is left to pay the debt."

Joel's lips parted in a smile that did not reach his eyes, "Don't count on it."

Jessica reached her hand toward Joel, fear in her eyes, "Joe, he'll kill you. If the captain is a friend of his, you'll have no help. You'll never make it to San Francisco."

Joel smiled at her, his smile tender, forgiving, "The captain of the packet that arrives tomorrow is Captain Fred."

Relief washed Jessica's face of humiliation and fear, "Dear Captain Fred."

"Yes, Fred, an honorable man of the law who will demand justice. We will have a satisfactory resolution to this problem by the end of next week. And I think the authorities will be interested in how Mr. Kinsey does business, if they don't already know. Until then he will remain tied up on the floor that he claimed was his until the packet leaves."

Captain Fred, delighted to have Joel on board, secured his prisoner in a cabin with bars designed for unruly passengers. He accompanied Joel and Kinsey to Carl Smithwick's office, an attorney whom Fred had recommended. He held his weapon at the ready in the event he needed it.

The attorney was familiar with Kinsey and the tales that surrounded him. When Joel finished recounting the whole story, the lawyer demanded that Kinsey produce the promissory note. He dispatched a young courier to Kinsey's home to retrieve it. The attorney's eyes widened when he read the document, commenting, "Kinsey, this is the most exploiting loan that I have ever encountered. How did you ever get these men to agree to these terms? It would be nigh to impossible to satisfy these obligations."

"That's none of your business. Now just get my money out of this dandy, if he really has it and let me be on my way."

"Not before the marshal has a look at this and Joel tells him of the threats that you have made against him and the Isaacs family. He has every right to press charges against you."

"I have no wish to do that." Joel replied.

"Wouldn't be legal, anyway, because he don't have any jurisdiction in Oregon." Kinsey sneered.

"Nevertheless, the marshal will have it on record in the event something happened to Joel or his friends. Obviously you've taken advantage of the lack of a legal system in more ways than one, Mr. Kinsey. Joel, do you indeed have the money to satisfy this unreasonable debt?"

"Certainly, I have already prepared a bank draft for the amount he said the Isaacs' owed. My employer secured an unlimited line of credit at the bank in order to transact his business while I am here. This included the purchasing of large tracts of land. I have already been to the bank and made these arrangements."

"You know this is ten times the market value of that property?" Smithwick asked.

"Perhaps, but the location is the key to accessing the harbor as Kinsey well knew."

"Yea and he has acquired the land surrounding it. Maybe you need to look at what he's gonna do with it. I'd say the Isaacs will never see ownership of this property again. He's doing the same thing as me—excepting he's sweet talking his way into it to get his hands on it." Kinsey accused.

"At a very high price." Smithwick reminded.

"It is a fact, Joe. The Isaacs will never be able to pay you back." Fred mused.

"We will cross that bridge when we get to it. Perhaps the brothers will have great success in their prospecting." Joel suggested.

"That's a joke. Last I heard they were nearly destitute and ready to come home. They lost all their gear trying to scrape together enough money to make it home." Kinsey sneered.

"So you moved in, Kinsey, before they could get home." Fred accused.

"Wouldn't matter whether they were home or not."

"Oh, yes. You came when you thought Jess was unprotected. You didn't count on Joe, here, and her friends that little Jay rounded up," Fred chuckled.

"I guess I underestimated the little tramp and how many favors she had given out," Kinsey sneered.

Fred barreled out of his chair and whacked Kinsey across his mouth. "Watch your dirty mouth when you speak of that little lady."

"Settle down, Fred." Smithwick admonished as Joel caught his friend's shoulder to restrain him. "Just sign here, Kinsey, and we will conclude your business."

Kinsey signed the promissory note and pocketed the bank draft made out to him for the sum of $10,000. When he rose to go, Joel stepped in front of him, "Kinsey, your business is complete in Oregon, and don't you ever bother the Isaac's family or their property again. If you do, I can't vouch for your safe return again. Do you understand me?"

"What do I want with that God forsaken land anyway when I have San Francisco at my feet?" He blustered as he pushed Joel aside and hurried out the door.

Fred walked Joel back to the dock to catch his packet north. When they parted, Joel spoke, his voice husky, "Fred, I can never thank you enough for all the assistance you have given me."

"Think nothing of it, my boy. But, Joe, I have to ask it. There was no truth in what Kinsey accused you of was there?"

"What are you talking about?" Joel puzzled.

"That land is yours now, and he said that was your intent all along, that it just cost you more than you planned."

Joel turned his head looking out over the busy harbor, struggling with the conflicting emotions that rioted in him. When finally he could speak, he answered, "Fred, believe me, all that I desire is the best for the Isaac family."

"I knew in my heart that must be true, but I had to ask. Those boys deserve to forfeit that property for leaving a good woman and their invalid father at the mercy of that shyster, but Jessica and Jacob deserve better. I worry about what will happen to them now."

"Believe me when I tell you they have a home for as long as they want it. Perhaps the brothers have learned a lesson."

"I only hope as much. But what will become of them now?"

"Here is another bank draft that will cover their passage home. Would you look for them?"

"I will start today. I'm sure they are on the waterfront somewhere. I'll put out the word that I am looking for them."

"Thank you, my friend. How different my life would have turned out if it had not been for you." Joel smiled and turned to board the ship, leaving Fred to puzzle over the meaning of his farewell.

CHAPTER 19

Jessica had a roaring fire beneath the black pot filled with water and clothes that she had collected from the men in the settlement. John Henry had taken Jay and Jacob on an outing, giving her some time to focus on the pile of laundry. She welcomed the extra money that it brought in and felt grateful to John Henry for his occasional help with Gramps and Jay. Jessica wished she could feel differently about her neighbor, but the thought of marriage to him repulsed her.

Suddenly reality set in. If not marriage to John Henry, what then? As she pushed and pulled the battling stick stirring the clothes, her mind ran to and fro. Anxiety creased her forehead. How would they survive and where would they live? The euphoria of Kinsey's defeat suddenly evaporated when the realization that they no longer owned the cabin crashed in. Joe owned it. He had paid the debt that they could not pay nor could they ever pay it. Their future rested in his hands. He seemed a fine gentleman, but he was a total stranger. She shook her head. She didn't even know his last name. What a strange thing for him not to tell her his last name. It was not unusual for a person to take a different name, but to mention no last name? Many were running from a past they would like to forget. She had always taken a person at face value, never delving into their past, considering her past and theirs were private. That is until today. None of her acquaintances had her tomorrows in their hands, Joe did. His real identity and his secret past might vitally impact hers and Jay's life.

When was he returning? The sooner the better. Winter approached and if she had to leave, better now than later. She still had the money she had saved for that last payment. Joe had refused it when he left for San Francisco. Maybe that would get her and Jay passage to California, but what about Gramps? She couldn't leave him and who knows if those sons of his were even alive. On and on her mind went exploring every possibility until exhaustion overcame her and she sat down beside her grueling task and buried her head in her hands, tears threatening.

Joel found her thus. So intent in her anguish, she never heard him ride up. "Jessica?" Joel asked as he touched her head.

"Joe!" she exclaimed as she wiped away the telltale tears and attempted a one-sided grin. "You caught me napping on the job."

"Napping? More like crying, I'm thinking," he observed as he held out his hands and pulled her to her feet.

"Crying? Who, me?" She shrugged. He stood his ground, remaining much too near.

His finger traced the tear that had traveled down her cheek and he put his arm about her pressing her head to his shoulder, encouraged gently, "Now tell me. What's the source of these tears?"

Her body turned toward him and her arms went about him as a deluge of tears wet his shirt and her whole body shook with a lifetime of suppressed hurt and fear. He stood with her in his arms for a long time just letting her cry. He patted the fiery locks, now loosened and cascading down her back.

When finally the explosion quieted, he replied in a soft voice, "Come in the house, we need to talk."

She nodded and pulled away. Locating a handkerchief in her pocket, she wiped her eyes and nose, moved toward the house.

Inside the cabin, a welcoming aroma of cinnamon and apples wafted from the pie Jessica had baked before she began the day's wash. He marveled that she could accomplish so much in a day's time. She never complained and was always busy. Sometimes she reminded him of the woman in Proverbs. The thought startled him.

This was Jessica, a betrayer, whose virtue was lost in her teen years, a woman of the streets who sold her favors to the highest bidder. How could she then be the epitome of a Proverbs 31 woman? He didn't know, but one thing he felt sure about, now was the moment of discovery. He would find out the mystery.

She fixed them a piece of pie and a cup of coffee. She busied herself until she gained some self-control.

Joel stirred the fresh cream into the dark brown liquid turning it a warm caramel. "Jessica, tell me about those tears."

"Just a moment of weakness, I reckon. Nothing to concern yourself about." The tremor in her voice gave away her attempted bravado.

"Tell me. Maybe I can help." His voice held a kindness in it that threatened Jessica's composure.

She sighed, her shoulders drooped. The burden proved too heavy for her to bear and she blurted, "I don't know what we're to do."

"What who is to do and what."

"You know--where we will live, what will become of us."

"Are you worrying, Jessica? You? That doesn't sound like you."

"If it were just me, I wouldn't, but I have to consider Gramps and Jay."

"Surely Gramps isn't your responsibility."

"What do you mean, not my responsibility? Who is to look after him if I don't?" Her tone indignant as if she couldn't believe Joel could entertain such an idea.

"His sons. They are the ones responsible, not you." Joel leaned back and crossed his legs in front of him, his tone matter of fact.

"I don't know their whereabouts, or if they are ever coming back."

"So? He's not your father." Joel commented, adding honey to his coffee, averting his eyes lest she see the raging emotions that his calm voice failed to betray.

"I love him and I want to take care of him. That's the only reason I'm afraid. If it were just me then I could manage." Her voice rose.

"What would you do, go back to San Diego?" Joel probed.

Jessica's face turned ashen. "You believed what Kinsey said."

"It's not that I believed what Kinsey said, I know for a fact who you were and what you did."

"What did you do, spend your time investigating what Kinsey said?" Anger fired her eyes.

"No, I've known for a long time."

"Yet you never mentioned it."

"No, I was trying to reconcile the other Jessica with this Jessica." He explained quietly.

"Joe, or whatever your name is, that is precisely my predicament."

"There are two Jessicas. You have a twin?"

"No, there is an old and a new Jessica."

"How so?"

"The old Jessica did shameful deeds, the new Jessica would rather die than go back to that other life."

"What brought about the change?"

"It's a long story."

"We have all evening."

"What about my wash?"

"I'll help you with it when we finish."

Jessica shot him a puzzled look. "You'd do that? You with all your wealth?"

"It isn't my money, it is my employer's."

"You spend it mighty freely." She accused.

"He told me to use it at my own discretion. I give an account to him for all the money I spend."

"So it is he who will dictate what's to become of us."

"No. I will. I will explain later. But we are getting away from the subject. I want to know about the two Jessicas."

"Kinsey was right. I earned a living with my body. I hated every minute of it and vowed when I could break free I would."

"Obviously you did. How did that happen?"

Raw pain darkened her features, "I've never told anyone what happened. Only Jacob's sons know."

"Not Jacob?"

"No, never. It would break his heart."

"So? I'm waiting. How did it happen?" Joel's dark eyes hard as flint.

Jessica twisted the handkerchief in her hands, anguish written in every line of her body. Tears began to stream down her face. "I betrayed an innocent man to win my freedom. That knowledge has tormented me for six years."

"Who was this man?" Joel probed, his heart pumping.

"My husband's brother." She whispered, a shudder enveloping her body.

"Tell me about it."

"Aaron promised to marry me and take me away with him if I would arrange for his brother to be shanghaied."

A muscle twitched in the side of Joel's face as he fought to control his emotions. "Why would a brother treat another brother like that?"

"Aaron was impulsive and I have to believe that had he lived he would have regretted his actions. I know that his brothers have. That's one reason why they left to prospect; I have called them irresponsible at times. I know that really isn't the problem. Especially with Ben. Guilt has driven them until it had become more difficult each day to face their father. The brothers are very different. Jim is quiet says little, but the regret saddens his eyes, Ben is open with me about his anguish, now Simm, well he is all bluster, but I believe deep inside, he carries a double guilt."

"Obviously you haven't experienced the same suffering." Joel's voice held an edge.

"You don't know what you're talking about."

Jessica snapped, "I see that young man's face every day that I look into Jacob's eyes and witness his unrelenting sorrow. Tormenting that's what it is."

"So your care for Jacob is penance?"

"No, it's love. There is nothing good enough I could ever do to undo or make up for the wrong I have done. I tried that until I nearly lost my mind. Nothing eased the guilty torment that I was going through. I would have taken my life, but I had Jay and I knew I had to survive to take care of him."

"What happened?"

"Jacob taught me to read."

"You learned to read?" Joel gave a mirthless chuckle.

"The Bible, the Holy Scriptures."

"And?"

"I found the Savior. The One who died for my sins. The One who could forgive me and cleanse me. I cried out to Him in my anguish and He forgave me. The scriptures tell me that I am a new creature in Him that old things have passed away. I am the new Jessica because I have been cleansed and forgiven by the only one who could. The consequences of my sin will follow me to my grave. I have to bear the burden of not telling Jacob what really happened to his son and that he might still be alive somewhere, although I doubt it. I heard that the ship Joel was on went down because it was overloaded and all of the men were lost."

"Where did you hear that?" Joel marveled at the misinformation available. How much pain and suffering he had endured because of the lies he had been told.

"A sailor on another ship said he had heard when he was in the Falklands that the ship was full of contraband. When the real owner caught up with them, he confiscated the ship, killing many of the men on board. His crew was too small to handle the overloaded ship and it went down in a gale." She shuddered again. "So you see, I could not confess to Jacob to relieve my own guilt and raise false hopes that his son might have survived. It would only double Gramps' sorrow to know of mine and his sons' betrayal"

Joel sat up, turning toward Jessica. Her head was bowed, staring at her hands, now clasped in her lap. He reached over and placing his finger beneath her chin, lifted her head, "Jessica, look at me."

Wide and sorrowful green eyes met his, questioning.

"Joel survived, Jessica." Joel said quietly

"What do you mean? He's alive? How do you know? Have you seen him?" Excitement fired her eyes erasing the sadness.

"Because I am Joel."

"YOU?"

Joel chuckled, "Yes, me. I am Joel Isaacs and Jacob is my father."

"But how, what-----? Why didn't you tell us? I

thought sometimes that something was familiar about you, but I couldn't put it together with where I had been and obviously who you are. I can't believe it." She babbled and then stopped; sudden fear transfixed her face.

"I was told that my family was dead. That is why I am only now returning. If I hadn't met Captain Fred, then our paths might never have crossed. Some people would call it a coincidence but I know it was God's grace."

"He answered my prayers. Oh, my dear, how I have prayed that somehow, somewhere I might beg your forgiveness, but I thought you were dead and I had as good as killed you."

Jessica leapt from her chair and dropped on her knees before Joel, tears streaming down her face. "Forgive me, please forgive me. I deserve nothing more than to be cast out of this house which is only a little of what I deserve. I know that you will see after Jacob so now I can leave in peace."

Joel threw his head back and looked upward, his heart breaking.

Jessica watched his anguish. Dropping her head, she murmured, her voice pleading, "Would you extend mercy to Jay? He is a little tyke, and the apple of Gramps' eyes. It would kill Jacob to lose him now. He is the delight of his life. "

With a sigh that shuddered his whole body, Joel

looked down at the head of flaming hair that bowed at his knees and he wept.

Jessica felt his tears as they dropped on her head and mingled with her own. She looked up, uncertainty filling her eyes then dropped her head once more.

It took several moments before Joel could bring his emotions under control, but when he did, he reached down and tenderly took Jessica's face in his hands, lifting it, and whispered, "You are forgiven, my sister."

In the days that followed, Jessica and Joel formed a bond that only a shared secret can weld. They anguished over how they should tell Jacob that the son he thought was dead had come home. How would the knowledge of the betrayal of his sons and the lie they had been living affect his health. Could his heart stand the shock?

Joel refused to compound the situation with another lie which might exonerate Jessica and his brothers, yet how could they tell him? And then what about his other brothers? If they came home how was he to deal with them?

Jessica was sworn to secrecy until he worked his own issues out. She basked in Joel's attention. After Jacob and Jay went to bed at night, they talked some nights into the early morning hours.

Joel assured her that her position in the home

was secure and that the cabin was hers and his father's for a lifetime. She questioned him about his unusual relationship with his employer and feared that he might not agree to Joel's plans for his family.

He told her of the opportunity that awaited him back in Boston, if he should return.

"If you decide to return?" Alarm fired her eyes as she whispered. "How could you not return when such a wonderful future laid out for you?"

"My family is here."

"Brothers and a sister-in-law who betrayed you?"

"You're forgetting about Pa."

"No, I'm not forgetting about Jacob. You could easily take him with you back to Boston."

"Pa would not be happy there. It is another world. Besides to rip Jay from his life would be another tragedy, one he does not deserve and perhaps could not survive."

"I think you are wrong. Gramps would not want to stand in the way of this opportunity. Jay and I could come see him, perhaps move there. I know there would be something I could do in Boston. I'm quite good with a needle and thread. Those rich women are always in need of a good dressmaker and Gramps could use a housekeeper." Jessica's eyes glowed at the prospect.

"It's not that simple, Jess." Joel murmured, as the memory of spun golden hair, wide, sparkling eyes, and lips like full, pink rose petals that he longed to kiss inundated him. Pain dagger like in its intensity erupted, as the recurring vision of another claiming her returned to haunt him.

Sadness touched Jessica's green eyes as she observed the agony in the dark eyes that held hers, "You've yet to tell me the real reason you can't return. Don't you think it's time to ease your burden?"

The winter wind whistled outside and cocooned them inside beside a roaring fire. Jessica made them a cup of hot cider and sat down beside him on the new couch that he had ordered sent up from San Francisco. Taking both his hands in hers, she gazed intently into his eyes, hers encouraging him to share his heart. It was then that he told her about Melody.

She listened quietly and then sighed, "I knew there must be more. I'm so sorry you have been hurt, Joel. What a poor, foolish girl!"

Joel quirked an inquisitive eyebrow toward her.

Jessica's voice grew husky, "How could she turn you down, Joel? To be loved like that is every woman's dream."

Joel shifted, suddenly uncomfortable with her beauty, her nearness. Longing filled him as the memory of what he had lost and what he could never have transported his mind back to Boston. "She didn't exactly turn me down."

"What happened?"

"She never knew how I felt until the last time I

saw her."

"Why in the world did you not tell her? She would have fallen in your arms."

"You don't understand. She looked on me as a brother."

"But you are not her brother. Why did you not pursue her? Let her know your heart?"

"Had I known that her father would have considered me a suitable suitor I would have. Alas I learned too late and she had already made her choice."

"Circumstances could have turned out so differently." Jessica mused. "You might never have found us."

"Perhaps, but I don't know if she would have ever looked on me as anything but a brother. Somehow I must have reminded her of the brother who died. That's why our last meeting was so devastating to her. I stepped over the boundaries."

"Are you sure that's why she ran away? I'll wager that if you had given her any inclination that you felt differently, she would have forgotten all about your being her surrogate brother." Jessica declared.

"You think so?"

Jessica gave a chuckle that failed to reach her eyes, "I know so."

An unspoken message passed between them, an invitation in the eyes that held his. Joel stood up and moved away from this beautiful temptation who invited him to forget the one who could never be his. But even then could he forget?

One of the packets which braved the winter ice arrived with fresh supplies and two letters for Joel. One was from Captain Fred informing him that he had located the Isaacs' brothers and they were all alive if not well. Suffering from exposure and hunger, they had fallen ill. Fred found living quarters for them and with the money Joel had left him. He had also found a woman to look after them until they were strong enough for the trip home. Joel knew that only Fred could pull off a miracle like that in San Francisco. Once again he was thankful for his friend.

Fred told him that he had had a hard time explaining his help, but since their alternative was death, they accepted the funds. They promised full repayment when they were fit enough to go home, back to their livelihood of trapping and lumber. Fred said that he didn't have the heart to tell them they no longer owned a property to go home to.

The second letter bore a Boston postmark and Joel retired to his room so that he could read it in private. His heart raced as he noted Mr. Wilkin's familiar scrawl. He wondered if he would have a word about Melody in it. Instead his ever thoughtful benefactor wrote how encouraged he had been to receive the letter

Joel had sent to him so many months before informing him that he had found his family. He never mentioned the probable end of his own dreams for Joel nor a word about his daughter, only that the future Joel had described in Oregon looked promising. It was his prayer that God would richly bless Joel in every endeavor, reminding him that one half of the west coast business belonged to Joel. He closed the letter by telling Joel that someday he hoped that he could make the trip and see for himself the grand land that proved so exciting. Meanwhile Wilkins had begun procuring workers and their families to make the long journey west while outfitting two ships, one for the equipment and supplies he needed and one for the passengers.

He charged his young protégé to continue his wise investments and not to forget that all work and no play could harm him in both body and spirit.

Joel chuckled when he read that admonition. Wilkins knew little about the wildness of the frontier. Beyond hunting to put food on the table and an occasional barn raising, there was no play or anytime for it.

Winter had tightened its grip on the Isaac household and Joel spent much of his time hunting, chopping firewood and reading. He had long conversations with his father and at times Jacob would turn his head and try to see Joel better with a sideways glance. Now and then a puzzled look would cross the older man's face, then he would shrug or shake his head.

Christmas proved a festive affair as Jessica prepared a meal of wild turkey and venison for all the men in the sparse settlement. Since there were no other women around, she hoped a good meal with a family might stave off the loneliness that plagued the settlement during the holidays.

Joel observed the men as they devoured the delicious meal and cast longing eyes toward Jessica and Jay. Without a doubt, the key to a successful enterprise here would be the introduction of families. He had high hopes that Wilkins would see the wisdom of his advice to make a way available for families to come. He understood the loneliness of these men. Within him a hunger to have family of his own, a wife to share his dreams and children to carry on after him tugged at his heart.

CHAPTER 20

The long winter finally broke and with the warmer weather, packets resumed their schedule, arriving regularly with supplies, mail and a few settlers. One of the first arrivals brought Joel's three brothers home.

Joel had spent the day riding the land acquisitions he had made and arrived home tired and hungry. Mounting the steps two at a time, anticipating one of Jessica's succulent suppers, he paused just before entering as he heard masculine voices inside. He opened the door to stare into three pairs of vivid blue eyes fastened on him.

"And just who is this, Jessica? Have you made a new friend in our absence? One who is familiar enough to come into a man's home without knocking?" Simm asked.

"He is the reason you have a roof over your head to come home to." Jessica snapped.

"And how has that come about, missy?"

"I have rented room and board from Miss Jess.

With the harsh winter, income proved mighty slow."

"Not to mention the mortgage you put on this place to outfit yourselves for that wild goose chase."

"How did you know about that?" Ben asked.

"Did you think Kinsey would wait to collect his money until you would find your gold mine?"

"He said he was in no hurry."

"No hurry? You weren't gone a week before he was out here snooping around."

"Yea, and he told Ma, he'd collect one way or the other and she'd have to be the one to pay."

"That wasn't our agreement." Simm protested.

"Did you ever read what you signed, boys?" Jacob asked.

"Shore. Do you think we'd sign something we hadn't read."

"All of it?"

"Couldn't read that little bitty print and figured it was not our concern."

"Well that little bitty print said that at his discretion he could collect the whole amount when he pleased. Jess finally got him to agree to monthly payments. She took in laundry, boarders and roomers to pay for your foolishness."

"Well, pardner, seems we owe you an apology. Thanks for helping Jess out. Since we're home and need our rooms, guess you'll be needing to find other sleeping arrangements."

"I don't think he'll be the one to find other arrangements, Simeon."

Simeon raised an eyebrow and looked from Jessica to Joel. "Am I missing something here? What's going on between you two, and right under the nose of Pa."

"Nothing is going on between us, but what you are missing is that he didn't just pay rent, the very floor you are standing on belongs to him."

"What did you do, sweet talk my sister-in-law out of our property, stranger?"

"Sweet talk? Sweet talk?" Jessica practically shouted. "He could have gotten himself killed defending me and this property."

"Shore 'nuff. That still don't give you a right to our property." Simeon blustered. "perhaps you better tell me the whole story, mister."

Joel slowly took off his mud incrusted boots at the door, his head bent avoiding eye contact with his brothers, "I'll be glad to after I have had a bite to eat. Miss Jess, that stew smells mighty good."

Jessica lifted the heavy pot and dropped it on the table with a bang, anger written in every line of her body. "Well here it is if you are a mind to break bread with these ungrateful slobs."

"Now, Jess, Simm didn't mean nothing." Ben pleaded. "This is our homecoming and ought to be a celebration, not a fight."

"Then Simm should act more appreciative, not accusing."

"You're right, Jess, and he will mend his ways, won't you, Simm?" Ben asked, his blue eyes turning steel gray.

Jim spoke for the first time, "I think we need to give this fellow----?"

"Joe," Jessica proded.

"Yea, Joe, a chance to explain and tell us his side of things."

"Maybe when I hear the whole story, I'll see things different." Simm nodded, realizing he had lost his brothers' support.

"And indeed you shall. If Joe won't tell you the whole story, I will."

Joel cast a questioning look toward Jessica, wondering what she meant.

As the men took their places on each side of the long harvest table, Jay patted the place beside him and next to his mother, "You can sit here, Mr. Joe. Ma don't care and we might have some things to talk over."

"Now what would that be?"

"You know, where you went today and if'n I can't go with you the next time and maybe take your rifle and hunt some."

"Sounds like a winning idea to me, Jay. I did see some interesting tracks today." Joel was glad for the distraction. His heart still hammered and his head sought an answer to his dilemma. He wanted to reveal himself to his brothers, but not just yet. He needed to know more about them, what made them do the things they did.

"Joe, why don't you give thanks for this bread we are about to partake?" Jacob asked, diverting Joel's attention from his nephew.

Joel bowed his head, "Lord, we thank you for this meal, the hands that prepared it and for providing the food that we are to eat. We also praise you for keeping Jacob's boys safe and bringing them home."

"Thank you for your prayer, stranger. And it is a miracle that we made it home safely. We have learned our lesson and desire nothing more than to settle down here and make a decent living and home for Pa, Jay and Jessica." Jim observed softly.

"That may be difficult to do, Jim. Jess was right, this place don't belong to us anymore. Kinsey saw to that. Or maybe I should say you boys saw to that." Jacob reminded.

"There is nobody to blame but us, Pa. We acted foolishly and my only regret is that you and Jessica will have to suffer for it." Ben agreed.

"Jessica has already suffered for it. Do you have any idea how hard she has worked with Kinsey's constant threats over her head, just to make the payments."

"No. We thought the payments were delayed until we returned."

"You should have known who you were dealing with."

"Nobody else would stake us." Simm confessed.

"Did you ever question why he was willing to?"

"Not really."

"He wanted this land, the resources for his ship building business. He knew you would never be able to pay him back, especially with the exorbitant interest he was charging. Jess was only paying the interest each month."

"So what happened? She didn't have the money for a payment and he foreclosed?"

"No, she had the money, thanks to Joe. Kinsey wouldn't accept her payment and called the loan."

"So the place belongs to him?"

"No, it belongs to Joe."

Three pairs of eyes impaled Joel's, "So where does that leave us?" Simm asked.

"That depends on you, I reckon, Simm." Joel drawled, his voice steady, his eyes hard.

"We're in a spot, you know. Pa can't travel."

"Perhaps you should have thought of that earlier, before you signed away this place."

"We were wrong, so wrong, but knowing that doesn't give us a future." Ben murmured

"Could be a new beginning, you know." Joel observed.

"I would give my right arm to turn the clock

back." Ben said

"Way back," Jim added, his countenance tortured.

"I might have a use for that strong right arm of yours, Ben. So don't be giving it away just yet."

"A job, you mean?"

"That is exactly what I mean. It is true I paid Kinsey off but I have plans for this land, plans that include you, if you're interested.

"What kind of plans?" Simm questioned, suspicion darkening his eyes.

"My employer is an entrepreneur who is involved in every phase of the shipping industry from ship building to hauling. He needs the timber on this property and the harbor to build a shipyard here."

"So that was the plan all along, take our land from us."

Joel shook his head, "It is true, I did come here to explore expansion opportunities for our company, but I paid for the land I did not take it."

"All the same it's yours, not ours."

"Simm, how can you be so stubborn about this? Joe paid many more dollars than it was worth and has promised us a place to live as long as we want to stay." Jessica all but shouted.

"That's right, boys. Now if Joe has a proposition for you, we need to listen." Jacob stated, frustration lining his face.

"All I can say, Joe, is whatever way you can help

us, we are more than blessed." Ben stated, dropping his head but not before Joel could see the immense sorrow in his eyes.

"What about you, Simm?" Jessica asked.

"Well, if the other boys agree, I'll go along. But first I gotta know what it is we're gonna do. We don't know nothing about this here Joe and for all we know he might want us to do something illegal. I won't go along with anything that ain't lawful."

Jessica laughed, relieving the tension around the table, "What law? Joel had to take Kinsey all the way back to San Francisco trussed up like a pig for market to get this mess straightened out legal like."

"Did you? I mean he can't come back agin, can he?"

"Legal and signed." Joel assured.

"OK. So what's up? Pa and Jessica can continue to live here. What'll we do?" Jim asked.

"And what's in it for you?" Simm added

"We have the resources for a great ship building industry here, our only problem is manpower. I want you to work for me."

"Ain't no logger alive that can out cut me." Simm swaggered.

"But maybe me and Jim." Ben added with a grin.

"Good, that's what you'll be doing at the beginning, but I have asked my employer to provide for families to come here from the east to settle and work.

If they do I'll need knowledgeable men to teach them logging skills and to oversee the production."

Both Jim and Ben nodded their heads, Ben added, "We'll do whatever we need to do. We know what it's like to be without work and money."

"No, we don't ever want to be without again. If it hadn't been for Captain Fred down in San Francisco providing fer us, the three of us would be dead. We quit prospecting before our money run out so we could get home. Somebody robbed us of everything. We didn't even have our gear to sell. Couldn't get home, no food and no job. We went without food for days and got real sick. For some reason that kind man helped us, right out of his pocket, I reckon." Simm confessed.

"It was the Good Lord." Jacob said.

"No doubt about it, but he used that good captain as His instrument. However, he told us it wasn't his money, but someone else instructing him to do it. Wish we knew who it was so we could thank him properly." Jim murmured.

Jessica looked at Joel, tears welling up in her eyes.

Joel cleared his throat, conflicting emotions tearing his heart apart. His voice, husky, he replied, "Perhaps someday you will meet him."

"How did he even know about us? That is the mystery, I would like solved." Simm blustered.

"Life holds many mysteries, especially why

some people treat others as they do. It even happens in families, people who are supposed to love and care for each other do strange and devastating things to one another. Why do you reckon that is, Ben?"

Ben dropped his head, but not before Joel saw the anguish in his eyes, "I don't know, Joe, but I do know that they will suffer for it the rest of their lives."

"Actions do have consequences." Joel agreed with a sad smile.

Jim stood up and stretched, smiled at Jessica, "Jess, that was the best meal I've had since I left home. Let me and the boys clean up before we head out."

"You want to help me in the kitchen, Jim?" Jessica's eyes widened in surprise.

"You bet. I've had a lot of time to think and we've never done right by you. From now on, Pa's gonna have a new son and you're gonna have a considerate brother."

"The good Lord works in mysterious ways." Jacob murmured, marveling at his usually uncommunicative son.

"Shore does, Pa. It's about time your sons grew up and shouldered their responsibilities like men." Ben added.

"Son, if leaving for the gold fields has brought about this change in you, then I'm thankful you went no matter if we did lose this place."

"It was God using hard circumstances in our lives to change us. I know He's not finished with us yet, but if He'll give us a job and a chance, I'm willing to take a lifetime making it up to you."

Joel turned his head before the men could see his eyes brighten with tears. He could see the miraculous change in Jim and Ben. But what about Simm? Had his heart hardened beyond redemption?

As spring made its way toward summer, the brothers floated logs down the streams toward the harbor where they piled up waiting for the delivery of machinery and men.

Joel told his brothers to pull out logs suitable for housing and soon they were adding bedrooms to the cabin, enlarging the kitchen and adding a broad front porch that looked out over the verdant valley.

With the expansion completed, Joel cleared a level, fertile spot by a fast moving stream and began the construction of several small cabins. He had faith that Wilkins would recruit the needed families and he would get a head start on providing for them. He worked alongside his brothers, with Jessica's friendly neighbors pitching in, and relished the hard physical labor that cleared his mind of the turmoil and longing that pursued him most of his waking hours and disturbed his dreams.

At times memories of Melody would catch him unawares as he built a cabin. When he thought of the living that would go on within the walls, the deep yearning for her would once more overtake him.

As he pounded the logs, he mused over his other dilemma. He saw the question in Jessica's eyes and watched as agitation claimed her. She wanted a solution, one that would work. He knew she dreaded telling Jacob as did he, fearful of how he would receive it, if it would be too much for his heart. To live the rest of his life in bitterness against his sons was not an acceptable alternative, yet he had to know. Needed to know that the son he thought lost to him, had come home.

Working with his brothers had given him an opportunity to observe them. However, a satisfactory resolution of the situation still eluded him. Of one thing he was certain, Jim and Ben lived in regret. Simm was another matter. They had made progress in their relationship. His initial distrust of Joel's motives had abated and they worked together amicably. However the warm intimate fellowship that he enjoyed with his other two brothers was missing. He recognized that his older brother often covered his real feelings with bravado, so he continued to search for the real Simm beneath all his bluster.

One evening, just at twilight when the western sky was streaked with gold and purple, Joel took an after supper stroll. He stopped, closed his eyes and took a deep breath, savoring the fragrance of fir permeating the air. When he opened his eyes, he noticed Simm just down the hill from him. The older man was seated, leaning against a tall tree and unaware of anyone nearby.

Joel observed his brother in silence.

Simm stared at the horizon as if in a trance. Amazed, Joel watched as his brother jerked off his knit cap, sending his wild red hair flying in all direction. He buried his head in his cap and Joel saw his shoulders begin to shake as a deep muffled sob gushed from him. Joel turned to leave, not wanting to intrude on his sorrow when he heard a pitiful cry for mercy emanate from his brother. He froze as he listened to his brother pour out his heart, confessing the dark sins of his past. When finally he had emptied himself he lay prostrate on the ground, still weeping, his face wedged in the soft carpet of needles.

Not knowing what to do, but as if compelled to go to him, Joel moved forward and knelt, placing a gentle hand on the giant's back. Simm raised his head and saw Joel, "You heard?"

"Yes, I heard."

"I'll leave. I don't deserve a second chance."

"None of us do, it's not what we deserve but what God has provided for us. Forgiveness through Jesus. You have been forgiven, Simm. I heard you ask for it."

"But how can I ever forgive myself. If I hadn't lost that money, Aaron and Joel wouldn't be dead and my pa a heartbroken old man."

"Joel's not dead, Simm."

"You're crazy. They told me his ship went down. How would you know anyway? You're just trying to make me feel better, that I'm only responsible for one death, not two.

"In the first place Aaron is responsible for his own death. He planned the whole betrayal."

A frown creased Simm's forehead, "How do you know about Aaron and who planned what? Did Jessica tell you?"

Joel smiled, "She filled in some details for me, but I knew most of it already."

"How?"

"Because I'm Joel."

Simm's face twisted in shock and bewilderment, leaving him speechless for a moment. Then with a loud shout, he jumped to his feet, pulling Joel with him and enveloped him in a bear hug. "Oh, my little brother. God has brought you back to me."

Then Simm dropped his arms and stepped back, joy turned to fear, "Have you told Pa. What are you going to do to us?"

"I haven't told Pa. My plans for you are good, not evil."

"You don't want any revenge?"

Joel shook his head, "I have no desire for revenge. What happened six years ago was ordered by God. You meant it for evil, but God meant it for good. He has placed me in a position to bring opportunity to our whole family. Something that we would never have known had I not been sent away on that ship."

"How can you forgive me?" Simm's eyes

questioned his in the last lingering twilight.

"Because God has forgiven me."

The Isaac brothers enjoyed an exultant reunion; the only thing marring their complete happiness was how they were to tell their father. They spent hours with Jessica and Joel exploring ways to break the news to him, all to no avail. There was no easy way to reveal their dark secret. They knew they had to do it. They were committed to put the lies behind them, but the method had yet to present itself.

One morning Joel delayed going to work to spend some time with his father. He popped into his room just before daybreak with a pot of coffee and a tray of hot biscuits. "Hey, mister, I think it's time the king bee around here got breakfast in bed, how about you?"

"Well, I don't know any king bee, but breakfast in bed sounds pretty good to me. Especially if you're going to eat with me, son."

Joel's heart constricted at the word son. How he wished his father could know that he truly was his son. He sat down on the edge of the bed and arranged the tray so that Jacob could feel where his cup and biscuit were because his eyesight had deteriorated monthly.

Jacob leaned back against the patchwork quilt, closed his eyes and grinned, "If this ain't the life. Biscuits that melt in my mouth and a son to wait on me hand and foot."

"Sir?"

"A son couldn't be any better to me than you are, Joe. You've almost got my son's name. Joel, that's what I called him. You sound a lot like him. Sometime when you are talking, I think it's he. I still miss him, but you kinda filled in the gap."

Jay ran into the room and climbed on the bed, grabbing one of the hot biscuits.

"Jay, you be careful now and don't spill my coffee. What' got you up so early this morning?"

"I had a hankering to sing some of my grandma's songs. What do you say we teach Joe some of them?"

Joel's heart hammered. The memory of his mother holding him on her lap, singing to him captured his mind. "Why I think that's a great idea! Why don't you start and I'll follow."

Jay's sweet little voice carried through the house as he sang the songs his grandfather had taught him. Joel joined in and soon they were singing harmony on the old tunes Joel had almost forgotten.

When they finished one, they would go into another until Jay requested that Joel sing one by himself. He began to sing it in his clear baritone drawing Jessica from the kitchen. He shut his eyes as the pleasant memories of his mother wafted through his mind, prompting him to sing verse after verse. Finally when he finished, he realized a hush had fallen over the room. He looked at his father and saw a tear trickling down his cheek.

"Joel, you are my Joel." He whispered. "That last verse your mother made up for you. You sang it with her."

"Yes, Pa, I am Joel."

"How have you come back? Where have you been? What lies have been told me?"

"I have come back. I went far away by ship. I was told that you were dead. That's why you didn't hear from me. By God's good grace I found you."

"Why was I told you were dead?"

"I think that they thought I was dead." Joel hedged.

"But they brought me your clothes. Is Aaron alive, too?"

"No, Pa, Aaron is dead. At the hands of robbers."

"They told me you were too. Did you escape?"

"In a way, I did. God sent me away so that I would be spared that encounter."

"It was us, Pa. We lied to you." Simm's deep voice spoke from the doorway.

And so it was that the truth spilled out while Jacob lay on his bed, his sons and Jessica on their knees surrounding him.

When it was over, his heart had survived and in the end he extended forgiveness. Reaching out his arms toward Joel and his sons he exclaimed, "If you have forgiven them, how can I do less for once my son was dead, but now he lives. Glory be to our God who works

His miracles in His time."

The next few weeks were a glorious reunion for the family. With all dark secrets revealed, the family, brothers and father made a new beginning. Joel experienced an intimacy and acceptance from his brothers for which he had always longed. His family seemed complete for the first time in his life.

Jessica blossomed in the new consideration given her by the older brothers and Jacob spent hours listening to Joel's tales of adventure and the opportunities that Mr. Wilkins had offered him.

"Son, I would have a hard time giving you up again, but I'm an old man and those opportunities waiting for you back East are too good to pass up."

"Pa, I can make a good living here, maybe I won't get rich, but that's not important."

"What is important is that you take advantage of the opportunities that God provides. We're responsible to be good stewards of our gifts and talents. He has blessed you with a winsome spirit and a keen mind."

"Which I can use here."

"Perhaps not to the ultimate advantage."

"Are you trying to get rid of me, Pa?" Joel chuckled.

"No, I'm trying to be what a Pa's suppose to be, encourage their children to achieve what the good Lord has in mind for them to achieve."

"I'll just have to do my best here, Pa. I've just found my family and I'm not willing to lose them again."

"Even if God's will is for you to go back to Boston?"

"I have a hard time believing that God wants me to return."

"Why? Is there something you're not telling me?"

"I have already written Wilkins that I won't be returning." Joel replied, evading his question.

"Something fails to add up here. Have you left out part of the story?" Jacob persisted.

Joel dropped his head, pausing to bring his errant emotions under control. "Yes, the woman I love."

"What woman?"

"Mr. Wilkins' daughter."

Jacob frowned, confusion wrinkling his brow, "She didn't love you?"

"She belongs to another."

"You love a married woman?"

"Yes."

"I can't believe you would do something so foolish."

"She was not married when I fell in love with her. That's why I left. She was to be married and when I confessed my feelings for her to her father, he suggested that I take this trip in order to give my heart time to heal."

"Has it?"

"The memory of her haunts me night and day."

"That's not unusual. When I lost the boys' mother, I thought I could never love again, but I did. Time heals the pain, but we don't forget."

CHAPTER 21

Captain Fred's ship arrived mid-July with Joel's first order of saws for his mill and a letter from Wilkins. His employer had procured a vessel to haul all the equipment Joel would need to set up his operation. He also promised him that his much needed workers and their families would be on a ship bound for California within the month. Wilkins had done abundantly more than Joel had dreamed or expected.

Once again, his dear friend had put action to Joel's dreams bringing them to reality. How his family would rejoice at this wonderful news, for his brothers had also caught the vision of the wealth awaiting hard work and diligence in these abundant north woods and had committed themselves to the tasks.

The letter was dated three and a half months ago. Joel's heart raced with excitement. The ships carrying equipment and workers would be arriving in California within the month. His vision was about to become a reality.

The long days provided extra hours to finish

the cabins they had started. Joel and his brothers took advantage of every daylight hour hoping to have completed housing for the families when they arrived. They built a bunk house with an attached kitchen for the single men and ten cabins for the families they hoped would arrive. Wilkins had not been clear about how many people were coming or what the mixture was, but Joel knew that if they had built too many, others would come and if they had built too few, families could share until they built more. He was just excited that a community was about to be born.

Mid afternoon in August, they placed the last step and finished the final cabin. Tired and hot from the long hours under the summer sun, the brothers left to go home. They planned to take a cool swim and bath in the crystal clear pool at the base of a waterfall back in the woods and urged Joel to join them. He declined, telling them that he would join them later when they went to catch Jessica some fish for supper.

Joel sat down on the steps of the final cabin and viewed the settlement. Voices of children played in his mind as they waded in the babbling brook that would bring water to the houses. Dreams of his own future, perhaps a cabin like one of these, a home of his own with someone to share it filtered through his mind. That someone took on the face and form of Melody and he chuckled. How incongruous! He could hardly picture Melody, who had known only luxurious living conditions and fine clothes, being content with these rustic conditions and wearing homespun? Yet only her face and her voice echoed through his mind, making the cabin of his dreams a home. When would these tormenting thoughts of her cease? His pa had told him that he would heal but he wouldn't forget. Must he take the image and longing for her to his grave?

Jessica found him there, vacillating between joy and pain. She sat down beside him and looked at him, her excitement bubbling over as she took in the settlement. "Housing's not enough. You're going to need a church right there and maybe a school over there. I hope there is a teacher in the bunch. A child should know how to read."

Joel laughed at her enthusiasm, dispelling some of the former sorrow that had intruded on his moment of triumph. He looked at her and marveled at the change God had wrought in her. She was dressed in a new green calico frock. His brothers had especially ordered the yard goods from San Francisco and she had made it the night before. It fit the upper part of her body like a glove accenting her tiny waist while the green fired the emerald lights in her eyes. The small cameo, which Ben had purchased for her, rested in the hollow of her slender neck. An inner glow radiated from her and a contented smile parted her full pink lips as she dreamed of a future emerging in these lush green forests.

Joel had to admit, she was more beautiful now

than the pouting temptress he had met on a dusty San Diego street. Joel's return and confession to Jacob had released the torture that had plagued her and now she had a future to cherish, one free of guilt and dread, one that might offer a chance to love and be loved.

Joel stood up, "I better get back. I promised the boys that I'd help them catch you a few fish for supper."

Reaching a hand out to help her up, they walked hand in hand toward the cabin as the evening shadows lengthened and a soft breeze wafted in from the harbor bringing the scent of freshly cut wood.

"I love that smell." Jessica said.

Joel looked at her and smiled, his voice tender, "Why do you love that smell, little one?"

"Because the future is in it. I just know that something great is going to come out of this, Joel."

Touched, Joel squeezed her hand, "I'm glad you share my vision."

They entered the edge of the clearing where the cabin perched beside the cascading stream. She paused and gazed up into his face, a heart stopping smile on hers, "I believe in your dreams."

A warm affection for her flooded Joel and he bent down and kissed her cheek, "Thank you for your help and encouragement."

A voice hailed them from the cabin porch, "Hey, Joe, the bad penny has returned."

Jessica shouted with glee, "It's Captain Fred and he's got someone with him."

Joel squinted, the sinking sun's rays blinding him. "I believe you're right. I can't make out who it is."

"It's a stranger." Jessica replied shading her eyes.

Suddenly Joel started to run, leaving Jessica behind, and shouting, "It's no stranger it's Mr. Wilkins!! The ship must have come in and he was on it. I can't believe it!"

Joel took the steps two at a time and instead of offering his hand to his mentor, he enveloped the frail man in a bear hug. "I can't believe my eyes! What a wonderful sight, you here. How I've wanted to see you, talk to you, share my dreams with you. Are you all right? Was the trip too rough?"

"Whoa, Joel. One question at a time. I'm fine, a little tired, but happy to be here." Wilkins responded before turning to Jessica who was making her way up the steps, "And this is?"

"Jessica Isaacs, my sister-in-law."

"Your brother's wife?"

"His widow." Jessica corrected.

"Oh, I see. Then you must be the mother of that fascinating little tyke in the house."

"Yes, Jay is mine and my most notable accomplishment."

"Truly children are a gift from God." A sadness briefly dimmed the sparkle in Wilkins eyes.

"Let's go inside and I'll make us a pot of tea. I think I might even have a fresh batch of cookies to go with it." Jessica suggested as she opened the door and moved inside.

Wilkins paused before going in and gazed across the broad expanse of forest. "I can see why you have developed an attachment for this place. The land is glorious and," Wilkins inclined his head toward the door, "I take it your personal life has taken on a new track. The healing process we discussed has taken hold."

Joel's eyebrows rose, "What? You mean Jessica?"

Wilkins nodded, a strange sadness dimming his bright blue eyes.

Joel gazed toward the edge of the forest, his back to the door. "No, I have a warm affection and admiration for who she has become and what she has done. Nothing more. As for the healing process, I'm still waiting for it to begin. I am tortured with a yearning that only your daughter could fill. I struggle daily with the guilt of wanting with all my heart and soul someone who belongs to another. What can I do?"

"Keep on loving me for a lifetime, my Darling," spoke a cherished voice from his past.

Joel whirled around and dream became reality as a vision of golden loveliness hurled herself into his open arms.

He enfolded her in his arms, forgetting for a moment she belonged to another. Clasping her to his heart, he buried his face in her fragrant curls while emotions overrode logic and reason. How many tortured moments had he dreamed of this, but reality far exceeded imagination. She was soft and fragrant, yielding and sweet. How could he ever let her go? Suddenly reality intruded, and with a groan, he pushed her away.

"What is it, Joel?" Her angel voice asked, eyes wide, tears threatening.

"You belong to another and the love I have for you is not that of a brother." Joel confessed, his fists clinched, his arms stiff by his side lest he take her in his arms again.

Melody's laugh tinkled. Relief cleared her eyes, "Is that all?"

"Is that all? Who do you think I am? A man can stand just so much. Why do you think I ran away?"

"Why did you run away?" Mischief sparkled Melody's eyes.

"How could I stay when you belonged to another and I still wanted you?" Joel demanded.

Melody moved in closer and placed both arms about his waist, drawing him to her, "Do you not have a kiss to welcome me, Joel?" She asked as she turned her face up to him, her lovely mouth soft and inviting.

"Melody, you are another man's wife." Joel all but shouted.

"Oh, but I'm not. I shall belong to you or no one, my Beloved."

"But wha, how?" Joel shuddered and kissed the lips he had dreamed of, forgetting Captain Fred, her father and anyone else who observed. The only thing that existed was Melody, his vision of happiness clasped in his arms and to be his.

Finally sanity returned. A chagrined Joel lifted his head and noticed the group of observers who surrounded him which now included Jessica, Jay, and his three brothers. His face flushed, he stepped back, pulling Melody under his arm, not willing to release her. She held him around the waist and placed her head on his shoulders.

"Family, this is Melody Wilkins."

"Why little brother, you've been keeping secrets from us. We're mighty glad to make your acquaintance, ma'am. I'm Simm, this here is Jim and that one over yonder is Ben. You've already met Jessica and Jay."

"Glad to meet you all."

"Ma, no wonder he warn't yore prince. He was Miz Melody's prince. Guess we'll have to find you another one." Jay piped up.

Melody gave Joel a sideward glance, "What's this about a prince?"

"My ma said someday her prince would come."

"So you thought it was Joel?"

"I hoped so. But my ma said it wasn't so. Now I know why."

Melody's eyes misted as she looked from the little boy up into Joel's eyes, "That's right, Jay. Joel is my prince, it just took me a little while to figure it out."

Joel pulled Melody hard against his side, "You've got some explaining to do, young lady."

"Why don't you two go for a stroll while I cook these fish. Give you time to talk and maybe get some answers, Joel. Melody, I've got a notion, you are just the medicine he needs."

"Medicine?" Melody asked.

"Yes, the kind that cures a broken heart." Jessica explained.

Joel and Melody climbed up the knoll behind the cabin and followed the stream to the base of the waterfall. Joel spread his jacket on the ground for Melody to sit on and sat down beside her. "Now tell me what happened."

"You remember the day that I came to your room and you kissed my hand?"

"You ran away because I scared you."

"No, I scared me."

"What do you mean?"

"When I saw the look in your eyes and felt your touch, I suddenly realized that all that love for you I thought was brotherly affection was something much more. Here I was promised to another man and loving you. I didn't know how to deal with it, so I ran away. When I found out you had left, I was devastated. That's when I confessed to father how I felt about you."

"What was his response?"

"He said I couldn't marry Peter and I asked him

what would we do about all our wedding plans, the invitations had all been sent out. He told me not to worry, we would just send out notes canceling it. I told Peter. Oh, Boston is abuzz with my scandalous behavior. You know Peter was the cream of the Boston crop. Of course all of my girlfriends were relieved."

"Did they know why you canceled your plans?" Joel inquired.

"You mean did I tell them about you?"

"Yes."

"No. I didn't know how much you loved me or if you might find someone else. When I saw you with Jessica and saw how beautiful she was, I was afraid."

Joel gathered her in his arms and she dropped her head on his shoulder. "You had nothing to fear. My love for Jessica is truly like a brother. You're not jealous of Jessica, are you?"

"Not really. When I overheard what you said to Father, I thought my heart would explode with joy."

"When you catapulted into my arms, I couldn't believe it was really happening. I had dreamed, much to my guilt, about holding you like this. When it happened it was a fantasy come true, but better than the fantasy." He chuckled, delight warming his whole body, remembering.

Melody tugged at her sleeve and murmured, "I might be a little jealous of Jessica."

"How's that, my love?"

"She had all these months to share your dreams and visions and I'm only just beginning."

"But we shall have a lifetime to dream together. You will marry me?"

"The sooner, the better."

"How soon do we leave for Boston?"

"I don't want to wait. Couldn't Captain Fred marry us?"

"Fred?"

"He's a ship's captain and a minister. Did you know that about him?"

"No, but I'm not surprised. But what about a big wedding with all the trimmings?"

"All I want is you." Melody squeezed him as if she never wanted to let go.

"That's music to my ears. Want to get married tonight?" He laughed.

"Could we?"

"Don't you want to make some plans?"

"Maybe we should wait until tomorrow."

"Did you come in on the ship with the workers?"

"Yes, and they are waiting for you down at the harbor. I forgot all about them. Don't you need to welcome them and show them their accommodations?"

"I do need to welcome them, but I bet Fred and my brothers have already taken care of showing them the settlement. How many came?

"Nine families and about ten single men. Fred

said that you had provided for them nicely."

"I think so. I'll be pleased to show you. Understand this is the wilderness and homes are primitive, nothing like Boston."

"Are you planning to stay here?"

"I was. Now I don't know."

"Why?"

"I'm afraid you wouldn't be happy here."

"You don't think I'm equipped to handle hardship?"

"It would be so different. You've never lived in an environment like this."

"Meaning I'm spoiled and privileged?"

"You said it, I didn't." He chuckled.

"I want to live wherever your dream is, Joel. I'm tougher than you think."

"There is a cabin available."

"Then claim it for ours."

"There is no running water or servants to do your bidding. The winters can be harsh and cold. We live under a constant threat of Indian attack. It wouldn't be easy."

"I'm not asking for an easy life, just a life spent with you. Joel, I am not willing for you to sacrifice your dreams, abandon your family and live in Boston because of me I'm not willing to risk your love turning to bitterness."

Joel smiled at her, amazed at her wisdom and

maturity. He had so much to learn about her, so many delights to discover. "The truth is, Melody. I'm not sure what my dream is or my future holds. I love the country here, rejoice in finding my family but I planned to stay because I knew I couldn't go back to Boston and see you belonging to another man. Your father offered me an unlimited opportunity there, one my father has urged me to take."

"Then we have some big decisions to make."

"Decisions that will affect a lifetime, but the first decision is when do we get married? Did you bring your dress?"

"Yes, I had high hopes."

"Then we'll corral Captain Fred and have him tie the knot." Joel frowned, "What about your mother? Won't she be upset, not being at your wedding?"

A radiant smile dimpled Melody's cheek, "She's already given her blessing."

"That settles it. The sooner the better."

The sun was sinking low on the horizon when Nate Wilkins made his way through a hastily constructed arch adorned with wild flowers. Clasped on his arm was a glowing Melody, her eyes fastened on the tall, broad shouldered groom that waited impatiently beside his brother, Simm, and Captain Fred. Joel's eyes drank in her beauty and radiance, his heart thundered with anticipation. God's goodness overwhelmed as his most glorious dream was about to become a reality.

The new community surrounded them and from somewhere the lovely strains of a violin accompanied Melody's procession toward Joel.

Nate lifted Melody's veil and kissed her cheek, then placed her hand in Joel's and they pledged their sacred vows to each other before God and the settlers that He had provided to carry out Joel's vision.

As twilight descended torches were lit and the wedding guests and family enjoyed a feast of venison and fish provided by Jessica. As evening deepened other instruments appeared and lively dancing in the level clearing began.

Joel's brothers each whisked the bride away for a dance and Joel looked for Jessica. He smiled as he spotted a tall, handsome newcomer whirling her around to the lively tune. He paused, just watching her. He sighed, painful as the journey had been, had it not been for the awful deed that Jess had perpetrated, he would not be standing here tonight, and a future with Melody would not be his.

He smiled. Maybe Jessica's "prince" was here somewhere in this new wave of people just waiting to claim her. Wherever or whoever he was, Joel knew in his heart that God had someone out there for Jessica to love and to be loved by.

He grabbed Melody as Ben spun her around the

floor. Grasping his wife's hand, he led her toward the door of their honeymoon cabin, where he had prepared a bed for them.

Turning to wish the well wishers goodnight, he picked up his blushing bride and carried her over the threshold into their private haven and toward the fulfillment of all his longings.

The End

www.ingramcontent.com/pod-product-compliance
Lightning Source LLC
Chambersburg PA
CBHW030013180626
46810CB00001B/19